WITHDRAWN

# Of Men and Ghosts

Kofi Aidoo

LONGMAN

Longman Group UK Limited,
Longman House, Burnt Mill, Harlow,
Essex CM20 2JE, England
and Associated Companies throughout the world

First published 1994

**British Library Cataloguing in Publication Data**
A CIP record is available from the British Library

Set in 11/12pt Baskerville
Produced by Longman Publishers Pte Ltd
Printed in Singapore

ISBN 0 582 22871 9

# Biography

Kofi Aidoo was born in the 1950s at Sagyimase in the Akim Abuakwa Traditional Area of Ghana. The first of nine children he had his elementary education there and at Asiakwa. His father's work as a touring Senior Officer in the Ghana Prisons Service allowed him to see all of Ghana even as a child. He began writing short stories about the various regions when he went to the Anum Presbyterian Training College. Some were read on the BBC-African Service. Working as a teacher in Accra, he studied at the Ghana Institute of Journalism, and published his first work *Saworbeng*, an anthology of stories interspersed with lays to mimic the traditional mode of story telling.

In the late 1970s, he went to the United States to study at the College of Wooster, Wooster in Ohio, where, in addition to the regular Liberal Arts program offered at the school, he had tutorial classes to bring 'color and vibrancy to raw talent' under the keen supervision of Professor Raymond McCall, Head of Theater and Drama Studies at Wooster. From Wooster, he went on to the University of Maryland at College Park. Studying for his Master's degree, he taught writing skills to Freshman students as a Graduate Assistant, fusing motion picture/ television images with literary forms and themes to promote descriptive writing by Telling Fact method.

His greatest interest is travelling by road, driving.

Currently unmarried, he has a son and several nephews and nieces from some of his five brothers and three sisters.

For
My mother
Abenaa Twum
And my father
Kwabena Nkrumah
And to the memory
Of my dear grandmama
Obaa Juliana Frempomaa
And to a great man of love
Okunini Nii Ashitey of Sekondi
A friend in need is a friend indeed

# Chapter 1

Thin mists of smoke filled the small kitchen, but thicker twirls hung near the low slanted roof. They twiddled toward the door and dashed outside, just below the lintel. The haze in the large shaft of sunlight through the doorway pronounced the shadows of floating silkweed floss, and they appeared like two pikes striking at Entea's feet which held the wooden stock of a Winchester between them. He was polishing the rifle. He had the barrel in a strong left-hand grip while his right hand moved a piece of damp cloth vigorously up and down the barrel. The movement kept shifting the butt to and fro, and it waved a dull reflection of the sunlight on the darkened surface of the rough-cast mud wall.

Entea paused in his work. Why had Minta not yet returned from his errand to the next town, he wondered? The sun was about mid-sky. By his calculation, the time was about noon. Or had Minta taken him for a fool and bolted with all the proceeds from their business deal? Minta dared not! Entea swore to shoot holes in Minta's roof and leave town that evening if he had not returned by then. Entea looked outside from where a sudden burst of noise had come to interrupt his thoughts. In the gravelled small yard, two stray dogs were yapping and growling and clawing each other as they fought over the entrails of game they had retrieved from the trash basket. He picked up a small clay bowl beside him. It had contained the oil with which he had polished the rifle. Without any regard to it, he flung it at the dogs, barely missing them. The bowl broke on impact. It sent shards flying in all directions. The dogs scampered and bounced over the low fence around the yard, dragging the entrails between them in their snouts. They kept going and going, as if they were headed yonder for the Atewa hills in the distance.

'Damn you animals,' Entea said. He rose and leaned the rifle against the wall carefully. In a stride, he was by the fire. He pushed the ends of the wood together inside the tripod clay hearth over which a slab pile of game was cooking on a wire mesh. As he turned the meat over, a steady stream of fat began to feed the embers which sent up a small leaping flame. However, the flame soon fizzled out. Thick acrid smoke rose to engulf him and he walked outside to the yard.

In the sweltering heat, the stench of decaying animal matter had overpowered the effluvium which, earlier in the day, the air had carried from the community pit-latrine in the bushes somewhere behind the house. Entea held his nose, his attention riveted on the bluebottles flying in dizzying whirls above the offal bits strewn about the gravel. Then, he let go, laughing. Why was it at all necessary to fight the putrefaction, pretending he found it disagreeable? Was it not his own doing – an addition to an already fouled atmosphere? Of course, someone could make an argument that the pollution by the community was a necessity. As offensive as it might appear, it was indispensable to the survival of the people. In fact, it was an attribute of nature. Mother Nature who was the source of all the beautiful flowers was also the source of that putrid smell. And so the community had had the decency to tack it away from sight at the outskirts. But what was the difference? It was foul smelling all the same, just like the putrid pieces of meat and all other rottenness, hidden or otherwise. Entea laughed.

He looked expectantly along the path that ran past the house to the community latrine in the bush. There was nobody in sight. And it was all quiet too. Only the corrugated iron sheets dramatized the effect of the relentless heat by intermittent snaps. Then he saw Minta ride into view around the corner of the building in the distance.

They had known each other from their elementary school days at Nkonsia. Because they were the oldest and biggest students, the school children had dubbed them *sukuu papa* and *sukuu wofa*. One day, Minta had a scuffle with his teacher over homework and the teacher tripped over Minta's foot and fell. The whole school was assembled immediately to witness the punishment due insolent students – twenty-four lashes on Minta's bare back. But he did not show at the assembly. He walked away never to return to the school again. He took residence on the other side of the Atewa hills at Pusupusu, the town of his ancestors, as he put it.

Minta and Entea maintained their friendship. They visited each other on some weekends. They set traps in the bush and in the streams. One day, Entea said that he found primary school stuff too boring for his age. He left town for the city. Rumours seeped back to Nkonsia that he had joined the army. Months passed. Entea did not come to visit. The hearsay died. Then, seven years later, Entea suddenly appeared in town, dressed as a soldier. He claimed he was on long leave after operations with the United Nations Peacekeeping Forces in the Middle East. On his first hunting expedition, he crossed the Atewa hills from Nkonsia to visit Minta at Pusupusu. Together, they went into the forest to hunt, operating from a dilapidated hunter's cottage. Entea explained to his friend that they could make some extra money by selling some of the game. And so, after some days in the bush, they came down from the hills to dispose of some of the game, fresh and smoked antelope, buck, deer and all.

As his friend got closer, Entea breathed in deeply, as if in the stench he found something magical, something invigorating. 'What took you so long? I was beginning to think I'd seen the last of you,' he said as Minta dismounted and leaned the bicycle against the worm fence.

'Adjeiwaa was away. I had to wait for her. Her assistants don't pay as much as she does.' Minta brought out a wad of cedi bills from his pocket. He handed it to Entea while he kept waving his left hand before his nose in a futile effort to drive the bad smell away. 'It stinks here.'

'Ironic, isn't it? Sweet smell of success.' Entea laughed, showing Minta the money. 'You know how terrible fermented cocoa smells. But as kids, when we struggled under its weight carting it home from the farms of rich people like Kani, we were told it was the smell of success. Rottenness translates into richness for some people. See how much we have here?'

'This smell breeds sickness –'

'Look at you, healthy and all rounded, like giant edible mushrooms grown in human manure,' Entea said, grinning. 'Where does your house stand but in the shadow of the air from you-know-what.'

'That isn't fair. The city does do strange things to people. You didn't use to talk like that. And I thought the army built people of cha – '

'Determination?' Entea slapped the wad of bills against his palm. Minta walked past him to one of the rooms to get a bottle of kerosine. He sprinkled it on the gravel. The flies and bluebottles dispersed. Some of them flew to perch on the roughcast mud wall of the kitchen wing, moving around slowly as if dazed. Entea was now engrossed in counting the money, making the additions of the various denominations on his fingers.

'Eight hundred and fifty-three cedis.' Minta volunteered.

'Good money, but lots of expenses to pay.' Entea counted off fifty-three cedis and gave it to Minta, who studied it and swallowed audibly.

'I stay with you in the bush. I carry the load on my bicycle. I ride the distance of six miles to do the selling. And this is what you give me?'

'There's plenty where this came from,' Entea said. 'Remember, this is only the first in a series of plans I have to make us rich. If you can sell the rest of the meat this evening, I could give you some more money.'

'What will you give Kani if you sell all the meat?' Minta asked. Entea looked up at the sky, smiling, as he pocketed the money. Then, he spoke.

'Don't worry, my friend,' he said. 'I have everything planned. In the game of checkers, we say never make a move if you don't have your rear covered. I know the farms in the bush. I know the springs and traps that fringe them. I'll find something for Kani.'

'Kani is a good man,' Minta said. 'Please, don't send him game stolen from other people's springs. I don't want to be part of this any more. You go to Adjeiwaa yourself and sell your meat. Don't come back to visit me any more if it's only to steal from others.'

'If only children know what adults know, there'll be few contentions in this world,' Entea said, laughing. 'Why would a royalty show favours to a pauper if the royalty has nothing to gain from the pauper? Kani needs me in his home.'

'It's all right for you to enjoy your fantasies. Just don't translate them into hurting anyone physically,' Minta said.

Entea was a child when his father Bonsra hobbled home on one leg from the war in Burma. Bewildered as he was, Entea remembered Kani vividly trying to make meaning out of Bonsra's injury by telling Entea that his father fought to bring freedom and dignity to several people nearly at the expense of his own life. As nonsensical as it all sounded to him, Entea accepted the trauma of living with a one legged father who barked instructions at him all the time, striking or poking him with the crude wooden crutch when the boy did something contrary to his father's expectation.

Years later when Entea banded with a group of rascally boys, Kani pressed upon Entea to learn how to command respect instead of demanding it through intimidating people. To earn respect, Entea had to get involved in noble causes. Kani further stressed that joining the army to defend his country if the need arose was an exemplary way to win honours. The army, as Kani emphasized to him, made men out of weaklings who, in their ignorance, roamed around bullying the innocent and the defenceless under the guise of manliness. The bold were never boisterous or threatening; the courageous and the powerful were always respectful and helpful.

And so, believing that the army would make a man out of him, Entea went away and joined it. No doubt, Kani had been grooming him for a special purpose in Kani's family. Minta's not knowing about that unique condition, Entea thought, was making him jealous of Entea's good standing with Kani. Minta might relate to the situation better if Entea explained the high stakes involved to him.

Entea went to the kitchen. When he emerged, he had the rifle. He raised it high in the air. 'If Kani can trust me with his gun, it means he's ready to accept me as his right-hand man. He's rich. Why would he whine or fuss over carcasses? We have serious business going, Kani and me. I intend to marry his daughter.'

'You aren't talking about Kani's daughter, Ayowa?' Minta chuckled. 'Where do you come from entertaining such thoughts? What has happened to you? Think, my friend, think. The gods don't look favourably on people who go for things out of their reach.'

'I do positive thinking. I believe only in constructive planning of my life,' Entea said. 'It's time I moved into the spotlight. And I have the means now. I have the power. It's aptly put in the game of checkers. The fellow who plans ahead wins the game. If a man makes a good move, he's assured of success. However, one must accept and deal with the consequences too, if the move is faulty. I'm making all the right moves so far. Have you ever heard of the song "Only the strong survive?"'

Minta reached for a broom and began scooping up the offal pieces on a shovel. He dumped the trash in the wicker basket. 'I didn't know you had become a philosopher as well. I wish you all the best.'

'Kani said those words to me when he gave me his gun,' Entea said. 'And now, it's I who have power. Kani knows it. He sees it as a meeting of great minds. His and mine.'

'How can you talk about Kani like that?' Minta asked. 'I'm beginning to get sick. Can we go and wash ourselves? You have a long afternoon ahead of you if you really mean to go and sell to Adjeiwaa. You've got another long trek ahead of you tomorrow, if you're going to return to Nkonsia.'

'Yes. Ayowa may be dying to see her future husband,' Entea said. Both men crossed the yard to the main wing of the building, where each went into a separate room. Entea left the rifle in his room. Minta left the bottle of kerosine in his. When he came out, he had two towels slung across his shoulders. Both men secured the doors and left the yard. Entea walked ahead. Minta rode idly on his bicycle behind Entea. And they went along the path to the river in whose pool young men took dips naked and washed themselves.

Far away on the other side of the Atewa hills, in the small town of Nkonsia at the foot of the hills, Kani was sitting in his hammock chair outside his house when a schoolboy brought him news that Master Darko wanted to see him. Kani immediately left to see him. Headteacher and Catechist of the Presbyterian school and church, Master Darko served as Kani's private secretary. His head bent a little forward, his big eyes staring down a few feet ahead of him, Kani took long strides on his way to the school. Like most renowned men of influence, he always appeared to be thinking while he walked. Unlike Kopra the-town-crier, whom children made fun of because his shorn head reflected the sun, Kani's baldness added more dignity to his personality. Some people in the town even called him *Nana*. They said that he looked more like a King than a friend of Kings. The very old said that he was the reincarnation of his matrilineal great grand uncle Kan-kanfo-the-general, who had been at the head of a long

7

line of wealthy men. The general, legend had it, was so powerful that he marched to the coast with his men and captured a fort of slave traders, set the chained people free and looted the fort. So plentiful was the booty that some of it had passed to Kani many years later. But that story distracted from the hard-working Kani who, as a young man, and after his demobilization from the army after the Second World War, had travelled extensively in West Africa, trading. Sometimes he was gone for three to six months speculating and hunting for gold and diamonds. He only settled down after his wife gave birth to his only daughter, Ayowa, after three sons.

When he reached the school compound, he avoided the gravel-paved avenue lined on both sides by tangerine trees. Too many yellow and red fruits weighed down the branches and they were close to touching the ground. He cut across the green playing field to enter the first classroom. The children rose to attention immediately. The boys saluted. The girls dropped a curtsy, their hands behind their blue uniforms. 'Good afternoon, Noble Kani,' they sang.

'How are you today, my children?' Kani asked.

'We're quite well, thank you,' came the children's choral response. They then sat down. An older pupil went closer to Kani. He reported that Master Darko was in the school garden and that he would be told of Kani's arrival.

Kani looked round the classroom, the children subdued into silence by his presence. Some busily scrawled on their slates. Except for the long blackboard, the rest of the yellow walls were posted with pictures of cocoa and pastoral farmers or gold and diamond miners, all gleeful at work. The alphabets, arranged in a pictorial parade, told the story of the letters. Scanning them, Kani paused on D, then at G. The two letters colourfully displayed their wealth in diamond and gold jewellery. He smiled. The boy who had gone out to Master Darko returned and said that the headteacher would meet Kani at the office. Kani left immediately. He went along the veranda in front of the chool block. Apart from classes One and Two, all the other classrooms were empty. The children were all at work in the school garden or on the pineapple plantations.

Master Darko had not arrived when Kani got to the office, so he waited outside. The ground before the office veranda had whitewashed stones laid out in the form of the country. In the centre of the map, a hoisted but tattered national flag flapped slowly. The crotons around it were clipped low, and butterflies and bees hovered and buzzed over the cosmos, zinnia, mimosa and the silver-bells. Master Darko appeared around the corner of the office building in an all white outfit, a fountain pen stuck between his calf and hose. His hair was parted in the middle to reflect the fashion of the strict disciplinarian teachers of the late sixties. He tapped his leg with the cane he held as he opened the office door. Kani instinctively bowed his head to avoid the door's crossbar and followed the schoolmaster into the small room.

Master Darko went behind his Odum desk, gone black with age, and sat down. He put on his reading glasses, picked up an envelope and took out a letter from it. All this time, he had not deigned his visitor a direct look. Then, with his cane, he indicated to Kani a rattan wing chair before his desk. But Kani remained standing, his huge frame bearing on the schoolmaster. 'Please, have a seat, nobleman,' Master Darko said. He proceeded to read the letter silently.

Kani sat down in the rattan chair. It was too small for his size and it squeaked as he shifted his frame in it to feel comfortable. His eyes stayed fixed on the schoolmaster. Then Master Darko pursed his lips in a pensive mood. He removed his glasses, rubbed his eyes with the back of his hand and stretched himself backwards on his chair. He put his glasses in their case and dropped it into his pocket. It's from Owiredu,' he said.

Kani drew a silk headkerchief tucked between his cloth and his chest and rubbed his shorn head. 'Has his illness turned worse?' he asked.

'He says nothing about that.' Master Darko paused and sighed. 'But you got your wish. Owiredu has agreed to your request. He's asked Baah, his son, to marry Ayowa when he gets out of college next year.' Master Darko pulled out his pen and poised it over the bottom of the letter. Looking at his wrist-watch he wrote down 'two p.m.'. 'What should I write back to him?'

'Nothing yet.' Kani grinned. Getting up, he wandered to the window. 'What a splendid day. I must visit Owiredu some time this week. Time is of paramount importance in all of this. The sooner we get the marriage going, the better it is for us both. I don't want insolent eyes pouring over my daughter any time she's out.'

A business associate, Owiredu was a wealthy man at Betomu, the right-flank administrative town of the Abuakwa state. In fact Owiredu's son was the heir apparent to the right-flank throne. That was principally why Kani wanted him for Ayowa. Since Kani could never become a king because he did not come from a royal lineage, he reckoned that if he married Ayowa to Owiredu's son, he would be compensated by the royal heritage of his grandchildren. And from the time Ayowa turned ten years old, he had been discussing the prospect of such a marriage with Owiredu. There were times that he let Owiredu's son, Baah, come to spend weekends at his home, so Baah would become familiar with Ayowa. However, Owiredu would not give a definite answer to the issue. Kani's fears mounted when his friend was suddenly taken ill six months ago.

Kani kept nodding his head and talking to himself as though he were alone in the office. 'Yes, for a man who has eaten from the same bowl with the King of the State of Abuakwa, custodian of all the land east, west, north and south of the Birim River, only a would-be chief's home is appropriate for my girl.'

'I don't like this.' Master Darko rose from his chair. He began to tap the top of his desk with his cane in emphasis. 'You should send Ayowa to secondary school. What is the

10

need rushing her into marriage now? She's young. She can still get a young man to marry even after ten years. These are the modern times. Women are competing with men for positions of responsibility.'

Kani just stared outside, where the school drums, their hide surfaces torn and held together by adhesive bands, were propped to sun against a sweetsop tree. Half-dead near the base, pressure-pad polypore fungus threatened to push the bark of the tree open. In the sparse and sickly leaves, however, was a solitary green flower. Kani beckoned the schoolmaster to come closer to him. He pointed to the flower. 'When all around me seem dead, I still have a sucker plant I can count on. The children of my sons will be mine only in name, but those of Ayowa will be mine in blood because of our matrilineal inheritance. Long before I had Ayowa, I had made plans for her –'

'To pawn her for royal blood that will never ascend to a throne?' Master Darko asked. 'You're smothering the potentials of that wonderful young woman.'

Kani chuckled. He turned to face Master Darko, who had returned to his seat. 'Sometimes you disappoint me,' Kani said. 'In fact, all scholars disappoint me most of the time. You fall into the trap of believing only in what you learned, not from experience, but from what you have read, and so you fail to see or comprehend what is so close to you. Yet you believe you understand everything out there far out of your reach. Owiredu's daughter recently came home to divorce her husband. As I understand it, she studied to become a doctor. A doctor who can't administer injections?'

'She's what we call Ph.D.' Master Darko corrected Kani.

'Whatever you call it. But my point is, a few years back, what young woman would divorce her husband? Now that's in vogue. You know why? Because the women have too much education. They're forgetting our values. They're forgetting their role in our system. Owiredu's daughter was dressed like a man, in a shirt and pants. She would not let her husband finish even a sentence without

11

her cutting in. Yet she couldn't say just one sentence correctly in her own language without slipping in an English word. You call that good education? And you should have seen her fingernails. Long and flaming red with whatever they call that paint.'

'Times change –'

'For the better, not for the worse.' Kani rubbed his face with the silk headkerchief, then paced to the wall and back to the window. 'I'm marrying Ayowa into a royal home. Her children will grow up articulate in the lore of our land. They'll interpret their learning to suit the needs of this country. Everything has a purpose. And too much of everything can be bad. Especially too much education for a woman. End of conversation.' He dipped his hand into the pocket of his velvet loose shorts and pulled out three red bills. He tossed them to the schoolmaster, who scrambled to catch the floating three hundred cedis. 'That settles matters.'

'Tha-thank you,' Master Darko stuttered.

'And remind me two months before independence anniversary, I promise the school a brand new set of marching drums,' he said.

Master Darko folded the bills and put them in the case of his reading glasses. He then rushed past Kani to hold the door for him. It was sunny, but large patches of shadows from the isolated clouds above spotted the greenery of the Ajapomaa hills to the east. In Kani's ears, the distant chirps of the weaver birds at the market area sounded like a harmonious song. 'Palm wine tastes excellent on such beautiful afternoons as this one,' he said, 'You want to come with me?'

'I can't go to the shanty in my uniform.' He took Kani's massive hand, and bowing a little, shook it in appreciation. 'Though the patches of clouds don't make it a near perfect day, I think the wine will be great. Have a good afternoon, noble one.'

Kani waved his hand. On the return walk, he took the gravel-paved avenue with tangerine trees on both sides.

The sun was behind him and his long shadow went ahead of him on the ground.

The large shadow cast on the Atewa hills by the tufts of white and grey clouds glided like a band of marauders toward the small town of Nkonsia at the foot of the hills. The menacing descent of the shadow across the bluish-green foliage of the hills increased Ayowa's anxiety. As she walked along the lane, a linen-covered enamel tray of items balanced on her head, she wished that she had reached Obaa Panyin's place already. She shut her eyes; she did not want to see the threatening shadow. But how far could she walk with her eyes closed? To her, the shadow seemed to embody the anguish tearing at her heart.

As definitive as the pain was, she knew that it was no more physical. That aspect of it had stopped. It was its counterpart, that horrible feeling that had developed after the sexual assault on her six weeks ago, that was killing her. What would she do if she were pregnant? It had been a week since she missed her period. The initial pangs she had felt at the thought that she might be pregnant had been growing each day. Now, she could feel it lodged inside her chest like a balloon with hot air inside it. On a couple of occasions, she had poured cold water on herself, hoping that would curb the burning sensation inside her.

Intangible as it seemed, she simply could not wish it away. It felt real, just like that shadow which she could not grasp, yet she could see it in its swoop upon the town. She stopped walking. She closed her eyes tightly as it approached, but it was a wave of cool relief from the sun that she felt sweep over her. When she opened her eyes and turned round, she saw the huge shadow harmlessly scudding away over the buildings and along the lane.

She quickened her pace to get to Obaa Panyin's. An elderly woman who lived by herself on the outskirts, her true name of *Nyameche* – God's gift – had been taken over

13

by the accolade and title of Obaa Panyin imposed on her by the elders of the town when they realized that she had developed psychic powers. In fact, they thought her the servant of the gods and so appointed her priestess of the Twafoor fetish – the oracle which from ancient times had protected the people in times of war, and from plagues and floods, and gave them peace, prosperity and happiness.

Immediately she was made the priestess, she issued new directives. She condemned the use of alcohol in oblations. She asked the elders to stop the slaughter of sheep and chicken in purification rituals. Completely at variance with the norms of the people, the whole town was stunned. Some of the townsfolk said that she had indulged in witchcraft which had led to her becoming possessed by powers of the dark. Others said that she was indeed out of her mind. After all, she had been brought home from a mental asylum where she had been sent after she proved unable to teach secondary school students in the city.

The elders rejected her directives. And she, in turn, refused to have anything whatsoever to do personally with the Twafoor shrine. She said that if the people were not ready to break with superstition and seek the truth, she was not ready for them either. In embarrassment, and also not to rescind their decision by overturning their own appointment because it was against the dictates of tradition, the elders appointed a deputy to be responsible for the Twafoor shrine – performing the duties that Obaa Panyin, daughter-of-the-gods – had refused to perform. But the elders and the catechist, the mullah of the small mosque, continued to consult with her quietly and individually. And so, the title given her as Obaa Panyin had stuck, and only a few people referred to her by her true name of Nyameche – God's gift. One of such people was Ayowa.

She had been friends with Obaa Panyin ever since Ayowa learned fourteen years ago that Obaa Panyin had peen instrumental in Ayowa's birth. Their friendship had become greatly intensified recently, however, since Ayowa was raped in the bush. Obaa Panyin was the only person in whose presence Ayowa felt assured of inner security. Though she had not breathed a word about the incident to anybody, Obaa Panyin's demeanour had suggested to Ayowa that the elderly woman already had knowledge of it. That was after the four days within which Ayowa did not venture outside her parents' home – four agonizing and tormenting days she deceived her parents that she was experiencing a painful period, a lie her mother had subscribed to by proffering that such terrible pains were natural for some women. When Ayowa visited her, Obaa Panyin appeared taken aback and curious about her. Silently, she felt Ayowa's upper arms. She pressed the flesh hard, even to a point of discomfort for Ayowa, who winced. Then, Obaa Panyin looked her up and down and smiled. Tapping her reassuringly on her back, Obaa Panyin said, 'Don't worry, my Pearl. Nobody can harm you any more. Nobody will hurt you any more.'

'What are you talking about?' Ayowa panicked. She backed away from Obaa Panyin. 'Nobody has hurt me,' she said. Obaa Panyin casually waved her hand at Ayowa, as if to indicate that Ayowa's surprise was only a feint. Ayowa stared in disbelief, frightened. Then, just as she thought she had espied a glint in the large bright eyes of the elderly woman, a mild shock wave ran through her. Before she could bring herself together to think and make meaning of what had been going on, she found Obaa Panyin smiling. In a strange manner, Ayowa began to feel relaxed.

'You don't believe as the others do, do you?' Obaa Panyin asked her. 'You of all people must know, not just believe. You don't think I'm insane, do you. Don't be afraid. Don't give yourself away. Just be as always. Everything will turn out well.'

It was inexplicable to her, but Ayowa felt reassured that she did not need to worry about anything anymore, and that she did not have to be afraid of anything whatsoever anymore. Her conviction was bolstered by the fact that she had indeed experienced something uncanny about Obaa Panyin. And since realizing that her being close to Obaa Panyin was like a soothing poultice on a throbbing boil, Ayowa always desired to be in close proximity to her.

Obaa Panyin never asked Ayowa prying questions. Instead, Obaa Panyin always reassured her. Frequenting Obaa Panyin's house these days allowed Ayowa to avoid her parents as much as possible. She did not know how she would explain the incident to them if they started asking questions. Would they believe her if she told them the truth? Would the town not say that she brought it on herself, enticing the men with her seductive moves at Odenchey dances? What about the taunting questions her peevish age group girls would ask: Was the pencil long or sharp enough? And the women jealous of her mother's good fortune, they would ask, not in her face and yet not out of earshot: Did she scream or chortle? Did she find adult games more appealing?

Ayowa quietly stepped through the small gate and latched it behind her. Even though the kitchen was just to her right, she waited. She did not want to go into the kitchen, at least not now. She did not want to deal with any indeterminate kitchen odours right away. Since the terrible ordeal, she had become shamefully aware that she tended to think that foul odours emanated from her, especially if she could not find their source. So she stood by the bamboo fence, the tray still on her head, and watched the flock of pigeons and mourning doves scoot around Obaa Panyin, pecking at bits of millet and sorghum and maize she tossed them. She then went down on her haunches and began talking to the birds, stroking some of them. Her back to the gates, she had not noticed Ayowa, who realized that she might end up waiting near the fence for a long time. Not to frighten the birds away, Ayowa took a wide turn to reach the open veranda where night-blooming cereus grew in the pebbles near the dwarf

16

wall. Though the buds were closed, the air was still redolent with their residual fragrance. She let down the tray on the short wall and exchanged greetings with Obaa Panyin, who stood up slowly, mumbling something about her waist. When she got her bearing, she walked slowly toward Ayowa, favouring a slight limp in her gait.

'I sometimes forget about these decrepit bones of mine,' Obaa Panyin said. She noticed the covered tray. 'And what do we have here?'

'After my visit this morning, I went on a ride in my father's car with Sanyo.' Ayowa removed the linen covering the tubers of *pona* yam, *zomi* cooking oil, and the egg-plants, among others. 'Koforidua is a good place to get you some nice provisions and gourmet stuff to prepare you some cuisine of the gods.'

'Gourmet stuff indeed,' Obaa Panyin said. 'These are wonderful, my Pearl. What will I do without you?' She picked up the bundles of Regal mushrooms and inspected them. 'I'm glad I don't have a kingdom to lose while I enjoy these.' They both laughed at the wry humour in the legend of the chief who had forgotten he was at war while he enjoyed the delicacy of mushrooms with broad-gilled-caps and long thick brittle stipes. He did not know that the special food had been sent by the concubines of his enemy-chief. When he realized what was happening, he had lost his kingdom. 'Don't shed a tear for me when you hear of my death. Thank you, my Pearl.'

'You aren't going to die any time soon. You'll bless my grandchildren on your lap. You deserve the best, Ma Nyameche. You're the true Royalty. I'm going to use them in peanut butter soup for your dinner.'

'I'll live long enough to see three of your own children, my Pearl. Your grandchildren I'm not so sure of.' Obaa Panyin laughed. 'You may as well move in here to stay with me. But how can I take Kani's "Walking Stick" away? These items must have cost you a fortune.' She turned over the plump tomatoes, avocados and egg-plants, overcome by sheer delight. 'Don't worry. I'll cook something myself. Sometimes I find the urge to cook irresistible.'

Ayowa's intention had been to pass the rest of the afternoon at Obaa Panyin's, cooking for her; but she appeared to have plans of her own. Disappointed, Ayowa remained quiet, thinking of something to say to persuade Obaa Panyin. Meanwhile, some of the birds fluttered to perch on the bamboo fence, cooing and ruffling their feathers. Others flew to the royal palms at the fringes of the town, where some pigeons kept their nide. Obaa Panyin noticed that Ayowa was sullen. She said that she hoped that she had not said anything upsetting to Ayowa. Ayowa then spoke, softly at first, as though she was afraid of her own words. 'Shall I forever be Kani's so called "support?" Ma, it can be stifling living with him sometimes.'

Obaa Panyin put her index finger on her own lips, cautioning silence and giving Ayowa an admonishing look. 'No, my Pearl, don't talk like that. Your father cares a lot about you. Even if it's to the extent of being overbearing for you sometimes, just remember that you're his world. Look, if you had come as my daughter, there are some desires you couldn't fulfill in your life. And so God, being all wise, sent you to Kani. Even so, you might as well be taken as my own daughter. Now, go home...'

'Ma!' Irritated, Ayowa snapped. But she paused quickly enough, catching herself to lower her tone. 'There's nothing home for me to do now. Maybe I can fetch your drinking water. There's very little water left in the pitcher. I couldn't fill it this morning when I came here.'

'Go ahead, if you insist.' Obaa Panyin suddenly had an expression of deep concern on her face. 'Well, now I remember. Something important you can do for me on your way to the stream. There's a satchel of food items in the kitchen. Give it to Konadu. She's been ill for some days now, and she hasn't been able to go to the farm to get food. Tell her that I'll visit her.'

Ayowa carried the tray of items to the kitchen, feeling

riumphant inside. Any moment spent away from her
parents was worth it. Her greatest fear was her father's
finding out that she was pregnant. In the kitchen, she
rranged the items in the cubicles inside a big cupboard
knocked together from packing cases. She found the pad
for her head atop the pile of firewood in a corner. Placing
the satchel of food items in a sunflower tin converted into
a container for carrying water, she carried it on her head
and went out. Far away from the Christian section of the
town came the toll of the church bell that the school used
to tell time to the town. It was three o'clock.

At that time of day, traffic along the bush path was usually
that of people returning from their farms. Ayowa did not
meet anybody on her way to the head pond of the stream
which, emerging from beneath a throng of water-canna,
cascaded over a boulder into a clear pool. It churned up
bubbles that danced above the shallow bed of white
pebbles. As some of the bubbles bobbed with widening
ripples, others drifted away and got caught among a mass
of besmirched froth held by dead snag where the pool
narrowed into a rivulet and escaped downstream under
clumps of Elephants' ear and Pickerel weed.

The air smacked of a crustacea in the early stages of
decomposition, but it did not bother Ayowa. Her fears
and worries had dissipated in the wake of her visit with
Obaa Panyin. Ayowa was now spirited. Sitting on her
upturned sunflower tin under a kola tree, she held a
bunch of mistletoe flowers at which she dealt light blows
to punctuate the lines of a fantasy game in which she was
engaged.

> When your mom touches you
> > You weep
> When your dad touches you
> > You scream
> But when your lover slaps you
> And slaps you hard on your waist beads

You giggle.
Smile for me too.

And under the impact of the last severe blow, the littl
black bud burst open, revealing the whiteness of i
insides. She chuckled at a childhood memory. It was
fight between Ayerakwa and Baah over her. The Nkonsi
school had travelled to Betomu to play Baah's school in
soccer game. Ayerakwa who was captain of the visitin
team, became involved in an argument with Baah eve
before the start of the game. It was a silly argument ove
nothing important, but it developed to centre aroun
Ayowa as each of the two boys claimed her as h
girlfriend. It came to a head with blows. Ayerakw
punched Baah in the face, and he had a bleeding nose
Even though Ayerakwa was kicked out of his team for th
game, his team won, and Ayowa was secretly delighte
that Ayerakwa won the fist fight, too. Ever since then, sh
had always looked forward with amusing curiosity to th
day of her marriage, always wondering which one of th
two men would be her husband...

Suddenly she remembered her horrible experienc
with a pang. And with her remembering it came th
realization that she was no more a virgin and that neithe
of those men would be her husband. With that know
edge, she found the insidious odour around becomin
poignant. In a strange manner, it reminded her of egg
plant stew that had too much stink fish in it, mixed wit
the sickening smell of sweaty armpits full of human hai
that had gone unwashed for days. She looked around fo
the source of the horrible smell, and she found it –
stinkhorn set by itself a little away from a not-ye
blossomed lonely stalk of a Blood lily. A stinkhorn? Th
sudden realization that she had been sitting close to it a
along without knowing it brought her the full knowledg
of its fetid odour.

She stared at the stinkhorn, its stem thicker at the bas
with small clods of broken earth against it, as though it

20

emergence had of necessity been a violent thrust from the bowels of the earth. The stipe curved just slightly in the middle to become erect. And covered with a slimy brown substance, its conical cap swarmed with bluebottles and flies in a feeding frenzy on the oozy stench. The revolting smell nauseated her, triggering a horrific thought in her mind. Had she unknowingly brought this on herself? She turned away and stepped into the underbrush behind the kola tree and vomitted.

As little children, she and her brothers, and Ayerakwa, who was living with them then, had engaged in a foolish game. She could not remember who had cooked up the idea, but they all had come to believe that the kigelia fruit had magical powers to accelerate their growth. So, any time they went to their farm on which there was a kigelia tree, the boys hit their thighs with the pendulous cylindrical fruits, believing that would give them big penises. And she, a little innocent girl, impatient with the slow natural process of maturity, rubbed the brown grey fruit against the tiny nipples on her flat chest, hoping that would grant her large breasts in due course. Had she actually hastened her own growth only to suffer such a brutal fate?

The day it happened on the Ntanoa farm, she was bent over digging up cassava from the wet soggy ground; there had been a torrential rain during the past night. Busy with her work, she did not hear anybody come behind her, but all of a sudden she found herself tossed up into the air. She fell flat on her back and over her stood – Entea? The man Kani had defended strongly when the elders of the town accused him of attempting to attack an old woman sexually in the bush? Ayowa fought back. The more she struggled and protested, the harder and more painfully he pinned her in the sod. She could not bear the body-odour from his armpits and so she held her breath. The veins on his forehead, like a three prong fork, throbbed and glinted with his sweat as he hissed through clenched teeth that he would kill her if she told anyone about it. In

the end, she gave in; her not breathing had drained her of
any energy to resist.

The tearing pain in his penetration of her was so
excruciating that it knocked her out into a world of total
darkness. She felt or heard nothing, though she strangely
remained conscious of herself in that ocean of darkness
passively watching a crystal chalice rolling on its side. And
when she came to, she was alone, pressed into the horrible
smelling soggy ground, her hair wet and matted by the
dung mud, her blouse torn, and her wraparound stripped
off. She lay flat on her back, facing the expansive blue sky
way up in the heavens, a witness to her shame and pain.
Fortunately, when she got home, there was nobody
around to see her shame...

A bluebottle circled her furiously before it went to
perch on her vomit. But as if it had no awful smell to
sustain the interest of the bluebottle, it flew away just as
suddenly, arcing down to Ayowa's left behind the kola
tree to join its kind on the slimy cone head of the
stinkhorn. Ayowa got up and went to her kerosine tin
container, picked it up and walked away from the drone
and buzz of the flies. She waded through the clear pool to
the area where it churned up bubbles. She filled her
container, and carrying it on the pad on her head, she
began her trip home to Obaa Panyin's house, wondering
if it was necessary at all for the stinkhorn to smell so foul
just to make the flies and the bluebottles happy.

# Chapter 2

High above the path, the crowns of the tall trees joined together and almost blocked out the sun. The few shafts of sunlight seeping through the foliage dappled the sparse undergrowth like a myriad of blinking eyes. When the wind moved through the tree branches, they sounded as though they were in a whispering conference. The only consistent noise around was Entea's footfalls along the path. The clumps of his cobbled boots echoed through the woods. He brushed his chin against his left shoulder to wipe off sweat on to his military fatigues, tightened his grip around the handle of his machete in his sweaty left hand and began to swing it to the beat of a refrain of a route march song.

> I didn't say goodbye to my mother
> I didn't say goodbye to my father
> And I'm going to die
> To be killed in this bloody war.

His dripping right hand lay on the barrel of the Winchester on his shoulder. About an hour's walk later, he found the height of the forest becoming shorter. Portions of it had been farmed before but left to lie fallow now. In the apparent haze engendered by the diffused shadows, the vines that had over the decades turned into wood, looked like large white serpents twisted around and choking the trees whose generosity had enabled the climbing plants to reach sunlight.

Entea started the gradual ascent of the hill. His body slightly bent forward, he shrugged on to his back his

23

stuffed haversack that kept slipping off his left shoulder. The path was turning wider and more tortuous. It had begun to follow the boundary lines of cultivated lands of cocoa, plantains and cocoyams. Rounding a bend in the path, he heard a loud warbling noise from a clump of secondary forest. He paused and listened, his eyes fixed on the upper branches of a wild pepper tree. Some leaves were trembling up there. He took a few cautious steps almost making an arc and stepped into the bush to get a better view. About the size of a pigeon, the bird flitted from branch to branch, pecking at the red berries. It then perched on a limb and began to coo. Entea slipped off his haversack, letting down the machete at the same time, his eyes still on the bird. It began a song in plaintive babble at first, then raised it to a sprightly trill interspersed with short bellowing sounds. Lowering it into croaky pauses, it turned the song warbling high again before the bird terminated it in little undulant echoes of uh-uh-uh.

Entea placed the rifle beside his stuff and brought out his slingshot from his back pocket. He quickly inspected and decided that the leather strap that adjoined the rubber slings was not big enough to carry a big missile. He put the slingshot back. He picked up the rifle and released the safety catch. The bird had begun its hop flight again, dashing from branch to branch and uttering intermittent coos. Entea stalked it around the clump of bushes, cautious not to scare it away by the muffled rustling under his boots. When he found a better angle beside a tree, he crouched, set the wooden stock against his right shoulder, and trailed the bird with the front sight.

Reverberating through the woods and down the hill, the loud report tossed the bird into the air in a scarlet spray before it began to drop, limp. It got caught in the branches, its iridescent blue wings spread out in a frozen flight. Entea leaned the rifle against the trunk close by, went for his machete and whacked his way through the clump to the berry tree. He climbed it in his boots to

24

etrieve the bird. The head had been blown off just above the nape, and the stump of a neck drained blood into the white and yellow feathers on its chest and belly. Entea cut leaves and wrapped it up, shoving it into the haversack. He carried it on his back and crossed the rifle behind his neck so that his arms were bent at the elbows and rested on it. He went along the path at a slower pace now, whistling.

When he reached an intersection of paths, he turned eastward. He began a descent, going down through the brushes to make a detour, his steps hurried by the gradient. Clouds had blocked the sun and that side of the hill was in the shadows. Large beams of sunlight shot across the sky to spread over the trees in the valley. Soon he reached a narrow track overgrown by grass on its sides. He went uphill for a short distance and came to a boulder under a large Mahogany tree. He let down his load, climbed on to the boulder and looked downhill, his hands on his hips.

The township of Nkonsia basked in the sun. The houses stood in rows like match boxes separated neatly by straight lanes. From one end to the other, and dividing the town in halves, was the highway looking like a grey ribbon, bubble-like vehicles crawling along it every few minutes. Sometimes two vehicles emerged from the opposite directions appearing as if they were heading for a collision. But they passed each other without incident. Entea smiled. Amid the surrounding bluish vegetation, Nkonsia, with rooftops of old and rusted ironsheets mixed with a few shiny corrugated aluminium ones and dark shingles or thatch, interspersed with shady trees, was like a large checkered fabric of yellow and blackish hues spread out in a field to air.

'Just like a piece of cloth. All of that will be mine. In due course, I'll wrap it around myself. People will bow their heads to greet me when they meet me in the streets,' he said. He jumped down from the boulder, carried his stuff and started downhill toward the valley.

It was late afternoon when Entea reached the outskirts of the town. The thump-thump of *foo foo* being pounded for evening meals filled the atmosphere. The weaver birds in the royal palms and the acacias at the open market place had settled into low sporadic chirps, except when occasionally the crunch and groans of a passing large truck sent them into a brief frenzy. Entea veered off the main path on to a narrow track. It ran along the northern fringes of the town past the refuse dump. Two young women, their baskets of refuse in wooden trays balanced on their heads, stepped out of the way for him. He had now slung the rifle on his shoulder and it tumbled against his side.

The track led to the start of the main east-west lane in the middle of the town. So straight were the rows of houses that even from that end, he could see a group of men on the veranda in front of Okuma's store. They were enjoying a game of checkers. As he neared them, he could hear bits of the commentaries and flatteries the excited onlookers offered on one player's good move, and the boos and suggestions on the other's disappointing play. One of the spectators looked in Entea's direction, and Entea saw him walk quickly to the other side of the onlookers. Abruptly, all the others looked briefly in Entea's direction and began to disperse. The urgency with which they broke up increased as Entea got closer to the store. Soon, only one man was left. He thrust the game board inside the store, leaped down the short steps before the veranda and darted away behind the corner of the building. Then, pulled from inside by hands Entea could not see, the double doors swung inward. The store was closed.

Entea bounced up the stone steps on to the veranda. There were two checkers on the floor, one black and the other white. He collected and put them in his pocket, then went to the doors. He tapped on them with the handle of his machete. 'Open up, Okuma. I know you're

n there. I'm tired. I don't want any argument with you
low. Give me what I need and I'll go away quietly.' Entea
aid. But there was no response.

'You don't want me to break down the doors.'

'I've closed to take stock.'

'Nonsense.' Entea kicked against the doors, but they
lid not give. Just as he retreated near the edge of the
eranda, he heard a click. He turned round. Okuma stood
)ehind the counter inside the store, drumming its top
vith his knuckles. His right arm was beside him and Entea
ould not see what it held behind the counter.

'I didn't come for a fight,' Entea said.

'Leave the rifle and the machete where you stand,'
)kuma said. Both men stared at each other. It was as if,
)etween them, the margin of triumph over the other at
hat moment depended on whoever maintained a sus-
ained stare. Then Entea blinked. He put down the rifle
ind the machete. 'Now, you can come close,' Okuma said,
ind Entea heard a machete clank against the cement
loor behind the counter.

Entea approached the counter with a casual gait, trying
o diffuse the tension with his demeanour. Bending his
)ody halfway, he looked over the small boxes of assorted
)uttons and spools of cotton thread, bars of carbolic acid
oap cut rectangularly and looking like pieces of cheese in
he counter glass. Broken in several places, the glass was
leld together by yards of Scotch tape. He then straight-
ned his body and scanned the dusty bottles of Philip's
nilk of magnesia and the bales of khaki and grey cotton
)n the shelves fixed to the back wall behind the
storekeeper.

'What do you want?' Okuma's knuckles drummed
larder.

Entea laughed, shaking his head. 'If I wanted a store to
oot it wouldn't be this pesewa-pesewa one of yours. Give
ne Tusker for men.' He inspected the wooden tray built
ike a small case of steps with assorted cigarette tins on it.
)kuma reached for the red can with a picture of an

elephant's head on it. Before he could open it. Ente
placed his hand on the top. 'I need a whole packet.'

'There's only one left. I have to ration it.'

Entea pressed Okuma's hand against the tin. The
storekeeper winced and looked up at Entea's face, on
which a sneer played. He let Okuma free, and Okuma
pulled a drawer from which he brought out a soft packet
of Tuskers. He handed it over to Entea, who brought out a
wad of bills from his fatigues. He picked out a fifty cedi
bill, then put it back together with the others. 'I'll settle
the account when I get paid by Kani,' he said. 'I don't
know when, but as you can see, I don't have any small bills
on me. I could get them changed at Kani's. Or I could
come here with him to play checkers.'

'You mention his name as if you're of the same age with
him.' Okuma frowned. 'Don't think because of its size
your moustache is older than your eyebrows.'

'You couldn't have said it any better. They're both on
the same face.' He slid the packet of Tuskers into one of
the pockets on his fatigues, then indicated the rifle. 'Kani
owns the gun. He buys the cartridges. I do the shooting.
As it's said, the child who knows how to wash his hands
well dines with prominent people. Good afternoon, Mr
Storekeeper.' He picked up the rifle and the machete and
went down the steps. Okuma just stared after him, shaking
his head in disbelief.

Short intermittent crunches approaching like the measured steps of a combat boot on gravel, made Kani turn his
head to look. On seeing Bonsra hobbling toward him on
old wooden crutches, Kani rose from his hammock chair
and offered it to his visitor. Bonsra waved Kani to keep his
seat. He then scooped up a portion of his cloth and
rubbed away the sweat on his brow. Had it not been for his
casual lean forward on the crutches, he would stand an
inch taller than Kani. Bonsra kept scratching his hair
gone grey with scrawls of yellowish brown and black kinks,
his gaze cast down to avoid Kani's direct look.

'You must rest your leg while we talk,' Kani said.

'I won't stay long, noble one,' Bonsra said.

'*You* must never address me noble.'

'You're joking.' Bonsra laughed, baring his kola-stained teeth. 'Master Darko couldn't keep your secret. I came to thank you for your noble gesture to me again. A trip in our car to the Military Hospital in Accra for me to be fitted with a rubber leg, and get me sophisticated adjustable crutches with foam cushions for my armpits? And I shouldn't address you noble? I salute you, Brave Warrior.'

'I miss you at council meetings,' Kani said. 'I'm aware of your discomfort when you venture out in that wooden piece of a limb. It's time you stepped out with more dignity.'

The two men had fought side by side in the Second World War in the jungles of faraway Burma. Much older than Kani, Bonsra made himself a big brother to Kani who was just past his twentieth birthday. Then a landmine blew off Bonsra's leg. What nobody in his platoon could ascertain was whether Bonsra had seen the device before the incident, for just before the explosion, he jumped and pushed Kani aside. Bonsra adamantly refused to talk about the incident, and even when he knew that he was returning to a broken home because of his missing leg, he insisted on keeping the experience quiet between him and Kani.

While Kani remained obliging to him, Bonsra did not demand any favours, except when he asked Kani to straighten out Entea. Kani had since then become unwittingly embroiled in the affairs of Entea. Much as they were uncomfortable for him, especially as Entea turned a young man, Kani realized that he had become inextricably tied to him because of the secret bond between Kani and Bonsra. In Entea's late teens, when he banded with the notorious Youths for the Advocacy of Vices, it was a great relief for Bonsra when Kani managed to send Entea away to join the army.

29

Bonsra took a couple of light short hops, as if seeking to steady his crutches for a balance. Having cleared his throat, he said: 'I know you tolerate Entea because of me. But his head isn't on right. If he drags your name into disrepute again, I'll shoot him dead. You know I was a marksman.'

'Don't talk like that,' Kani said.

'O, I promise you. I'll kill Entea if he disdains his affiliation with you.' Bonsra pointed to the dusking sky, then hobbled away, mumbling something about why it was said that the inside of firearm barrels was pitch dark. Kani slumped into his hammock chair, staring after Bonsra, who disappeared around the corner ahead.

Kani sat up in his hammock chair. He fetched a piece of tobacco from a small round tin, and fed his pipe. Reclining all the way back in the chair, he placed his pipe beside a large box of matches on a small table beside him. He sat at one of the outside corners of his house and so he could see as far as the ends of the two lanes intersecting where he sat. The lanes were empty; most people were inside their houses at meals. He was waiting for Benoa, his brother-in-law, who lived on the other side of town, so they would eat together. Kani usually invited him to share his evening meals.

The clucks of a hen scratching the ground nearby made Kani look skyward across the Atewa hills. The trees had turned scarlet from the shimmering orange disc of the sun hanging a few yards above the hills. 'A hen and chicks out at this time? What is the world coming to?' he asked amazed at the chicks that skittered around their mother. Tweeting, they pecked at the upturned gravel for food. The hen suddenly stopped scratching. It uttered a draw of a cluck, and the chicks, twittering, dashed and scrambled under her. It sat on them. Yet, it darted its head, cocked to one side, around in little thrusts at the sky, still clucking in drawls.

Kani looked up in time to find a hawk swooping at the hen. He scooped up a handful of gravel and threw it at the hawk. But he was too late. The mother hen took a hop-flight at the hawk. The frightened chicks scattered. Three of them ran for cover under the canvas seat of Kani's hammock chair. In a moment, the air combat of the two birds was over as the hawk fell in the agitated dust, flat on its back. Just as suddenly, it scrabbled over on its wings and flew away with mewing caws.

'My heart bless my soul.' Kani gazed after the hen. It fluttered around in circles and gathered together all of its little ones. They hurried behind her through the metal gates and went inside Kani's house. Still staring after the hen and its chicks, he did not notice the arrival of his visitor.

'A hen of prowess?' Entea placed the rifle against the wall. He opened his haversack and took out the bird he had shot earlier. 'That hawk got thrown flat on its back.'

Kani felt a pinch in his chest. His appellation was the Hawk, and he wondered if the incident with the hawk and the hen had any significant meaning for him. He contemplated the subtle smile on Entea's face, puzzled if the young man knew of the implication of what he had just said. Then, Kani drew the haversack closer and inspected its contents of smoked carcasses. 'Almost a week of hunting, and you bring me two grasscutters? How do you account for all the cartridges?'

'Your hunter's cottage has fallen into disrepair,' Entea said. 'All my provisions got soaked from the rain. On top of that the animals seem to have gone into hibernation somewhere. Sometimes, I walk all day without any sighting. And at night, only rodents come out.'

Kani sat back in his chair. He reached for his pipe and the oversized box of matches. He struck one, waited for the wood to catch, then applied the flame to the pipe's bowl. When it was lit, he waved the stick dead. After three quick puffs, he took out the pipe from his mouth. He held it at eye level while he contemplated Entea through the rising smoke. Entea, on the other hand, kept shifting his eyes and thus avoided Kani's.

'What are you trying to conceal from me?' Kani asked.

'Something you'll find handy some day.' Entea brough
out the checkers from his pocket and handed them over
Kani shoved them into his pocket immediately. Entea
chuckled as he fished for the packet of cigarettes from his
pocket. He tossed it up, caught and ripped off the
cellophane around it. Then, he tore the soft box open a
the top to one side of it. And as if trying to reassure
himself of his cordial relationship with Kani, he tapped
the other side of the top with deliberate slowness until the
filtered end of a cigarette shot up. He pulled it out and
squatted beside the small table. He picked up the box o
matches and studied it. 'Damp proof Ohio Blue tip
matches,' he read the print on it. He took out one stick
studied it before he struck it. 'The tip is brown though
Fanciful overseas product.'

'Look closely at it and you'll see it's blue-tipped,' Kan
said. Entea lit his cigarette. He opened his mouth wide
but he did not exhale. Instead, he popped out small ring
of smoke which grew larger as they floated up and
gradually diffused into the air. 'What are you waiting for
anyway?' Kani asked.

'Is my future wife Ayowa home?'

'Is your head screwed on correctly?'

'Can't you take a joke?' Entea laughed.

'I'm not your playmate.'

'We share an affinity.'

Kani studied him pensively, then he said: 'As long a
you're in town, if you want to keep working for me, ge
any silly ideas about my daughter out of your head. I ask
again: What are you waiting for?'

'Money. I need to buy more cartridges. As I said, i
rained in the hills. Most of the cartridges I had got wet and
became useless. I'll be careful how I keep them next time.

Kani gripped his pipe with his teeth. Leaning sideway
in his chair, he dipped his hand underneath the folds o
his cloth and into his pocket. He brought out his wallet
peered into it and counted some bills. He extracted three

:ed bills and extended his hand toward Entea, who looked away, scratching his head. 'I intend to be in the bush a longer time when I go into the forest next week,' he said. 'And you know our Ghana; prices go up each day.'

Kani put the money back in his wallet and stood up. A head and shoulder taller, he appeared twice the size of Entea. Kani swathed his twelve yard piece of cloth around him properly and lifted the haversack by its strap.

'I'll take it inside the house for you,' Entea volunteered.

'I never want you inside my house,' Kani said coldly. He dragged the load behind him through the wide open gates into the house. His wife was inside the kitchen chattering and laughing with her children. Kani left the load at the kitchen door and spoke through the door, saying there was something out there for Ofosuaa.

All whitewashed, his house was a majestic cluster of buildings with a patio. Each wing had three rooms. These he had shared among his family. Except the east wing which comprised the kitchen and the garage, the north and south wings each had a cloistral veranda barely separated from the patio by balustrade-railings. Facing this magnificent yard was the west wing, an open porch enclosed by a parlour and a sleeping-room. Exclusively for Kani's use, it was much higher in elevation because of the partial underground water tank hidden by a seven-step-stoop to the porch. Two lean columns flanked the topmost step to hold the entablature.

Three steps up the stoop, Kani halted. He looked up at the large lunette of a carved hawk in the tympanum. As he stared, the incident with the hawk and the hen earlier on came to haunt him strongly. To him, the hawk symbolized his soul, his manhood, his personality, his worth. Had he been thrown flat on his back by a mere hen? He felt something give way in his groin area, and pressure at his lower part intensified. He rushed down the steps and crossed the patio to the opposite side of the gates. He went through a small door, quickly stepped over a cement stool on which he and his wife sat to wash themselves, and entered a much smaller room. The floor boards echoed under the pressure of his steps. Raising his cloth and quickly lowering his loose shorts, he removed the cover of a hole in a box mounted on the floor and sat down on it. Humid and acrid air rose to caress his bottom. He shut his eyes tight, straining himself to push. After so much effort only a small hard turd came out, but it hit the bottom of the pit with the plonk of a heavy object.

He cleaned himself and went and washed his hands at the bathing place. He felt lethargic suddenly and he trudged up the stoop, not looking up at the tympanum this time. A small table stood in the middle of the open porch with his dinner set on it and covered with white poplin: two short stools stood on its opposite sides. He walked past them, oblivious to the small transistor radio blabbering some *Asafo* songs in low tone. Inside his room he went past the dresser to the highboy set against the wall on the other side of the room. He pulled out a middle drawer and fished for a wad of red bills underneath some cloth bound folders. He took out ten and returned the rest to the drawer. He then went outside and gave five of the red bills to Entea, who flipped through them and said 'Five hundred cedis. Good money.'

'Go to my farm at Cattle-town tomorrow. Cut down all the banana trees . I intend to plant that plot with oil palm seedlings.' Kani looked along the lane where a man was coming in the distance. 'That looks like Brother-of-man.'

'Yes, it's Benoa all right.' Entea chortled at the man approaching. His faded cloth appeared too small for his age, and as though any swing of his arm would cause the cloth to rip, his arms lay almost stiff by his sides to keep the cloth in place. Entea dropped his cigarette and stepped on the stub with the heel of his boot. He said 'I better leave before Benoa gets here. Ever since I came to town on leave, he's been stalking me. He thinks he can catch me on the wrong foot, then he can use the spittle from my mouth to wash his wounds from his impoverishment.'

'No wonder people say bad things about you.' Kani said. You don't think well of others. Use the rest of the money wisely. And don't come to me again with two grasscutters and tall tales of rain and hibernation. I was born long before you were even conceived as an idea by your parents. Good evening.'

Entea left before Benoa got there. When he greeted Kani, he just nodded his head in response, stroking his clean shaven chin, his eyes half closed and cast midway on the sky. 'I hope I haven't starved you,' Benoa said.

'Not really.' Kani collected his pipe and the box of matches from the table. 'Something that happened here a little while ago has drained me of all energy.' He recounted the incident of the hawk and the hen to Benoa. The coincidences are just overwhelming. Why should the hen and its chicks be out this time of day? And why did I help the hen against the hawk, my own soul mate? I can't for any reason understand why the hawk had to be defeated right before me.'

'Rest your soul, Brother-of-man.' Benoa laughed, coughing and making a noise like a cracked clay pot in his chest. 'I know you well. If you had told me you acted any differently, I wouldn't have believed you. Could you ever sit by and watch a chick snatched away in talons? Do you remember when we were teenagers, the missile from your slingshot, aimed at a bunch of oranges, accidentally hit a goldfinch? You buried it and planted a dracaena palm over it. That was the first and only bird you ever killed, and that day you didn't eat,' Benoa said, and Kani looked at him with a bland expression on his face. Benoa continued: 'Why do I still remember it? I do because that dracaena turned into a grove of the palm. I cut the small ones to repair the fence around my house.'

'Hawks prowling at sunset for chicks out at sunset?'

'If I hadn't been late in coming, you wouldn't have been here to see all that. You're thinking too much about something quite unnecessary,' Benoa said.

'I hope so. Let's go in before I lose all my appetite.'

Kani stood up, a giant of a man beside his skinny and medium height brother-in-law. And that was how far the differences between them went. They could be on opposing sides of an issue and argue it out in the strongest of terms. However, they never allowed such tension or disagreement to affect the amity in their relationship.

Between them, there was nothing more important than the cordiality between them and their families. There never existed the slightest hint of ill-will for or antagonism against the other. And there was a tacit recognition of each others pride: neither made unwarranted intrusions upon the others's privacy; even when Kani knew that Benoa was in dire need of cash, Kani never proffered it directly to his brother-in-law. Kani always went through Ofosuaa, his wife. And whenever Benoa thought he had had a bountiful harvest of plantains and so sent some to Kani's family as token, Benoa never mentioned it to Kani. And it had been like that for them since their childhood days. Their wives spoke of them as being spiritual twins – in other words, they had been twins in the world of spirits beyond. And as if the two men were confirming that, they addressed each other as Brother-of-man.

They went inside the house. Kani paused near the kitchen door and gave an instruction to one of his sons to go outside and bring inside the hammock chair and the small table. He then joined Benoa in the open porch. They sat on the small stools at either side of the table and washed their hands in a white enamel bowl of water. When they started eating, the radio was broadcasting the world news in the Ghanaian languages.

After supper, Kani repaired to his chair now set against the back wall of the open porch. Benoa sat in a Windsor chair near the parlour. One of Kani's sons came and cleared the bowls, the table and the stools from the porch. An aladdin on a tall stand lit the porch and the patio. From a room in the south wing came the low voices of children, some from the neighbourhood, learning mathe-matical tables under the direction of Misa, currently Kani's eldest son in the house. The radio, on a ledge in a corner of the open porch, was broadcasting 'Farmers' Forum'. Kani and Benoa sat silently chewing sticks and listening. They both nodded their heads frequently in agreement to points made in the discussion as to why the country could not produce enough food to feed the population, in spite of abundant fertile land.

'I made that point a long time ago,' Kani said at the end of the programme, standing up and going to the radio. He turned it off and went back to his seat. 'My children came home one afternoon from school, singing 'We'll study hard because there's dignity in being clerks.' I forbade them to sing that song ever again under my roof. Instead of emphasizing farming and fishing, the schools brainwashed our young people for the cities. Most of us who produced food years ago are now too old for any hard work. Some of us are dead.'

Benoa added: 'The younger generation who should have replaced us are in the cities, sitting in something they call air-conditions in offices. No work on Saturdays. Just sitting in bars and quaffing beer and nursing potbellies. As if the mattresses they sleep on are stuffed with millions. I doubt if they get the beer at reasonable prices at all.'

'During my travelling days, people left food beside the roads. Just for passing strangers to have something to eat on their way,' Kani said.

'Those days are gone forever.' Benoa shook his head sadly. 'These are the modern days of greed and confusion and cheating. I feel horrible any time I remember that even a hundred cedis cannot feed my family for a week.' He rose from the Windsor chair and carefully swathed his cloth around him. 'I must go now,' he said to Kani. Having walked close to the stoop, he hollered in the direction of Ofosuaa's room an old jolly saying, 'Dear sister, if you look for a threepence and don't find it, you must know it's gone into making change.'

Kani laughed. He knew that expression was a signal of 'help' from Benoa to his sister; any time he used it just before he parted, Ofosuaa later went to see him, using a visit to her sister-in-law as excuse. 'I know all your moves,' Kani said. 'From before you initiate them, I know where you're going to place your foot. You never can escape my traps.'

Benoa turned round. He scratched the back of his hand, then with a smile, said: 'Would you like a game tomorrow? I've beaten you three times in a row. The checkerboard will testify to it if you really can see through my moves. What do you say?'

'A good sport has never refused an honest challenge,' Kani said and stood up. He walked with Benoa to the edge of the stoop. 'When the tension in a spring is released, the rod always swings back to its original position. Sleep well Brother-of-man.'

'Good dreams to you, Brother-of-man.' As Benoa walked past the aladdin, his shadow, long and enlarged near his head, swung from behind him across the patio and the white walls to his right to be ahead of him.

# Chapter 3

From the streets the wind carried fragments of a merry song to the open porch. Kani stood gazing at the aladdin as his mind drifted from the recitation of the boys to the singing girls in the lanes. Like a wave, a leading voice rose above the others. He knew that soprano belonged to his one and only Ayowa. The toil was worth it, he thought, and smiled at the white vapour-like radiance of the aladdin which, though soft, brightened the patio and accented the whitewashed concrete walls of the house.

For seven years after their marriage, Kani and Ofosuaa could not have babies. Kani believed that the problem could be with either of them, and so he took her along on some of his travels in search of help. They went to Atebubu and Yeji, Salaga and Tamale, Lome and Abidjan, Illorin and Lagos, Axim and Abandzi, but they did not find the herb that could make them have babies. After years of fruitless search, they found the solution in their own backyard. An Italian doctor who had been posted to the Kibi hospital did what he called a simple surgical procedure on Ofosuaa. Then the babies started coming, three boys in a row. Then Kani realized that he wanted girls, too. And so, once again, he and Ofosuaa tried several potions and concoctions to no avail. Then, once again, they found the solution in their own backyard.

This time, it was Obaa Panyin. She had come home to settle after not being able to hold her job as a teacher. As it was explained, she was being troubled by ghosts and spirits that wanted to take over her body. A few months into her having returned to Nkonsia, she became stable.

And that was when she asked Kani to change the position of his bed if he wanted a daughter. At first, Kani would not do it; like everyone else, he thought Obaa Panyin had lost her mind. He gave in only after relentless pressure from her: he could no more withstand Obaa Panyin's persistent visits to his house every morning to inquire whether Kani had changed the position of his bed. Ofosuaa became pregnant soon after. And exactly nine months to the day she gave birth to a beautiful baby girl seventeen years ago.

The baby was so beautiful that Kani named her Ayowa – the bridal clay bowl – to reflect her lovely features. For him, there was nothing more eloquent of her beauty than a well-moulded and smooth bridal clay bowl, baked and polished with palm kernels by expert fingers so that on its own, the bowl shone with excellence.

Kani's eyes strayed from the aladdin to a portion of the kitchen wing and lingered there awhile. Were it not for that small area, all the walls of his house would appear stainless. That part had blackened from a pair of tripod clay hearths set against the wall. One morning four years ago, he had returned home from the palm-wine-drinking shanty to find his wife plastering red clay over the white walls.

'My heart save the soul of the Mighty Hawk!' He slapped his chest. 'What madness is this? What is going on here? What are you doing to my white walls? What has got into you?'

'Your walls?' Ofosuaa asked. 'Is the house for only you? Well, I don't have to be kept within four walls anytime I cook. I'll need fresh air sometimes. I insist on a spare cooking place outside the kitchen.'

'I'll buy you one of those things they call gas cookers – '

'So I blow up myself? Forget it, nobleman.'

Kani swallowed audibly as he watched her hands knead more clay, roll it into a ball that went to finish raising the third mound of the hearth. 'It isn't proper to have a fireplace outside to deface these beautiful white walls. What is wrong with you, my woman?'

'Progress for me is living my traditional lifestyle in a refined manner,' Ofosuaa said. She washed her hands in a bucket of water beside her. 'There's nothing shameful about our having a hearth outside the kitchen in this house. Until we came up with this house, I cooked most of our meals on similar fireplaces outside. End of discussion, nobleman.'

And so she had it her way. And the result was that perpetual black smudge which she made worse each morning with more polish of red ochre. In spite of all the whitewashing done twice each year, the fireplace remained an eyesore to him. As he listened to Ayowa's voice in the lanes, he swore silently to protect her with all his resources, unlike the wall about which he had given in so easily to Ofosuaa. Engrossed in thought about his daughter, he had not noticed his wife watching him from her doorway.

'My man,' she said, 'you usually aren't this pensive.'

Kani turned to her briefly, then began to pace to his seat. But his shadow, thrown on the back wall of the open porch, rose menacingly to meet him. He turned round again and almost bumped into Ofosuaa, who had climbed the steps to the open porch. Kani started, then he lowered his eyes. His wife stood an inch shorter than he. Her face was round and broad like his, with a straight nose set above her broad lips. Many people in the town said she even looked more like him than their children did, and that the similarities between them were as a result of their having been so close together for over thirty years. The striking difference between them, however, was that Ofosuaa was fair in complexion while Kani was jet black.

'What is on your mind?' Ofosuaa asked.

'My daughter.' He ran his hand over his bald head. 'It's always darkest before dawn. There's a little fear in me. The devil has been known to be alert all the time, waiting to pounce at the moment on unsuspecting innocent victors.'

'You don't think Owiredu will change his mind now?'

He shook his head. 'Just that temptations abound during the pitch-dark hour before dawn.' He sank into his hammock chair while she scooted one of the Windsor chairs closer to him and sat in it. She spoke softly and assuredly.

'If our tutelar spirits have protected her until now,' she said, 'I don't believe that they'll leave her to be destroyed by our foes. Yes, they've brought us this far not to disappoint.'

Kani looked askance at her. He picked up his pipe from a gateleg table and lit it. As he smoked, he looked outside the open porch. 'Akata Kojo-the-traveller was overtaken by darkness one day,' he also said in a low tone, as if to no-one in particular. 'He prayed to his gods and went to sleep, his back against a tree. When he woke up, he found his leg was being swallowed by a python.'

'Don't you ever have faith in anything?' Ofosuaa stood up and put a cotton shawl over her *kaba* blouse. 'Well, I promised Buaa a visit. I must go now.'

'Tell Benoa that if I beat him at checkers tomorrow, he'll buy me palm wine.' He blew out a cloud of smoke. Ofosuaa chuckled and went down the stoop.

Because of its elevation, Kani commanded a good view of the courtyard from the open porch, and long after his wife had left, he stared at the fireplace against the kitchen wall. A soup crock still sat on the hearth. He knew that it had not been cleaned after supper, to his chagrin, but that was how Ofosuaa liked it. They had had an argument over that too a few months after the house was built. He returned home from a meeting at the chief's to find that all the cooking utensils had not been washed. He demanded the reasons. Ofosuaa, who was plaiting Ayowa's hair in the open porch, calmly explained herself.

'The spirits of our ancestors must have something to eat when they come home to visit at night.'

'Absolute nonsense!' Kani blurted.

'You aren't insulting the spirits of the land, are you?' Ofosuaa looked at him hard. 'To whom shall we turn for rain and abundant crops, good health and wealth, if the spirits above desert us because we're abandoning them? People keep saying it's becoming tough living in the world now. They forget they arbitrarily change their relations with their Maker and His agents. They do what they aren't supposed to do, and they don't do what they're supposed to do.'

Kani swallowed hard, then ranted on: 'I'm tired of all this nonsense of traditional this, traditional that. Diseases are also a tradition when you breed germs. Those unwashed pots will breed germs. They'll make my children sick – '

'Remember, your own mother lived to the ripe age of eighty-six. She never washed her bowls after cooking in the evenings. And she never heard all your sweet talk about hygiene, either.' Ofosuaa did not even deign him a glance, but kept braiding Ayowa's hair. 'I'll wash the pots in hot water with lots of soap in the morning. And you don't have to shout when we're talking. After all, I'm only a couple of feet away from you.'

'I'm the head of this house, and no ghosts,' Kani thundered, stomping the floor with his foot. 'Listen to the radio. See how the world is changing. Stop clinging to stupid superstitions that don't generate any wealth.'

'Calm down, my man,' Ofosuaa said in a low voice that even astounded Kani. 'Not everything said on that magic box is the truth. You don't have to believe everything that comes out of it. You're indeed the head of this house, but without me, you alone couldn't have achieved it all. Let's have a compromise. I'll wash all my cooking utensils every evening, except the soup crock.'

Kani walked away to his room.

Still looking at the soup crock on the fireplace, he struck a match and lit his pipe which had gone dead. Through the smoke haze in the porch, he saw Benoa's son Opia coming up the stoop. Except Saturday when Opia came for story telling-sessions in the evenings, Kani usually expected him once each day in his house. Opia was the carrier of Benoa's good morning greetings. In reality, however, his message was an indication that Benoa had espied the palm wine tapper's return from the bush as he passed by Benoa's house and so Kani was to meet his brother-in-law at the drinking shanty. To reciprocate Benoa's gesture in the mornings, Kani sent one of his sons to give his good evening greetings to Benoa. On seeing Kani's son, Benoa understood it that Kani wanted to share his supper with him.

Opia saluted and held his hands behind him. 'Noble Kani, my father asks that you come to the chief's house immediately. He said there's a meeting in progress.'

Kani placed his pipe on the gateleg table. Why would the chief not send for him directly? And why would the elders start a meeting when he was not present? 'Did your father say anything else?' he asked Opia.

'Just that he would see you at the chief's.'

Kani rose to his feet. Opia stepped back from the huge frame towering over him. Looking into the big man's face, Opia asked 'Can I go now to greet my cousins?'

Kani nodded his head and wrapped his cloth around him. His body bent a little in the doorway, he went inside his sleeping room and took an electric torch. When he came out into the open porch he heard the yells of his children in their room hailing 'Opia, master-storyteller.' Kani smiled as he walked out of the house. He had not known that Opia was such an excellent narrator of tales until the boy told the story of the Raven and the Vulture and won the story-telling competition the town organized as part of the festivities marking the opening of Kani's house.

'Long, long ago,' Opia had narrated, 'Raven lost his mother from protracted illness. In her life-time, she had been very popular and so many friends and relatives turned up for a vigil in her honour. The hut in which she lay in state had several low burning clay oil lamps. They lit up the sombre atmosphere as the heartbroken mourners sat around the raffia bed on which the deceased lay.

'While the silent mourners believed that it was a relief for Mother Raven because she had suffered too much pain, her son did not think so. He cried so loudly that some of the mourners forced him out of the hut. Outside, he shrieked and struck pans together, causing commotion and screaming "I'll go with you, mother. With whom did you leave me?"

'Much as those inside the hut thought that sonny Raven was making too much out of his mother's death, they sympathized with him; that was the worst thing to happen to any one so young, they said. Vulture, who incidentally was anxiously waiting for the burial ceremony, went over to Raven and consoled him. "My friend," he told the bereaved, "you've got to muster courage and face life now that your mom is gone."

'Raven thanked Vulture and stopped crying.

'Some time after the corpse had been interred, Vulture flew to the burial ground. From the air he saw some activity going on near the grave. He flew closer to check it out. He did not believe what he saw at first, so he perched on a tree to have a critical look. It was Raven down there all right and busily pecking at his own mother's body. Vulture joined him to eat it in silence.

'Back at the hut, Raven began to cry again. This time, he flapped his wings about, slapping some of the mourners in the process. But none among them complained openly; they all knew that sonny Raven was in mourning. Then Vulture accidentally got slapped in the face. He became infuriated and snapped in Raven's face: "You ought to be quiet when you're asked to. After all, everyone here is aware that your mother is indeed dead!" And Raven ceased his disturbance at once.'

As Opia had concluded the story, Vulture had spoken to Raven in plain language, but Raven understood him proverbially. That intimation appealed to Kani and Benoa very much; between them, when one winked, the other knew what it implied. They began addressing each other 'Brother-of-man' from the day they heard Opia's story.

A cool breeze blew against Kani's face as he went along the lane toward the chief's house. The town was relatively quiet; the singing girls had taken a short break, and so he could hear low rumbles of thunder in the east. He looked up toward the Ajapomaa hills. The glow of the rising half moon betrayed outlines of dark clouds scudding toward the hills. It might rain, he thought. It always did when clouds gathered in the east.

Ahead of him behind a building, he saw two figures seemingly in a struggle. He thought of turning on his electric torch, but he heard an amorous soft protest of 'not here, please.' A ticklish laughter followed. Kani chortled. He turned into the next lane, whispering to himself what the chief of the town had told him when Kani presented the chief with the layout of the then to be established new township: 'Nkonsia won't conceal any bad deed.'

Because of his experience fighting in Burma with the West African Frontier forces and his extensive travels through the country and West Africa, trading even before he turned twenty-five years old, Kani had been given the privilege to come up with a plan for the new township. The chief wanted a new Nkonsia reflective of modern times. Kani consulted his friend the King of the Abuakwa State. The king had studied in England and Canada before. He therefore drew up a plan similar to that of some small towns he had seen overseas and gave it to Kani. The result was Nkonsia as it stood today – buildings in such straight rows that if someone were standing at the end of one lane, that person could see where the lane ended.

The original plan even had marked on it where electric light poles and public standing pipes would be – just in case sometime in the future, the town could afford these indices of civilization. But as straight as the lanes were, they had never been paved with bitumen. The drains on their sides were not trimmed with cement. And any time it rained, gullies formed and gushed away with the blood of the earth.

Kani flashed on his electric torch to guide his step over a wide gully to the broader east-west lane central to the town. When he reached the chief's place, two lanterns in the windows of the cloister-like veranda and low mutterings indicated to him that the meeting was inside. He walked past a group of onlookers in the entranceway and along the inner walls. He found Benoa and seven other elders sitting quietly. Their faces fallen as if they were in some funereal conference, they all had propped up their chins in their hands. The chief sat in a pillowed armchair. His spokesman stood beside him before the elders. Odikuro-the-chief raised his head and beckoned Kani to sit by him in a cane wing-chair.

'Your looks are disturbing,' Kani said. 'Has His Paramount Highness stepped at the heels of his ancestors?'

'No, but it's equally serious.' He sat up. 'Will Benoa tell us again what he heard in the streets this evening?'

Benoa smothered an almost burnt out Durbar cigarette under the cut-out-tyre-sole of his sandal and stood up. He drew up his cloth, but too small for his size, it would not stay in place. It kept slipping down his shoulder to reveal his rib bones that could be counted even in the low light. The small crowd began muttering. Amid twirling trails of smoke from his nostrils, he cleared his throat several times to quieten the crowd. He then gestured with his head at Kani. 'After I left you this evening, I met Entea.' He paused to let the murmurs that had risen again die, untying the threadbare satin headkerchief around his neck and dabbing his greying hairline blackened with soot from a lantern chimney.

'Silence.' The chief's spokesman yelled as the small crowd talked more loudly with chuckles. 'We're at the chief's house. And it's an important matter we have going here. Any one who can't stay quiet should go away. We have to hear Benoa.'

'Thank you,' Benoa said, an enigmatic smile on his lean

face. 'Entea had a bottle of *akpeteshie* which he was drinking in swigs. He was also eating some roasted bird – obviously someone's chicken that he had stolen – ' The chattering among the onlookers rose again. Some of the elders were talking in low tones among themselves. Baffled, Benoa tied his headkerchief around his neck, a strategy he had devised to hide his collarbones.

'Go to the point,' the chief's spokesman said.

'Entea was bragging before some young men. He said Nkonsia was like a clay bowl in his hands and that he could drop and break it at will.' Benoa nodded his head to emphasize the gravity of the charge about which the other elders were expressing ohs and uhms and arghs. Some young men broke out laughing. Benoa turned to them. 'I know some of you here heard him. Yet you don't want to step forward as witnesses.'

The young men booed. Benoa bit his lower lip in chagrin, then yelled in impotent rage: 'I won't let Entea destroy this town.' He sat down.

'And is it such a statement that has turned you all into mourning women?' Kani asked. All the elders sighed, an expression of shock on their faces. In this land, it was considered an insult to relate men to women in such an effeminate manner; it was actually like emasculating them. 'And Nana Odikuro, what do you say about that?'

'Coming events cast their shadows ahead of them, nobleman. That may be trite, but it's true,' Odikuro-the-chief said.

'O, no. Not again.' Kani sat back in thought, his *dumas* cloth vibrating with impact as he tapped his feet. He believed that the elders wanted to frame Entea for punishment. 'That young man has suffered too much at your hands. I hope you haven't been sniffing out for malefactors because of your insatiable appetite for mutton and schnapps.'

'More. More of those.' Some of the onlookers laughed.

A few weeks ago, just after Entea came on his leave, the elders fined him a fat unblemished sheep and three bottles of schnapps after they accused him of attempting to sexually assault an old woman on her farm, though the facts of the matter were never established. Believing that it was a miscarriage of justice, Kani stayed away from the sheep-slaughtering ceremony and the libation poured to placate the wounded spirit of the old woman. Moreover, as he protested, the brunt of the punishment fell on Entea's father who provided all the items of appeasement because his son said that he did not have any money. Nobody knew that Kani had loaned the poor old man the money.

It was after that incident that Kani called Entea and had a chat with him. Even though the elders had handled the case with their ears slanted, Kani felt sincerely concerned that his name was being smutched by Entea; it was only out of a strong sense of pride that he had deliberately refused to agree with the elders that his defence of Entea was a misplaced alignment. How could Kani ever let them in on Bonsra's saving his life in the jungles of Burma?

And so he sought one more time to steer Entea away from the path of notoriety to which he seemed to have been bewitched. Kani told him about his philosophy in life and what he had gained out of military life. To Kani, it was as if his dangerous and painful stint in Burma had scorched away thick layers of dross that had covered sterling qualities of courage, love and integrity in his personality, which by baring them, made his soul find profound pleasures in being in love with life. The irony of it was that for him, his war experiences deepened his appreciation for genuine human endeavours and sharp- ened his respect for human life. He shared affinity with everyone else. Every other person's joy was his joy. Every other person's sorrow was his sorrow. And in the wake of the military coup, it saddened him whenever he heard rumours of atrocities by soldiers. He did not want Entea to be like the greedy souls obsessed with the rabid acquisi- tion of riches by cheating and arbitrary seizure, but he must let the military make a true man out of him. Entea's goal in life was to do his best to bring happiness to other people.

Kani loaned him his rifle to use in hunting for two reasons. The first was that his rifle had been lying idle for years gathering dust in his attic. He had given up hunting because, as he put it, he was past the years of youthful bravado. The second was to keep Entea busy and so out of trouble. And now, this problem with a mere off-guard comment? The bias nature with which the elders had dealt with the old woman's case gave Kani the idea that the elders were definitely out to get Entea.

'Respectable elders,' Kani bellowed. 'I don't mean to sound as if I'm on the side of Entea. But can you, Brother-of-man, provide just one witness who heard Entea make that threat?'

'I blame you for his crazy actions, Brother-of-man.' Benoa looked at Kani. 'If he drinks and makes a fool of himself in the streets, we all know the sort of person he is. But after you gave him your gun, he began to assume he was a god. How can we take it as an empty threat when he claims this town is a clay bowl in his hands and he can break it at will?'

'Nobleman,' the chief's spokesman said, 'I heard a gunshot in town today. When I investigated it, I found that it was Entea firing shots into the air. For no apparent reason.'

'Is that why you want him punished?' Kani asked.

'No. As it's said, what goes up comes down. In other words, when such a powerful instrument becomes a plaything in the wrong hands, that can be cause for great concern.' The spokesman looked at the chief for approval, then continued: 'Mere whistling can create a tune unknown before. And a windstorm has always preceded a rainstorm. If we don't reprimand him now that he's firing shots into the air and making dangerous statements, he'll become complacent. By the time we know what is happening, he's firing shots through our windows. I remember the first insolence of Entea when he

50

ame home on his so-called leave. That was even before
ou gave him your rifle. He said he had charms to attract
ur wives into bed with him – '

'I suppose this meeting is for matured men?' Kani said,
little edge to his deep voice. 'Next time you'll say he's
aken away your manhood and hidden it under his bed.
lders, are we here because one of us is jealous of a young
nan's sexual prowess or what?' The young onlookers
urst into wild ribald laughter. Some whistled and
creamed obscene remarks.

'Quiet out there,' the chief's spokesman shouted. In a
nuch lower tone, he said: 'Nobleman, the chief and his
lders will pretend they didn't hear you on that one.'

'I insist Entea recant that statement about the clay bowl
efore us.' Benoa thumped his knee with his fisted hand.
We must ask him to apologize to the townsfolk. For all
he years he's been away, this town has been at peace. He
rrives here within a month and little children become
amiliar with awful vocabulary and terms not heard
poken in public before. He's a soldier and so what? Our
oil and taxes feed and clothe him. We don't buy him
uns and ammo to turn them on us. He's supposed to
rotect our way of life, not to intimidate us.'

'Excuse me, elders.' Kani stood up. 'I have things to do.
'm tired of people expressing their jealousies at the
uccess of others. I can't sit here listening to the whines of
vomen.'

'Brother-of-man, you know none of us here is a woman.'
Benoa nodded a finger at him. 'Be careful. You may
ecome the tree to which the vine we call the-devil's-beard
vill attach itself to for support to reach sunlight.'

Kani stopped in the exit-way of the cloister-like veranda,
iis head almost touching the overhead. He cast a wary
lance at Benoa. 'If you men are famished, you need
owerful rifles for bullock meat,' he said. 'Entea's noose
loes ensnare only rodents. I had hoped that Benoa in
articular would be understanding. Entea belongs to your
lan – the Asona.' He left the meeting.

Outside, he heard that the girls had resumed their singing in the area of the 'tree of threepences'. Kani smiled at the evolution the tulip tree had gone through in the minds of children. The pioneers of the town had let the tree stand to serve as the part of the town where all games and traditional festivities would take place for that was where the two main lanes in the town intersected. As the tree grew taller, the men truncated it. The stem thus grew fresh low branches all round it. On moonlit nights girls and boys played under it. Children dubbed it 'tree of threepences' because they thought it bore fruits of money; they did not know that the coins they found under the tree in the mornings were those the dancers did not see to pick up as admirers threw money into the open space or stuck them on their favourite's forehead. The tree was old now, and there had been a gradual dieback of the branches.

As Kani headed in its direction, he could hear the roll of thunder even above the frenzy of *Odenchey* music and dance. He looked up. The moon, hidden behind dark clouds, had etched an outline in murky yellow of a huge lion with something like a mouse in its paws. As the cloud swelled and twisted slowly, the lion grew mean and kept crushing the tiny mouse until there was no feline or rodent, but pouches of rain clouds with reddened gibbous ends pointing earthward.

All at once, the music in the streets stopped. In the silence that followed, some empty feeling settled on Kani and in a strange manner, he felt as though he did not belong where he was. It was as if he had never been part of the town before. And he wondered why he was there at all. It seemed to him that was not his place at all, and that he was lost. As profound as the experience was, it might have lasted for only a second. Kani looked around to assure himself of his surroundings. He heard the throbs of his heartbeat in his temples and in his ears. He felt confused that he should find himself a stranger in his own town, his own birthplace. For a moment, he thought he would go

ack to the meeting of the elders. He, however, decided
gainst it; he was the man who never went back on his
ord. He was the warrior who, when as a young man at
wenty, braved bullets in the jungles of Burma and came
ut unscathed. He was afraid of nothing. And nobody
nder these skies could hurt him. He was the man among
ien, the personality for whom people stepped out of the
ay.

Then, suddenly, a mellifluous voice so high and clear
iat it even trilled a note of sadness, rent the air from the
rea of the 'tree of threepences'. A loud applause greeted
and ceased just in time for the voice to warble again.
:hills mixed with tickles of delight sent goose flesh over
.ani's arms as he listened to the solo re-start of his
aughter's soprano voice.

> Wanderer, o wanderer
> Sojourner, o sojourner
> Where are you heading
> When the clouds seem to come down
> And you don't want to turn your back?

)ther voices joined her in a lively song to rhythmic hand
laps and the throbs of bongos and tom-tom. Yet the high-
owered echoing voice of Ayowa endured, weaving a
emulous lead around the hand-claps and in-between the
irobs of the drums.

The whole intersection was crowded with people when
.ani got there. The night hawkers had abandoned their
read and buff loaves and rice-porridge, and joined the
iass of spectators under the 'tree of threepences'. Some
f those behind the crowd were craning their necks or
tanding on their toes to catch glimpses of the activity.
)thers, with their lanterns, had climbed into the lower
horl branches of the squatting tulip tree. The dust that
ose from the dancers' feet had absorbed the glow of the
imps and hung in the air like a spray of gold dust from
ie tree. Kani could have watched the dancing over the
eads of the crowd, but he jostled his way through the

53

throng to the inner fringe. His arms folded across hi
chest, he beamed at the proceedings. He looked from
Ayowa in the centre of the open space to the nubile girl
including Mansa, Benoa's daughter, in a semicircle. The
picked up the lines of the song after Ayowa as in a
roundelay. Weaving intricate steps with their nimble feet
the girls clapped, then bowed their bodies and slapped
their elbows in rhythm to the throbs of the tom-tom and
the bongos between the drummers' knees. They sat or
short stools in a squat-like position, their bodies streaming
with sweat. In the flush of the lanterns, they both looked
as if red oil had been applied to their skins. Their hand
worked the tympanums briskly. Kani detected the cue
from the bongo drummer to change the beat of the song
and Ayowa's high vibrating voice started a solo refrain
again.

She stood akimbo, he body bent backward a little. The
lanterns in the tree lit her face as she looked up at th
clouded sky and restarted the solo refrain. In the same
span of time, she did the half-turn dance, wriggling he
waist so vigorously that even above her voice, the crowd
heard the jingle of the guinea beads around her waist.

'Adjoa-a-a!' A young man said in the crowd.

The people clapped their hands in appreciation.

Some young men in the tree whistled catcalls.

The women spectators sighed.

The older women turned their faces away, looking
down as though in search of something in the dust. Kani
felt nostalgic, too. His daughter's performance had
flooded him with past memories, when he had returned
home from a journey to find Ofosuaa, then unmarried
doing a similar dance at the same place, singing about
him. He married her three months later.

As was the custom, Ayowa had to face the four points o
the town and sing. She raised her hands as if asking the
skies for blessings. She then turned in the direction of he
father. On seeing him, her voice went dead and she
dropped her hands then walked around listlessly for a few

moments. Murmurs rose among the crowd. Eyes darted at Kani and moved away slowly, as though his mere presence was an awful intrusion upon the collusion of the youth.

Ayowa raised her hands and began to sing again, but the magic was gone from her voice. Desperate, she threw her hands in the air. Her cousin, Mansa, ran to her. The mutterings in the crowd grew louder. Somebody said something above the murmurs about a nobleman who would not stay away from young women's games. Kani looked around, embarrassed. It was atrocious for anyone to imagine that he was there looking for a mistress. In spite of his wealth, he had never sought for a mistress beside his wife, at least not at Nkonsia. Unlike many rich men whose reputation preceded them by their countless concubines, Kani did not like to have more than one wife at a time. He believed that men with two or more wives, and mistresses into the bargain were liars; they told lies to each of their women when it came to her turn to share his bed.

He walked away from the 'tree of threepences' and the dance and the music, but he could still hear the song of youth in the background even long after he had left the scene. Only that his daughter's captivating voice was missing. Thunder rolled. He looked up at the sky. 'The eyes of the clouds are down,' he said to himself. 'The rain may come to end the dancing in the streets presently.' He flashed on his electric torch and hurried home to his wife.

# Chapter 4

When Kani reached home, he found that Ofosuaa ha
already returned from her visit to Buaa. Smiling, h
withdrew into the partially dark inside-corner near th
gate, thinking it a good opportunity to rehash a game h
used to play with his wife. For seven years after they wer
married, and before the babies started coming, Kani an
Ofosuaa played a type of hide-and-seek in their bedroom
the winner made love to the loser.

Near the kitchen entrance, Ofosuaa had a lantern. Sh
had placed it in the doorway to guide her as she carrie
the soup crock inside. Because of where it was, the lanter
betrayed the aladdin blind spot Kani had chosen in th
corner, and Ofosuaa could easily have seen him on he
way out. She, however, did not. She was carrying befor
her a large cone-shaped wooden bowl to cover the heartl
outside to prevent direct assault on it by the rain. Kan
tiptoed toward her, silently and, because her back wa
toward him, she could not see him. However, as he neare
her, his creeping shadow thrown ahead of him because o
the aladdin behind, betrayed a presence to his wife. No
knowing who it was, she panicked and dropped th
wooden bowl, turning round at once.

'I got you,' Kani chuckled.

'You almost made me break my precious bowl,' sh
said.

'How much would it have cost to replace?'

'There are certain things no amount of money coul
ever replace,' Ofosuaa said. One of several assorte
wooden bowls, she used them to hunt for gold dust in th

56

Birim river-bed several years past. She picked it up and tipped it over the hearth. 'You don't have to bring into the open our secret amusement. Of course, we're too old now for nuptial games.'

'No, no, my woman,' Kani said. 'If we entirely stop playing our childish games, death might think we're too old to live. Thus he'll come for us. But do we have to go so soon? We must witness our daughter's wedding.' He squeezed the little bulge of satin underwear fastened to her waist beads under her wrap-around cloth. 'Your node seems to be growing bigger these days.'

'Stop it.' Ofosuaa tenderly slapped off Kani's hand. She walked away from him toward the open porch, the sideways movements of her hips a little exaggerated. 'It's going to rain.'

'It rained on the first night of our wedding.' Kani caught up with her and threw his arms around her. Ofosuaa put the lantern down on the short balustrade wall in front of her room, and picked up the aladdin. Together with her husband, she climbed the wide stoop into the open porch. She placed the aladdin on an etagere in a corner, then went to the half-folded gateleg table and collected a bottle from it.

'Sanyo brought you this.' She showed it to Kani.

'Splendid,' he chortled. Having placed his electric torch on the gateleg table, he took the bottle from his wife. He inspected the pieces of fresh roots and barks inside it and grinned. 'Sanyo tells me these are the most potent bitters he's ever concocted. He warns that I must always make sure you sleep with me anytime I drink just a shot of schnapps that have stood around them.'

'I'm not a young woman any more, you know.' She giggled.

'I'm always gentle with you, my woman.' Kani touched her on her cheeks. He knew that Sanyo, his chauffeur and also the local mullah of the small mosque might not have been joking about the bitters. Hailing from the Northern Region of the country Sanyo was excellent in his knowl-

edge of herbs, barks and roots. With just a wilte
bryophylum leaf plastered with other mashed herbs, h
was able to draw out, within an hour, all the puss in a larg
painful boil that had affected Ofosuaa a couple of year
back.

'You must try some now.' Ofosuaa winked at Kani. Sh
picked up the electric torch from the gateleg table an
went inside Kani's room. She flashed it on and searche
for a full-size bottle of schnapps in one of the drawers o
the chest beside the bed head. She then collected tw
glasses and went back to the open porch. Kani took th
drink from her, but just as he was about to open it, he wa
distracted by the clanking noises of the gates. He looke
toward the patio.

'That must be Ayowa,' Ofosuaa said. '*Odenchey* danc
and rainy weather have never agreed.'

'Remind me tomorrow,' Kani said. 'I must give her
full piece *Dumas* cloth from the bottom of my air-tight bo
She was simply wonderful at the dance until she saw me.

'But why did you go there?' Ofosuaa asked.

'What does it hurt if I'm a little nostalgic for the time
of innocence, my woman?' He uncorked and poured th
schnapps into the bottle of bitters. 'I miss those days o
quiet beauty.' The wind picked up, surging into the hous
and fluttering the lantern on the short wall. Ofosuaa wen
down the stoop, collected the lamp and took it inside he
room. Kani was strolling to the edge of the stoop to tal
with Ayowa when another windstorm whipped bits of rai
against his face. He retreated immediately as it brought i
its wake a patter of heavy single raindrops on th
galvanized roofing sheets.

'My Princess,' Kani called Ayowa as she ran int
Ofosuaa's room and refused to come out. 'I think she'
still upset with me,' Kani said as Ofosuaa joined hi
again. 'I know what it takes to pacify her.' Kani laughed.

He shook the bottle of liquor vigorously until bubble
rose to the surface. He poured her half a glass full, the
filled his own. In the background, the winds wer

eceding. He could hear them crashing through the trees
the outskirts of the town. He raised his glass to the
laddin and studied the little pieces of wood tossing up
nd down in it. With a wink at Ofosuaa, he set it to his lips
nd drank it all. He then winced and shook his head
iolently. Ofosuaa sipped hers, her face grimaced.

'It's bitter,' she said.

'Only when it's this fresh.' Kani dealt several light blows
) his massive chest, as if to force the heat down by that
nethod. 'I'm going in now.' He turned the wick of the
laddin down. The open porch became suffused with half
arkness.

'Remember to keep the adjoining door between our
ooms open,' Ofosuaa said and went down the stoop to
er room.

s he normally did, Kani had woken up at first cockcrow,
ashed himself and gone back to bed where he stayed
ntil the church bell tolled seven. He would then get up
nd make himself ready for Benoa's good morning
nessage. But at six o'clock this morning he awoke with a
tart. He was sweating all over. He turned to Ofosuaa, a
ild look on his face, his fingers pressing hard around his
hin. Ofosuaa only smiled. She buried her head under the
ed covers and he felt her hand groping for him. He
urned on his side, away from her hand, and stretched his
rm over the top of the chest of drawers to the small lamp
nd turned up the wick to brighten the room. He jumped
lown from the bed. Moving some feet back from the
lresser, he bowed his body a little until he saw the
eflection of his face in the mirror. He bared his teeth and
apped his incisors, one after the other with the nail of his
ndex finger.

They all felt strong. They were still white and evenly
rranged. He sighed and turned to Ofosuaa, who now half
at on the bed, her upper body partially covered by the
overs. She watched him with amused curiosity.

'Just a bad dream,' she said from his puzzled look.

'I hope so. It seemed so real.' He seated himself on the edge of the bed, breathing heavily. 'And a strange on too. I was chewing on a hard bone. While I broke all m molars, I lost the entire set of my front teeth.'

Ofosuaa embraced him from behind. She ran her han over his hairy arms and chest. 'You must have carried in your sleep the incident of the hawk and the hen,' she sai As Kani just sat, she let him alone. She pulled her blous and cloth from the crossbars of the fourposter and g down from it to dress. 'It's daybreak already. I must go my chores. Probably, you'll want to wash again.'

'Ask Misa to bring up my cleaning water,' he said.

'He beat you to it,' Ofosuaa reported in the doorwa Among his sons, Kani had shared certain househol duties, which he changed every week. Having woken u earlier than he usually did, he thought the items for h morning sprucing up would not be ready on the gatele table in the open porch. He put on a white jumper ove his long velvet shorts. From a drawer in the chest by th bedhead, he found a bottle of Milton antiseptic and small stick. He put the stick in his mouth and began t chew it, using the fluffy end to scrub his teeth. He steppe into the open porch.

Misa had placed the glass of water to wash Kani's mout in a saucer. Beside it was a small mirror placed fac downward to carry a packet of Gillette blades and a silve shaving stalk. Misa had also folded his face towel an placed on it a cake of Lux near a bowl of water. Kan smiled at the neat arrangement of the toiletry items. 'Mis will do this for another week,' he said.

He dropped some Milton into the glass of water an rinsed his mouth with it. Having hung the small mirror o a nail in the wall, he looked into it and shaved his face. H then washed his face and dried it, rubbing some dustin powder on his cheeks and chin. The mentholated tal tickled his face, drawing a little water from his eyes. As h stared at himself, he let his big eyes move down. The rested on his neatly trimmed moustache under his broa nose, pouring over the hair for foreign matters. His nostrils dilated as he picked out a white speck from the hair in one. Slowly, his eyes moved up to his bushy eyebrows. Greying where they curved and tapered off toward his temples, they stood out prominently because of his receding forehead and naked scalp. He twitched down the corners of his large lips in a satisfied smile.

Back in his room to dress up, his eyes moved slowly along the canopy frame of the brass bed, looking among the large pieces of cloth folded and hung on the crossbars. When he saw the cloth with many green leaves printed on a brown background, he leaned over the bed to reach it on the far side. He wrapped it around himself, slipped his feet into his king-size princeling sandals, taking a few steps about on the red Persian rug. Fairly new, the sandals made tiny squeaking noises. On hearing agitated gibberish in the patio, he looked at his clock. It was getting to seven. He stepped out of his room and stopped short of going down the stoop.

The lower steps were wet from the splatter of trickles by the overflow pipes in the sides of the partial-underground tank. In the patio itself, very little evidence remained of the past night's rain. Kani folded his arms across his chest and watched his two youngest sons. In their khaki uniforms topped with light sweaters, they hit each other alternately and stamped their feet to splash themselves with the water trailing on the concrete patio from the overflow pipes. Seeing Kapre who peddled *aprapransa* to his wife, Kani sought to discipline his sons immediately; he did not want Kapre to go spreading awful tales about him and his family. Dubbed 'Radio' by the townsfolk, Kapre was a gossip who added her own twisted versions to whatever stories she relayed along. If she did not start it in the first place, Kapre-the-Radio appeared to be a part in every hearsay at Nkonsia. Kani compared her to the indispensable smell of onions in most foods by calling her 'Onions' sometimes. She looked on amused as Kani's boys kept fooling in the puddle on the patio floor.

61

'Behave yourselves!' Kani bawled. The boys dashed into their room. 'Why didn't you send them away to school, Ofosuaa? If you can't discipline them now, what will you do with them when I'm gone from this world?'

'They'll be living on their own by then,' Kapre volunteered.

'Who asked you, Onion?' Kani asked Kapre.

'I just know it, Noble Kani.' Kapre hurriedly buttoned up her oversized sweater as Kani went down the stoop. A thin woman with a lean face, Kani had told her before that she could grow some flesh on her thin body if only she would stop gossiping. Apart from her petty trading in small-small items, she was reputed at Nkonsia to be the best cook of *aprapansa* – a delicacy made from ground-dry and toasted-corn cooked in palm-nut broth with ginger, black pepper, sweet basil and smoked herring.

Ofosuaa stood beside Kapre, eating the food she had bought, pretending to be oblivious to Kani's presence, her face distorted a little by the bulge of food in her cheek.

'Didn't you know they were late for school?' Kani asked his wife again. But she remained silent. 'Have you grown deaf now?'

'But why don't you address the children who wanted the food in the first place? Today's *aprapansa* is special. I have roasted shrimp and chunks of porcupine meat in it. You may want to try some yourself, nobleman,' Kapre said.

Her explanation seemed to infuriate Kani the more. He went toward the boys, who had emerged from their room carrying their books on their heads. 'I'm sure you've consumed a cauldron of cocoyams this morning. Are you both going to grow just thinking of food?'

'*Aprapansa* is food for the gods,' Kapre said.

'Tell me, Onions, if my wife or children have signed you on as their lawyer,' Kani said to Kapre. 'If they have, then I want you to know that I haven't contracted with any of my children for their feces to manure any of my farms.' He took a hard look at Kapre, intending his statement to serve as a warning to her not to broadcast any lies about his family. As he kept staring at her, his sons took advantage of the distraction from them and dashed away and out of the house. 'I dislike my children's squabbling over food. The world knows nobody is being starved in my house.'

Ofosuaa looked on, still mute. Any little thing the boys did contrary to his expectation threw Kani into rage at them. One evening, as he sat chatting with her, Misa, who was playing with a pop gun he had made from a pawpaw leaf stalk, mistakenly fired it toward the open porch. The dummy bullet, a piece of cassava pith forced out of the stalk by a stick, flew to hit Kani on his bald head. He called his son. After berating him, Kani slapped the boy so hard that the impact lifted Misa off his feet and landed him on his haunches.

'Please, never hit any of my children like that again. It sets my belly on fire. I carried them inside me for nine months. Alone,' Ofosuaa protested. Kani had never hit any of them since.

Kapre put her stuff together and left.

'Will you please talk to Ayowa?' Ofosuaa said. 'I asked her to go to the Ntanoa farm. Just to bring home a bunch of plantains. But she refused to go. It rained all night. Why does she rather go to the stream-side for water when I don't need it?'

Kani thought that Ofosuaa's remarks were intended to make him annoyed against Ayowa. 'You know for certain that you can't make me mad against my daughter, my woman,' he said. 'She's not here because, maybe Obaa Panyin needs stream water. You know, sometimes, you disappoint me. Why should a young woman destined to become the wife of a would-be chief go to the farm? Or for that matter, do any hard work?'

Not saying a word, Ofosuaa carried her small bowl of food near the tripod clay hearth. She sat down on a short stool and began separating better corn cobs for planting from those good only for consumption. She knew Kani would not tolerate any adverse report on Ayowa. When ten years old, she had come home from school one afternoon, sobbing. He asked her what the matter was. Ayowa showed him weals on her arms and at the back of her thighs. Without asking why she had been caned, Kani immediately went to the school and demanded the transfer of the teacher who had whipped Ayowa.

Just as he turned to walk to the open porch, Benoa's son entered the house. He greeted the people around and addressed Kani. 'My father asked me to tell you that the sun was a little late in coming up today.'

Kani forced a laugh. 'The rain might have cleared the clouds, but the streams in the sun's path might have got overswollen,' he said. 'Be careful on your way to school son. It may still be wet on the ground.' He paced to the edge of the stoop and looked up, above the kitchen wing toward the Ajapomaa hills. Thick fog rose from the woods on the hills to merge with the light clouds which the sun was quickly dissipating. That was a good sign for the day ahead. Kani smiled, reflecting on how children interpreted that sign: monkeys were toasting plantain; i implied abundant supply of food for the day.

Outside the house, Kani noticed that the downpour in the night had been the torrential type. In the old days, such downpour allegedly brought up tiny gold pieces from the earth and young children scampered about in the gullies looking for the precious metal. These days, apart from stripping the earth of its good surface fluids, such heavy rain brought only cold weather in its wake. The cold that morning appeared to have subdued the weaver birds. Except an occasional hop-flight as a result of passing huge trucks, the cassia trees along the lanes and the coconut and royal palms at the open market area hardly showed any signs that they accommodated the incessant staccato shrill of the birds every day. But the cold did not bother Kani.

His right shoulder was bare to his breast, but the rest of

his body down to his feet was swathed in cloth. Having passed a mass of it under his right armpit, he held the bulk in the crook of his left arm while one end trailed him on the damp red ground. He threw his right arm about like a man who had absolute control over all the space around him. As he rounded one of the corners of his house, he noticed a fairly deep hole at the base of his house. Through the water in it he could see the pebbles and stones in the concrete foundation of the building. He halted. Flabbergasted, he looked up at the jointed corner of the hip roof. The gutter along the eaves that carried rainwater to the tank below the open porch had come apart and the turbulent drop of water through the gap had dug that sizeable hole. From the opening in the gutters, drops of water still plopped into the clear pool at the base of the building. The drops raised particles of the earth, which whirled dizzily to the surface, then gradually resettled, only to get excited again by another plop.

Kani felt as if his own personality was being skinned. How could an overnight rain dig out and betray the solid foundation of his house? In thought he looked up again, wondering what it all meant. The hawk and the hen? That terrible dream in which he was battling the bone? And now this – a hole beside the solid foundation of his house? Were they all sheer coincidences? They definitely ought to be. He thought that there certainly must have been several of such incidents before; they did not bother him because he had not paid them any attention. Maybe, he was indeed worrying too much about unnecessary things, as Benoa had said the previous day.

As Kani went on his way, he found the lanes empty. Most people were around fires in their houses. The buildings stood solemn, like columns of dispirited soldiers. He could even tell what materials had gone into their construction; the soaked and splattered white or mustard yellow wash betrayed the outlines of adobe or blocks or wattle and daub structures beneath their stucco. He kept to the centre of the lanes; the eaves of the roofs still dripped. His feet clumped the ground as if in deliberate effort to crush under his princeling sandals anything small that crossed his path. He merely nodded his shorn head in response to a greeting from a boy, who quickly stepped to the side of the lane for Kani to pass.

'Noble Kani,' the boy said, running after him. 'The chief sent me for you. There's a meeting at his house.'

'Thank you, son,' Kani said. As he quickly diverted his way between two mud houses, he intoned to himself that if the elders brought up anything more about Entea, he would tell them something they would never forget. Nearing the chief's house, however, he heard laughter above the babble of noises. He found a motorcycle parked near the bamboo paling around the house. It must be a government official from Kibi, he thought, and hurried through the entrance in the fence.

The meeting appeared over. A couple of the elders were already leaving the house. Some of them stood beside the bamboo fence, talking among themselves. They patted their shoulders and laughed. The chief waved Kani to come to his side, where he introduced a young man in government khaki to him. 'Any time I see a forestry official here, I know some more of our land is gone into the forest reserve programme.' Kani shook hands with the man.

'I brought a new directive this time,' the man said. 'To increase food production, the government is allowing more portions of the forest reserve to be farmed. At fifty cedis a chain, of course.'

'Kopra will announce the good news by the gong in the evening,' the chief said. He walked with Kani and the government official to the gate in the bamboo paling and said goodbye. After the official had left on his motorbicycle, Kani tarried with the chief for a discussion.

'Nana,' Kani said, 'I want to register my displeasure with you. I'm concerned about how I've been left out at the start of the last two meetings. I know no decisions were made in both, but at least I must be present at the start of every meeting.'

'I shall bring your protest to the attention of the other elders,' the chief said. 'As you noted, neither of the last two meetings was formal or important. Your being absent at the start of them wasn't deliberate. Have a good day.' Odikuro-the-chief went inside his room. The other elders left behind were also leaving the house in two's and three's. Benoa walked over to Kani. In a ragged denim overalls too big for his haggard body, he clutched a machete under his armpit.

'Make time this afternoon,' he said to Kani. 'I won't stay long on the farm today. I hatched a new strategy in my sleep last night.'

'I'm the Hawk.' Kani laughed. 'You must thank me for having allowed you some streak of wins over me lately. From this afternoon, I'm putting a stop to your wins at checkers. But I must first share the news with you. I should have told you about it yesterday. Owiredu sent his word about your niece.'

Benoa gaped at Kani, his cheek bones jutting out of his gaunt face. 'But why am I surprised? Peacocks can only play hopscotch with their kind. This calls for celebration. Come on, Brother-of-man, I'm treating you to palm wine today.' The two men fell in step on their way to Nna Asaa's palm wine drinking shanty. The sun was bright now. Steam rose from the ground and the mud houses along the main lane.

Returning home from the palm wine bar, Kani smelled burning hair two buildings away from his house. The odour intensified the closer he got to his house. He smiled. The signs from the hills had been good indeed. It always had been like that for him; happy tidings usually came to him in sequences. On entering the gates, he found his wife smoking meat on a grill over the clay hearths. Near her was Sanyo. His chest bare and his feet in Wellington boots into which he had tucked the ends of his

khaki pants, he sat on the ground astride a spread o
banana leaves. On them he worked the carcasses of ar
antelope and a grasscutter. He looked up briefly at Kan
and revealed a set of kola-stained teeth in a grin.

'When it rains, crops release subtle fragrance into the
air,' Sanyo said. 'Animals come out of their dens to eat
But they don't know Nana doesn't want his food crop:
destroyed by them. And now, here they are, going to feec
Nana instead.'

'Where did these come from?'

'Entea brought them. From Ntanoa,' Ofosuaa said.

Kani looked down in thought, speaking in an incred
ulous tone. 'Entea? But the springs at Ntanoa have beer
dead for almost a year now. What is that man up to?'

'Noble Kani,' Sanyo said, 'some traps stay inactive only
because the animals fail to tread the tracks cut to the
snares. However, when the tracks overgrow and so shake
away the lingering scent of human beings, the animals go
that way. Then wh-a-m! They get caught in the noose.'

Stroking his chin in thought, Kani looked at the smoke
from the hearth, rising in twirls of dark fumes. He said
'It's something *that* I may not know of, or be aware of, bu
which could hurt me, that's what bothers me. That's wha
frightens me.'

'Nana.' Sanyo pointed at the tympanum above the oper
porch. 'You're the mighty Hawk. You can always soar
above troubles. You are the grandsire of the Awesome
Buffalo. You ram your way through troubles. Nobody car
pin your back to the bare earth.'

Kani went closer to the grinning Sanyo. Kani felt like
patting him on the shoulder, but he held back. 'Tha
earns you a raise of three hundred cedis, Sanyo,' Kan
said. Sanyo stood up and bowed his head. He was wel
built, but not to Kani's height.

'What must I do to justify the raise?' he asked.

'You deserve it. I have a good friend in you,' Kani said
Ofosuaa turned on her stool to Kani. Her eyes streamec
from the fatty smoke.

'Your dream didn't turn out bad after all,' she said, and Kani nodded his agreement. 'What one sees in a dream usually turns out to be the opposite,' Ofosuaa said.

Kani went inside his room, and when he came out, he had topped his long velvet shorts with a brown jumper. He came and held the carcass while Sanyo cut it up into several small pieces. Kani then passed some of the banana leaves to his wife, who hovered them above the fire until they became wilted. Having collected them back, Kani wrapped up several bundles of the meat. 'You know all the people you want to share these with. Make sure you give a bundle to Entea. We must share whatever curse there is with him if he stole these from somebody's traps,' Kani said to his wife.

'Nana, I agree with you,' Sanyo said.

Kani put aside two large bundles. 'These go to Nana Odikuro and Konadu. I hear she's been ill for some days now.'

'I'll send Ayowa to her with supper tonight,' Ofosuaa said.

'But where's Ayowa? I haven't seen her all morning.'

'She's at Obaa Panyin's.' Ofosuaa said in reply to Kani. 'Look for her at Obaa Panyin's these days anytime you can't find her here.' She turned the roasting meat over and placed a clay bowl over it. Just then Ayowa entered the house, a sunflower tin of water balanced on her head.

'Aha, my sister knows her name,' Sanyo said. Having lived at Nkonsia for a long time, he claimed to be a citizen and a son to Ofosuaa. He addressed Ayowa. 'Bring the water to your father so he could wash his hands and arms.'

Ayowa hesitated, then she went past her father toward the kitchen entrance. 'Didn't Sanyo ask you to bring me the water? Or Obaa Panyin has been turning you against me? Please, bring me the water,' Kani said. Ayowa paused in the doorway, then turned round and went to Kani. She let down the tin beside a silver basin, and used a calabash to pour water over her father's lathering hands. Kani could see that her hands were trembling. He felt her breath on his arms, too. And it was hot and it came out in gasps. As larger quantities of water poured on his hands, splattering him, he spoke.

'Slowly, slowly,' he cautioned. But Ayowa started at her father's voice and dropped the calabash, splashing the bloody water in the basin on Kani. 'Where is your mind?' Kani thundered.

'I'm sorry,' she said.

'I might as well go and wash down.' Kani stood up. 'Lest I forget, I've asked Entea to do some work on the farm you'll be going to today, my woman.'

Ayowa looked at her father with wild eyes. Ofosuaa also rose from her stool, an expression of shock and disbelief on her face. She stepped forward after her husband. 'Did I hear you right about Entea? Wasn't he the young man Asonchey accused of trying to sexually assault on her farm?'

'I don't subscribe to mere hearsay,' Kani said.

'Mere hearsay, you say?' Ayowa said, and everyone turned to her surprised. 'Can I say something here. Why is it always you, father, and no one else? I'm an individual. And whatever you do for me, it's I who must deal with my feelings. Why is it only your feelings and opinions that matter – ?'

'Don't question your father like that,' Ofosuaa said.

'No, no, allow her,' Kani insisted. 'Master Darko explains to me that's part of teenagers' growing up. I didn't see that rebellious aspect in my older sons because they were away at school. Allow Ayowa to vent hers out. She's a woman now, ready to go into marriage – '

'I don't care about that.' Ayowa snapped. 'I'm talking about Entea. Why do you try so hard to latch him on to your family? It's a misguided exercise if it's because he's of the same clan as mother. I'll never accept that. I hate him.'

'If my attempts to make him a worthy citizen of the town causes you such torment, I'll terminate it immediately,' Kani said almost apologetically. 'Right now, he

70

already has left for the Cattle-town farm. I'll cancel all arrangements with him as soon as he gets back.'

'It's too late indeed –' Ayowa said, but her father interrupted her.

'I'm the head of this house and family. If no one can hurt me, no one can hurt anybody under my roof. End of discussion.' He walked away to the open porch, not wanting to hear any more. Ofosuaa turned to Sanyo.

'Sometimes I wonder what manner of man he is,' she said.

'A strong and powerful one.' Sanyo grinned. 'Don't worry, mother. I'll be with you on the farm. There will be no trouble from Entea.' He pulled down his resin-stained T shirt from the copper line, and put it on. He picked up his machete. Carrying his own bundle of meat, he went out of the house.

'Ma, can I go and finish with what I was doing at Ma Nyameche's?' Ayowa asked of Ofosuaa.

'Pass on the bundles of meat to your uncle Benoa's house,' Ofosuaa said. 'And bring back Obaa Panyin's items for washing. Tomorrow is laundry day.' Ofosuaa carried her tray and set off after Sanyo. She swung her arm to keep alive a brand she held. She could have taken a box of matches to make fire on the farm to roast plantains for the workers and herself, but she liked doing it the old fashion way, just as her mother did all her life.

Kani sat in his hammock chair in the open porch and puffed at his pipe. These days, when he did not have to take business trips or go to see the crops or work on any of his farms, he sat in the open porch and listened to the radio. When it struck noon, he went to Okuma's store to play or watch the young men at the game of checkers.

# Chapter 5

On their way to Okuma's store, Kani and Benoa waited beside the highway for a truck groaning uphill to pass. As it shifted gears, its drone drowned the toll of the church bell in the distance announcing three o'clock. Benoa rubbed off the grit blown on his face with his palm. Kani cleaned his with flaps from his satin kerchief.

'It's dusky, as if it's already sundown.' Kani scanned the sky. Pitch-dark blotches punctuated the rolls of white clouds that had earlier spread the heavens. The obscured sun, like an enormous black hub with radiating spokes, sent out rays in all directions high above the town. He said: 'I feel terrible if I can't see my shadow during the day.'

'It isn't by a man's shadow that his essence is measured.' Benoa said and crossed the highway with Kani, walking abreast. He pointed to a section of the road. 'You know my house was bulldozed for this highway. It brought me a good compensation of ten thousand cedis those good years – those years when a cedi was worth forty cedis of today. My favourite saying then was "I'd shoot myself if at anytime I had only ten cedis in my pocket".' Benoa laughed. 'But here I am today, my cloth limp on my shoulders. We're never in control, are we?'

'I'm always.' Kani tapped his chest with his palm.

'Then, you weren't hinting at my going to beat you when you talked about dark days without shadows?' He cast a sideway glance at Kani. Kani felt the white checker in his left pocket. He had a black one in his right pocket; Entea had presented them to him in the past day. 'I'll defeat you today, even with my eyes closed. Instead of being appreciative of my having allowed you a string of a few wins, you choose to boast about your skill.'

'We'll see how you can beat me today.'

When they reached Okuma's store, they found six young men squatting in a semicircle on the veranda and in the process of determining which two players would have a first shot at the checkers. Addo-the-tapper – so called because he worked felled palm trees in the bush and brought home palm wine to the drinking shanty – was before the young men. His back to the steps, he did not notice the arrival of the two older men. Having climbed the steps, Kani and Benoa stood at the edge of the veranda and watched the proceedings. Addo showed a dice to the young men before him. He then threw it on the floor. The dice rolled and hit the wall, then lay still with 'six' showing upward. A teenager leaped into the air, saying: '*Seke*, my number.'

Addo threw the dice again. 'Two' was the winner.

Kani cleared his throat. Addo turned round.

'Actually, Benoa and I had already decided on those two numbers,' Kani said. 'Our eyes are failing. We need every little light to contemplate our positions and movements. As young men, you can play any time, even at night.' The young men started grumbling. Paying them no attention, Kani sat down on the chair against the short wall. Benoa reached for the checkerboard reclined against the wall. He sat on the chair opposite his brother-in-law. As Benoa tried to reach the small biscuit can containing the checkers, Addo-the-tapper pushed it away with his foot.

'This isn't fair,' he said.

'Just a small misunderstanding, young men. It can be settled fairly now.' Kani pushed down his cloth from his shoulder so that it formed a loose bulge around his waist and thus exposed his massive chest. 'Okuma, will you please give the young men a bottle of *akpeteshie*? And each of them a packet of his favourite brand of cigarettes. That settles matters, I believe.'

'Adequate compensation,' Addo said in an exulting voice. He picked up the can of checkers and gave it to Kani. 'Folks, let's express our appreciation to the nobleman.'

'Live long Nana,' they said.

They crowded inside the entrance of the store. For a little while, they quarrelled over the cigarettes as each of them tried to reach Okuma first for his cigarettes. Addo ordered them quiet. He received the items from Okuma and passed them around as the other young men called out their brand names. One of them went down the steps and around the corner of the store into the house proper behind. When he returned, he had lit a cigarette. Addo took it and kindled his own. Soon, each of the young men was smoking.

Meanwhile, Kani had picked out a black and a white checkers. He held them gingerly between his thumbs and his index fingers and showed them around. Benoa gestured with his head in agreement. Kani then hid his hands under the checkerboard and looked away at the young men. Addo-the-tapper brought a bottle of local gin and a glass toward Kani. It was the custom that the buyer always drank the first shot.

'Will Nana take the head?' Addo asked.

'Don't you know manners at your age?' Benoa cast him an angry look. 'A youth doesn't proffer a drink to his elder that way.'

'I haven't been to your tapped palm trees recently – that is if you have any.' Addo implied that he had not done anything to provoke Benoa. 'Looking at your lips, I can tell you want a drink. But I won't give you anything. The nobleman bought it for only us. Will Nana please accept the head of the drink?'

'Older folks are always at peace when our offspring are adequately fed. Go ahead and enjoy yourselves,' Kani said. As Addo clinked the bottle of liquor against the glass to serve the young men one after another, Kani's hand, under the checkerboard, slipped the black checker he had shown around earlier into his left pocket and brought out the white one already hidden there, so that he had two white checkers in his concealed hands. He closed his fingers over them and brought out his hands. Extending them before Benoa, he stared him straight in the eyes, his lips pressed tight together. Benoa looked back at him with no facial expression.

Addo paused in serving the drink. All the young men remained silent, looking on at the ritual to determine which of the two men would have the privilege to make the first move. Benoa tapped Kani's fisted left hand. Kani did not open his hands. Instead, he placed the white checker in his left hand before his brother-in-law. Benoa nodded his head in agreement to his own choice. Addo poured himself half a glass full of strong gin and gulped it down. To no one in particular but in obvious reference to Benoa's having chosen a white checker, he said: 'Once a loser, always a loser.'

'When a tiger falls into a pond, it just gets wet. Its stripes never wash away.' Benoa planted his checkers in the red squares in his territory.

'Tigers with no claws.' Addo clinked the glass and the bottle again. 'Insinuations have a curious way of betraying those for whom they're intended,' he said. The young men burst into laughter. Benoa swung his arm, intending to catch Addo with a vicious blow. The tapper, however, jumped out of the way.

'I can beat you to any woman anywhere, anytime,' Benoa yelled.

'Will you two stop gibing?' Kani said.

When Benoa was enjoying his propitious moments with his highway construction compensatory money, he took as mistress a young woman Addo had intended to marry. The palm-wine tapper's proposal thus fell through. Since then, a quiet animosity had developed between them; it came to a head with verbal assaults anytime the two met.

After both Kani and Benoa had planted their men – the white and black checkers on the red squares, Kani made the first move. He secured the farthest red square to his right. Surprised by this unusual move by Kani, Benoa retaliated by moving into the central square. Then both men initiated rapid movements for sometime. The young men stood on both sides of the checkerboard, not taking sides. They just watched. Benoa gave one of his men for Kani to jump free before he was able to capture one of Kani's. Then, in another rapid sequence, they grappled for the central squares, Benoa always after Kani. There was a brief pause. Benoa studied the positions of his men with intense concentration. His leading men were all surrounded by black ones; he had no room to advance. Making gesticulative calculations with his fingers in the air, he planned how to wiggle himself out of trouble.

'Working out strategies to build mansions in women's arses,' Addo said. Ribald laughter from the young men greeted that statement.

'Only a gelded fellow would speak thus about women,' Benoa said. He kept his eyes on the checkerboard. 'He doesn't even know how wonderful a woman is to be with.' The young men laughed even more loudly. Then Benoa raised his hand for silence. He had found a move that could infiltrate Kani's defences. Benoa initiated it. Rapid capturing of checkers for both men in the middle squares ensued. At the end of it, Kani realized that he was in a bind. He had only one move to make. And that would be captured freely, allowing Benoa to have a crown.

'I can't wait all day for your next move,' Benoa said as Kani studied the board for a long time. As he did not make any move yet, Benoa feinted standing up. 'Amateurs play this slow.'

'This game can go either way, according to how the men stand,' Addo said. 'If a man hasn't been affected by hydrocele, we don't rush out and look for special briefs to hold his distended balls.' The young men laughed wildly. Kani smiled.

'Light me a Consulate,' he said. 'And light another one for Brother-of-man, Okuma.'

As Okuma the storekeeper brought the cigarettes, there

as a reprieve. The young men turned round to take ngle shots of their drink. Benoa thrust his head sideways ) receive the cigarette with his lips. Kani quickly shoved is left hand underneath the folds of his cloth and into his ocket. He fetched the two black checkers he had hidden 1ere. Then, he placed his hand at the corner of the heckerboard and let one checker down. As he leaned )rward, practically covering the board with his body to eceive the cigarette with his lips, he slid the other black hecker along the edge of the board into the second quare of his back row. He then sat up and took a long draft. ienoa carefully smothered the burning tip of his cigarette etween his thumb and finger and pocketed the piece.

'Shall we go on now?' he asked Kani.

'I suppose so.' Kani blew out a cloud of smoke. 'Good igarettes can even be hard when a man isn't used to hem.' He gave his cigarette to Addo, then pushed the •nly black checker for which he had room to manoeuvre. ienoa quickly jumped two of Kani's men.

'A swift flight –'

'To where?' Kani asked as Benoa's hand froze in the air. Ie remained agape, staring at the black checker in the orner where he knew there had been nothing previously.

'I could swear that space was empty,' said a young man. I had even anticipated Benoa's jump to a crown.'

'Generation of today dare to accuse our elders of mpropriety,' Addo said. 'Go on your knees and tell Noble ani that you imagined what you just said.'

Benoa, on the other hand, just looked round at the aces of the people, expecting support. They only shrug-,ed their shoulders. The one who had attempted to be a vitness lit a cigarette and began to whistle a tune. 'Can I ount the checkers?'

'When did I plant new men on the board?' Kani asked ienoa.

'No, it isn't necessary to count,' Benoa said. 'It's a win or you. Let's give the young men a chance to play. We'll neet again at this checkerboard some other time, folks.'

'If you say so.' Kani agreed. Both men drew their chair back and stood up. The two young men who had won th dice toss earlier on took the seats and began to plant th black and white checkers on the red squares. As Kani an Benoa went down the steps, they heard one of the youn men saying that the nobleman might have mistaken played with more checkers. 'I put those two there,' Add countered the young man. Kani chuckled. When the were beyond earshot, Benoa spoke.

'Your first false move initiated the traps that ensnare you. Then you chose an undignified approach to wor your way out. I just didn't want to count the checker before the young men. You know Addo lied for you.'

Kani dabbed his brows with his satin kerchief. 'I playe resourcefully,' he said. 'I made certain there were me always in my rear flanks to provide me cover.'

'It's only a game we play each other all the time,' Beno said .'You didn't have to cheat. It robs the joy out of m trust in you. And the spirits don't look favourably on that.

'The so-called spirits cheat too.' Kani laughed. 'If the didn't, we down here wouldn't know how to do it.'

'Be careful what you say under the open skies about th spirits.' Benoa pointed to the sky. 'Everything good an beautiful was created by God. All evil and ugly things wer made by man. We shouldn't complicate God's work, fo this world may be more than what you see.'

'Spare me your sermon, will you.' Kani said. They ha reached the intersection where they would normally par They both paused, standing face to face. Kani the continued speaking: 'In the game of checkers, strategy i the essence, and the honour of the players is always a stake. I'll save my mother over my wife any time if the both were drowning.'

'It's good human beings don't have a communa stomach, like the air we breath,' Benoa said. 'Good day Brother-of-man. See you later.' He turned to go, but Kan called him back.

'Let's go straight to my place,' he said. 'Ofosuaa mus

have finished cooking by now. If she hasn't, there are strong bitters and E.K. schnapps. We could relax with them. That was an exhausting game we played. We haven't had schnapps together in a while.' Kani winked at him. Benoa winked back at him, smiling. He walked back to Kani. They fell in step and went along the same way.

As they ate, the radio reported that a severe thunderstorm and heavy rain had affected the coastal areas of the country and was gradually pushing inland. Ayowa and Ofosuaa were also at meals in the kitchen, together with her sons and three of Benoa's children. Benoa told Kani about the new course of action the elders wanted to take in reference to Entea's utterance that the town was like a clay bowl in his hands and that he could drop and break it at will. The elders first wanted to eliminate any curse inherent in the statement by Entea before they called on Entea to recant it in public.

The reasons behind the new action were quite logical, as Benoa was explaining them. Nkonsia was established by the Asona clan. Entea who had made that abominable statement also belonged to that clan. The State of Abuakwa was headed by the Asona clan. So the head of the clan at Nkonsia was to perform rites of absolution for the clan before the matter slipped out of town and reached the ears of some important person connected to the paramount stool of the Abuakwa state. However, Opong, the Asona clan head at Nkonsia, had refused to have anything to do with the rites. It was a matter for the whole town, and not one clan, he argued.

'He must be destooled if he won't perform the rites,' Benoa said as his fingers probed the palmnut soup for meat. 'Yes, he must be forced to abdicate so that someone like me, willing to absolve the Asona clan, will ascend the stool.'

'So you want some regal lifestyle?' Kani took his time to swallow a morsel of *foo-foo*. 'Well, I think it isn't fair for Opong to be used to wish away your fears. Besides, I don't think this is a case that merits the dimension being given to it. Only cowards take a mere statement by a drunk seriously.' With his cupped hand, he swished the soup into his mouth.

Benoa stared at him, his hand in the bowl of food. 'We would banish Entea from this town, if these were the old times,' he said. 'Who knows what motivates any person to make statements anywhere at anytime –'

'Will you take your hand away from the bowl so I can eat?' Kani said and coughed. He fetched the small towel on his lap and wiped away a trail of soup from his cheek. 'When a child urinates on his parent's lap, the thighs are never amputated. It's just the urine that is wiped away.' He ladled the *foo-foo* with fresh soup from a silver bowl beside the table.

'What about the derogatory statements he made about the Twafoor fetish?' Benoa fished for a piece of meat and ate it, sucking on the bone in it for a while.

'Those are new charges to me,' Kani said. 'Besides, if your so-called fetish had powers, all our young men would be rich. They wouldn't be elsewhere, working as cleaners and gravediggers.'

Benoa straightened his body and said: 'Being rich isn't the sole purpose of life. We all have roles to play. You as a young man used to carry some of the waters of Twafoor in a small bottle during your travels. Why? Because it ensured your safety. You told me you took some with you to Burma. Why? You said it ensured your invincibility. What has happened to you to change your beliefs?'

Having cupped soup into his mouth, Kani began to cough. 'Can we please stop this debate so we can enjoy the food?' he said. 'You know that eating and talking don't get along well –'

'They share the same passageway,' Benoa said. The two men then ate in silence. Only the radio kept babbling the world news in the Ghanaian languages.

After dinner, Kani sat outside his house, on a bamboo pew. Benoa had left for his house already. Ofosuaa sat lose to her husband, her legs stretched out and crossed before her. She was perched on a short stool, making a broom from palm leaves shredded from their branches. The section behind the house where they sat, faced the Atewa hills to the west. On bright afternoons, Kani repaired to the bamboo pew after dinner to watch the sun set. Few people walked by. He knew it was meal time in most homes. The redolence of spicy soup and bush meat from various kitchens hung in the air. Kani looked along the lane but he saw nobody coming in the distance. He made a sniffing sound and rubbed his nose.

'Did my soup lack anything you desired?' Ofosuaa asked.

Kani laughed. 'If ever I were to go hungry, I'd just stand in the streets at this hour and swallow mouthfulls of air. That alone could make me full because of the sheer density of the aroma. When, however, I'm filled by your delicious meals, the savour of the air makes me yearn for my pipe. Ayowa has stayed too long.'

'Maybe Kapre isn't home and Ayowa's waiting for her.'

'The Radio might have got caught up in gossiping –'

'She may be out selling or collecting from debtors,' Ofosuaa said. 'This is when a peddler is likely to find people at home.'

The sun hung above the Atewa hills. A huge glowing ball, its flush had bathed the trees in vague scarlet and even infused with a tinge of redness the long shadow of the coconut palm under which the couple sat.

'I didn't know that you wanted the banana trees to the north of Cattle-town farm felled.' Ofosuaa was refering to the farm she had been to. 'It's said that equal attention as we pay to plantains must be given to bananas. Who knows, banana may become the staple here if there's famine.'

'I want all that piece of land planted with oil palm,' Kani said. 'Oil palm is the crop for cash now. Everybody wants to stay clean. The soap industry will forever be growing. Do you know why Buaa is always insulting your brother?' He turned halfway on the bamboo pew and

faced his wife, a smile on his face. 'Buaa has poor opinio
of Benoa because he isn't rich. And he isn't rich becaus
he didn't plan his future well. A few minutes before yo
came out and joined me here, I watched an ant plan it
future. It was carrying an insect's wing many times the siz
of the ant. It amazed me how it avoided that obstacle
Kani pointed to a piece of stick close to Ofosuaa's fee
'The ant couldn't go over it, so it went all the way aroun
it to enter that hole.

'You know, I heard on "Farmers' Forum" that ou
government is going to establish two more soap factorie:
Oil palm farmers will soon have two big customers – th
people who buy it for food and the factories that will tur
out soap and detergents to keep us clean.'

'I have always admired your foresight.' Ofosuaa pulle
the palm fronds on which she was working closer to he
'You ought to have seen how seriously Entea took th
work. It was as though he were happy to be the person b
whose hands the banana trees suffered death.'

'I know he's a hard-worker. He only needs to channe
his energies while he's on leave.' Kani struck his palm wit
his index finger in emphasis. 'If I were you, I'd b
concerned about the things people say about him. He'
your kinsman, belonging to your clan the Asona as it is.'

Ofosuaa picked her teeth with the shell piece. She the
turned her head sideways and let out a chute of saliv
through the mid-gap in her upper teeth. The jet of saliv
splattered against small puffballs growing out of the bas
of the building. 'Each person has his or her own name,
she said. 'His is Entea and mine is Ofosuaa. Each perso
chooses to be what he or she wants. That says it all for me
Why not be the bee instead of the bluebottle that settle
on everything, filth and all. I wonder why you trust Ente:
so,' she said, adding a stripped spine of palm leaf to th
small pile of those already cleaned.

'Entea can't hurt a fly,' Kani said. 'It's the people wh
have created the image of a bully for him. You're my wife
You don't have to be afraid of any one. Fear is a bad thing.

Ayowa emerged from behind the corner of the next house. She stopped on seeing her parents, and she appeared to Kani as if undecided as to whether she should go forward or retreat. Then she went forward, heading for the gate, her face conspicuously turned away from her parents. Kani stopped her.

'I thought I sent you, *Me Buroni.*' He called her using the nickname of 'My-Fair-Lady.' Ayowa looked at him with pearly white eyes. 'Or you forgot? If you did, smile and shame the devil,' Kani said. Ayowa grinned, displaying a neat row of dazzling white teeth and her dimples. Kani recalled the joke by some old women in town about Ayowa's comely features when she had been born. They said that they had tried to mar her face by poking her cheeks with broomstick. But their efforts had been futile, making her more beautiful instead with those tiny dents in her cheeks. When she was a child, Kani usually placed her on his knees and told her funny stories or tickled her in her sides and armpits – just to make her laugh to show her dimples. Ofosuaa stopped him one day when she said Ayowa was too big for such games.

Now, she stood quietly before her parents, her head bowed. She only raised it to look up at a group of late parrots as they nonchalantly cawed out their evening greeting to the town while they crossed the greying sky in a crescent formation. They were flying free, not in a hurry to reach wherever they were headed even though nightfall was overtaking them.

'Is something bothering you?' Kani asked Ayowa.

Ayowa just put her thumbnail in her mouth, nibbling at it while she gazed at her toes bent to grip the insole of her sandals. She just wanted to get away from the presence of her parents, go and hide in a hole where they could not see her.

'The Mighty Hawk,' Kani said his own appellation. 'Isn't it my own daughter with whom I speak?' The silence that followed was only mitigated by the rattle of the coconut palm leaves as a cool breeze swept by.

'No need to fret,' Ofosuaa said. 'If you don't mind, can share my piece of Aduako's tobacco with you Turning to Ayowa, she continued: 'Could you please fetc your father the piece of tobacco on my window sill?'

'Bring my pipe and box of matches along too.' Kani said, but by the time he finished his statement, Ayowa ha already gone into the house. He threw a suspicious look a his wife. 'I think Ayowa knows about the arrangement with Owiredu involving Baah. I know she likes Ayerakwa but how can I allow her into such a dry home? It's Baal and no one else.'

'My man, you know I can't tell her about thos arrangements, at least not now. You know how happy I'n about the Baah plan.' Ofosuaa gathered together th stripped spines, which were sufficient to make one broom tied them into a bundle and started on another one Hoping to change the subject, she said: 'I heard there wa a government official in town this morning.'

Kani turned to face Ofosuaa squarely. A cheerfu disposition replaced the sombre one on his face. H always enjoyed lecturing his wife on new topics and idea in farming that he picked up from the radio or a Farmers' meetings elsewhere. 'We can now farm th *surveyor line* forest. As I was saying earlier, everything i planning. You plan well, you ensure a successful future The government wants to cultivate some trees to sell th timber overseas. The only resource it can use to get th forest cleared is the people –'

'We've always been the slaves of the government,' sh said.

'Without us the people, there can be no government. Kani agreed with her. 'After we've cleared the forest, th forestry officials will then come and plant the seedlings o the trees among our food crops –' Kani interrupte himself to receive from Misa the items he had aske Ayowa to bring earlier. 'But where is Ayowa whom I sent? Kani asked. He pushed a long thin metal in and out o the stem of the pipe. Bits of charred tobacco droppe nto the bowl, and he knocked it against the pew and cleared it. When it was clean enough, he tore the tobacco into two and gave one piece to his wife. 'I think Ayowa is deliberately avoiding me for some reason. If it isn't the Baah plan, then I don't know what,' he said to Ofosuaa.

'Don't make a big deal out of this,' Ofosuaa said. 'She just feels big enough to delegate someone else when you send her.'

'Did you notice how nervous she seemed earlier before us?'

'It was because she forgot to go to Kapre's to get you the tobacco.' Ofosuaa put her bit of tobacco in her mouth and pushed it far back where her molars were. Kani stuffed his pipe with the other piece and lit it. The smoke infused the air with a pungent odour like a stagnant pool of water filled with rotten garbage.

'How do some people dry their tobacco?' He coughed and spat out phlegm. 'This is terrible.'

'It's good for chewing.' Ofosuaa cocked her head, listening. 'I think I hear Kapre,' she said as they heard a woman greeting the occupants of the next house.

'If you had delayed just a little more, I'd have poisoned my system with some awful leaves,' Kani said as Kapre put in her appearance. 'Where have you been? Chattering somewhere, I believe. Have you considered changing your name to Onions?'

'I went to Betomu today, Nana.' Kapre let down her wooden tray. It had a medium-size silver bowl in it. 'Owiredu asked that you come and see him. His illness has shaken him badly.'

'The hospital at Kibi is too small for his illness,' Kani said. 'I've asked him to go to Accra. In these hard times, the bigger hospitals in cities have the best medicines and specialists. They can cure him in a day. I must advise him strongly on that when I see him tomorrow.' Kani tapped out the tobacco in his pipe. Trails of smoke rose from the smouldering bad tobacco on the ground. Their acrid bite got into his eye. Blinking and rubbing his eye, he smashed the burning tobacco under his sandal.

'Do you have something good for me?' he asked Kapre.

'Can I live at Nkonsia if I refuse my nobleman good tobacco? I have a special type from Nkwakubew.' She rummaged through her silver bowl of beads, cotton wool, camphor, arum, candles, and small bottles of codeine, phensic, and A.P.C. and dark balls of barks and roots. She found a tuft of tobacco tied neatly and gave it to Kani. 'Here you are, my Noble Kani.'

'Just keep supplying me good tobacco and we'll get along just fine. I may even drop calling you Onions.' He quickly untied the piece and stuffed a bit of it into his pipe. Lighting it, he took a long puff, then said to his wife: 'Could you give her ten cedis for me? I don't have little ones on me here.'

'Rest your soul, Nana.' Kapre put her wares together. 'I know you'll like its flavour and come to buy some more. The cost of that will offset this sample.'

'Just like Anancy-the-spider sharing two cobs of corn with the donkey and the cow,' Kani said and puffs of smoke escaped from his mouth. 'Anancy gave one to each of them. Then he asked them to give back to him half each of theirs.'

'May I go now?' Kapre asked.

'The lanes are all clear, Daughter-of-the-Land,' Kani said. 'Please, walk well with the coolness of the evening.' The sun had gone behind the Atewa hills. The grey dusk was turning into darkness. Kani got up and said that he had something to discuss with Master Darko. As he went away, he heard the metal gong sounding. The voice of Kopra-the-town-crier followed soon, announcing the news about the *surveyor line* farmland.

After Kani left her, Ofosuaa gathered her palm fronds into a bundle and went inside the house to continue with her broom-making. It was dark, but the patio was bright with the radiance of the aladdin on the short wall in front

86

f her section of the house. Reaching her from their room
were the voices of Benoa's and her children, studying by
their usual rote method under Misa's direction.

> Twelve nine one o eight
> Twelve ten one twenty
> Twelve eleven one thirty two
> Twelve twelve one forty four . . .

t always amused her to hear the children study. They did
t as if they were singing in roundelays. She put the bundle
of leaves down, then went outside again to fetch her stool.
On her return, she saw Ayowa, standing behind the
balustrade short wall of the cloistral veranda, her head
supported in her palms propped up at her elbows on the
wall. She was staring vacantly into the sky. Ofosuaa went to
her. 'Ayowa,' she called her. Ayowa started. Ofosuaa
patted her on her back to reassure her, but Ayowa turned
away from her. Ofosuaa was quick to catch the glint of a
tear in her eye. 'What is the matter with you?'
'You scared me, mother.' Ayowa walked past her to the
patio. Ofosuaa followed her.
'Where are you going?'
'To Odenchey dance.'
Ofosuaa watched Ayowa disappear around the corner.
She then went back to her room and brought out a
lantern. She took it where she had the fronds and
continued with the broom-making. The children's voices
reached her from their room.

> I'm going to sweep the dirt away
> I'm going to sweep the dirt away
> I'm going to sweep the dirt away
> Swish, swish, swish
> If anybody carrying some dirt
> Comes here to litter again
> I'll hurl that person
> On to the garbage dump.

Ofosuaa smiled. Starting with religious recitations, the

boys went through multiplication tables, names of place and historical events, then closed their studies with rhyme. She knew that they would come out soon and joi her in the patio to tell stories. Then, she thought sh heard her name called from outside. She remained seate though, uncertain whether she had heard correctly. Fron the lanes came the sporadic phrases of a song and th throbs of tom-tom. Then, she heard her name again Ignoring the boys' coming out to join her, she rushe outside. In the dim light of the rising moon, she sa Ayowa doubled over on the bamboo pew, so that her ches rested on her lap. She was drawing some marks on th ground with her index finger.

'You aren't stopping our princess from the danc tonight, are you, Ofosuaa?' the voice that had summone Ofosuaa outside asked. 'I found her here, sitting all alon like a widow. And she won't speak with me. What have yo done to her?'

'I di... didn't know –' Ofosuaa paused to think, tryin to come up with a convincing explanation to Kapre-the Radio, lest she go to broadcast something else. 'Ou princess had complained of a headache earlier. But didn't know she was sitting out here.'

'Hmm, I see,' Radio said. 'These are the dangerou times for nubile girls, especially when they start com plaining of headaches. Take her home and make he comfortable.'

'Thank you,' Ofosuaa snapped at Kapre. 'Our princes doesn't have the type of headache you're thinking of Good night.' Ofosuaa took Ayowa's hand and went wit her toward the gate. Ofosuaa could feel the gossip's eye still on her back. When she was about to enter the house Radio returned her goodnight greeting.

'Sleep well o-o-o, nobleman's wife.'

Hearing the noise from outside, the boys had come an stood near the gate and looked on. 'What is the matter mother?' Misa asked.

'Nothing. Go on and start the storytelling,' Ofosua

aid. 'Your sister has headache. I'll give her some 'hensic.' She walked with Ayowa to the open porch. )ccasionally, the breeze rose and clothed the bare throbs f tom-tom and bongos with swells of *Odenchey* music from he streets. Ofosuaa stood before Ayowa and spoke softly o her. 'I can feel there's something bothering you. Why lon't you tell me? I can only help if there's a problem and ou share it with me. I'm your mother.'

Ayowa studied Ofosuaa quietly, then she asked: 'Will ou believe me if I told you?' Ofosuaa nodded. Ayowa aid: 'Last week, after *Odenchey* dance, a man pressed my ›reasts. I'm afraid I'm pregnant.'

Ofosuaa let out a heavy sigh, then chuckled – a chuckle vhich gradually developed into a long hearty peal of aughter. 'You're so innocent and ignorant, daughter.' ›he hugged her and laughed more. 'When I asked you to ›e careful about men's touching you, I meant going to ›ed with them. Men's passes at you you'll have to contend vith, unfortunately, as you grow. We'll talk more about ;rowing up tonight in the room. Come and help me with he broom I'm making.' They walked where the boys ılready sat. Opia was just about to start a story as Ofosuaa ınd Ayowa sat down to make the broom.

'Who knows why the bat hides during the day and flies ›ut at night?' Opia asked.

'We're yet to learn it from you,' they said.

'Many many years ago . . .' Opia said and the storytelling ›ession began.

# Chapter 6

In a long blue velvet pair of loose shorts topped with white lace jumper, Kani stood on the steps to the open porch and watched the sun come up from behind the Ajapomaa hills. Ofosuaa had told him that Opia had already delivered Benoa's morning greeting, yet it seemed to Kani that the sun had risen earlier than usual that Thursday. He could not remember when in recent times he had slept till eight o'clock after his usual dawn bath. He beamed at the blue sky, then went outside to his garage.

Sanyo was in there already. In starched and well-ironed khaki pants, his black shoes clacking on the cement floor as he went from one side to the other, he briskly dusted the burgundy Mercedes. Kani went round it and in a sweeping glance, had inspected it. He opened the back door and smiled at the fresh white drill with which Sanyo had covered the leather seats. 'Splendid,' he said.

Sanyo grinned. 'Thank you for the pay increase.'

'Much better times are ahead.' Kani winked at him. 'I'm sure the car needs some fuel and engine oil before we set out. See to all of its other needs. I know the gas attendant will make noises because of the fuel rationing. You know how to silence him.' He gave him a wad of cedi bills. 'I also need ten full-size bottles of schnapps. Tell the GNTC manager I want only E.K. brand. You know where to find me on your return.'

'Yes, Nana.' Sanyo pocketed the money. He had to drive six miles to Kibi for the items and the servicing of the car.

Kani went back to his room. He took off his jumper and looked for the cloth dubbed *smiles* because of its designs

cowry shells arranged in a radiating cluster. Having
onned it, he pulled the bottom drawer in his dresser. It
ontained several small safe boxes – wooden and metallic.
e carried out a silver one and placed it on his bed, fished
or a bunch of keys under his pillow and carefully opened
. Its inside was lined with burgundy velveteen, and it
ontained gold jewellery. Kani picked out a big ring,
nspected the symbol of the hawk on it and slipped it on.
le then hung a royal-like chain on his neck and went and
ood before the mirror on the dresser. The hair on his
nassive chest made the gold chain prominent. He turned
is head casually and looked at the far side of the bed
here his wife had slept, smiling at the unmade four-
oster. Suddenly, the room appeared to have darkened.
When he turned round, he found Ofosuaa standing in the
oorway, watching him and smiling.

She had been outside all morning, cleaning the
urroundings of the house in anticipation of the sanitary
nspector's visit to the town. He came every Thursday.
Thursday was Mother Earth's day. Nobody went to the
arm. Nobody did any serious groundwork, lest the
oddess of fertility be disturbed. For the women, Thurs-
ay was a day of general cleaning, too. It was the day of the
anitary inspector, also. He knew nobody was supposed to
o to the farm, and so he came to see how well they had
ept their neighbourhoods clean. And after he had come
nd gone, the women did their laundry. Ofosuaa had
ome to collect from Kani's room the items that needed
o be washed.

'My man, you should have been born a king, instead of
friend of kings,' Ofosuaa said. 'Owiredu must feel proud
bout his would-be in-laws.'

'You couldn't have expressed it any better.' Kani threw
he folds in his twelve yard cloth on his left shoulder. 'And
ny footwear? What do you think of it?'

Ofosuaa stepped back, just to have a good look at his
rinceling sandals. Encrusted with symbols of the hawk
arved out of leather, the footwear shone with Balmoral

91

gloss. She said: 'Sometimes I entertain fears that sor
young woman may whisk you away from me.'

'Why should I sacrifice your oil palm nut soup for h
pepper soup?' Kani laughed. 'If I stuck with you for sev
years when we couldn't have babies, which young wom;
can snatch me from you now? I hear the young women
today hardly wear beads around their waists.'

'They say these are the modern times,' Ofosuaa said.

'Of infidelity. Of promiscuity. Of disloyalty,' Kani sai
'Some of the women look very much like men these da
They talk like men. They walk like men. My woman, I'
happy today. I don't want the maladies of the so-call
modern times to spoil a perfect day for us. I want to enj
a little sun before I go to the bar.' He went outside to tl
open porch.


Ofosuaa proceeded to take down from the canopy fran
of the four poster brass bed all the pieces of cloth Ka
had worn during the week. Some she would just air to su
Going through the open porch, she spoke to Kani. 'I m
be somewhere behind the house. If I don't see you befo
you leave, give my regards to Owiredu.'

'He'll hear,' Kani said.

Ofosuaa carried the load on her arms into her roor
left it there and went outside the house, behind tl
kitchen. Ayowa was inside the kitchen. Having cleaned tl
clay hearths of their ashes, she was using red ochre
polish them and the portions of the floor raised as sea
for children. The window was opened and Ofosuaa cou
carry on a conversation with her through it without seein
her. 'Your father looks as if he's going to be enstooled
king today,' Ofosuaa said. She resumed her scraping o
liverworts from the ground with a snail's shell.

'I thought he'd already left,' Ayowa said back.

'That was Sanyo, going to Kibi.' With her broon
Ofosuaa brought together into a small heap the weeds sh
had got off the ground. 'Your father plans going
Betomu later this morning.'

Ayowa had been wanting to go out of the kitchen to tap water from the tank under the open porch. She, however, had been delaying because of her father's being in the open porch. She was afraid of meeting him face to face. Much as her discussion with her mother in their room the past night had reassured her not to be afraid of her future, there was one thing that kept nagging her. She did not tell Ofosuaa about Entea's sexual assault on her at the Ntanoa farm. Worse still, she had not had her period since then. That was an undeniable situation. Therefore, as far as the truth was concerned, Ofosuaa's words to assuage her fears had not had any impact.

Ayowa fetched a rag saturated with red ochre batter, and daubed the hearth with the paste. Still warm, the pods gave off vapour, which ceased as the red ochre dried quickly. Now, the hearths looked new, as if they had never been used before. How long could they stay thus? Only one fire would blacken them again. Why then, was it necessary to go through the ritual of making them appear new each morning? To her, in their present apparent new form, the pods looked cold and horrendous, like something defiled but hurriedly made over to conceal the marks of blemish. How warm they always appeared each morning, unmade and natural?

She heard somebody greet her mother outside. Realizing it was Kapre-the-Radio, Ayowa listened for any fresh rumour the gossip was broadcasting this morning. 'Better hurry up, Ofosuaa,' Radio was saying. 'The inspector is already in town. On the other side of the highway. These days he doesn't let us hear his footfalls when he's coming.'

'He surely can't get anyone if he heralds his coming.'

'I say he'll put up a mansion soon,' Radio said. 'Last week he got Jamea for not covering her barrel of water. All the spittle in her mouth almost got finished with pleading for mercy. It wasn't until he took a bribe of a hundred cedis from the poor wretch before he tore up her summons sheet.'

'I heard it,' Ofosuaa said.

'I suppose that's better than Jamea's going to court. She'd pay five hundred cedis in fines,' Radio said. 'What we need even to buy food is hard to come by these days. Hmm.' A pregnant pause interrupted by a crack of her knuckles. 'Say, how is our princess this morning? Isn't it wonderful that you're going to become a grandmother soon?'

'From where did you get that idea?' Ofosuaa asked.

Inside the kitchen, Ayowa felt a stab in her chest.

'Well, as it's said, a teenager that will have an early childbirth attracts men by her every action.' Kapre laughed. 'I say, you must see her wiggle her waist at Odenchey dances. All the men go crazy any time she steps inside the circle.'

'Good day, Kapre,' Ofosuaa said. 'I've got work to do.'

Ayowa heard the angry swish-swish of her mother's broom, sweeping away the dirt the sanitary inspector must not come to see on his tour of the neighbourhood. Ayowa's paste, too thick now, had to be diluted. She grabbed a bucket by the handle and tiptoed near the door, stretched her neck to peek from behind the jamb and check the open porch. Her father was not there. She stepped out of the kitchen, but just then Kani appeared in the open porch from his room. For a moment, Ayowa was fixed to the spot. Glaring at her father, she decided to beat a hasty retreat into the kitchen. In her desperation, she tripped over the threshold. She dropped the bucket which rolled noisily away on the patio floor while she reeled back, falling over and crashing against the pile of firewood in one corner. A small piece fell down and scattered a mother hen and her chicks, one of which got hit by the wood. The twittering chick crawled on its side in circles dragging a flagged wing.

Ofosuaa pushed her head through the kitchen window. 'Are you all right? Put the injured chick behind the crock. It should get well soon,' she said. Ayowa picked herself up. Trembling, she drove away the furious mother hen, and squatted and picked up the injured chick. She placed it behind the crock, in the small space between the base of the pot and the inner corner of the walls.

Meanwhile, Kani still stood on the stoop, astonished by Ayowa's behaviour. And for the first time, for no definite reason he could think of, he knew that he was scared – afraid of something he did not want to think or believe could happen to him. 'Ofosuaa!' he bawled and went back into his room.

'What is it?' Ofosuaa asked through the window. Not getting any answer from Ayowa, she quickly left her chore. Ayowa knew that it would be best for her not to stay around. She picked up the bucket, grabbed a towel from the copper line and was rushing out of the house when she met Ofosuaa at the gate. 'What happened?' she asked. Ayowa just walked past her. Ofosuaa hurriedly crossed the patio to the tank. She turned on the tap and washed her hands under the spout. Swishing them in the air in a futile attempt to dry them quickly, she went into Kani's room. He was sitting on the bed, his head hanging. He did not appear to have noticed his wife come in as he only stared at the red Persian rug.

The intricate palmette motif designs in it played tricks on his imagination. In one moment, they seemed to be distending and assuming pregnant shapes of a human belly, and the next they dwindled and began to whirl round and round, until there was nothing to see but the fusion of the red with all the other colours into a hazy ball.

'I'm here.' Ofosuaa rubbed her hands in her cloth.

'Sit down.' Kani thumped the bed.

'Why do you make my heart beat so fast?' Ofosuaa barely perched on the bed, a considerable distance between Kani and herself. 'What is the matter?'

'You should know,' Kani retorted, his gaze still on the Persian rug. 'I wonder if you're a woman at all after your seven births. Have you noticed that there's something – something awfully wrong about my daughter?' He beat the bed with his fisted hands and the gold chain on his neck tossed around, clinking.

'Who, Ayowa?'

'I don't have a second daughter by another woman.' Kani turned to Ofosuaa. His mind still played tricks on him. At the thought of people assuming he might have gone to bed with his own daughter, nausea glutted his throat. He spat a glob of mucus on the rug. Ofosuaa rose from the bed. 'Where are you going?' Kani stared after her as Ofosuaa walked to the window. She leaned against the wall, in a partial sitting posture so that her lower back was against the edge of the sill while her upper body almost blocked the sunlight from outside. She eyed her husband with such apathetic calmness that it infuriated him more.

'Get away from the window and let in fresh air,' he said.

'If something smells foul in here, it's your sputum.'

Kani glared at her. 'Having seven children and going around boasting about them doesn't make you a woman if you can't tell what is wrong with my daughter. Gee, my only daughter. What creature would seek to hurt me like this? And my own wife can't see there's something wrong with my daughter?'

'Yes, I know,' Ofosuaa said. 'She only had headache – '

Kani growled and bulged his cheeks to spit again, but he did not. His face, however, contorted in a grimace as he audibly swallowed the phlegm. 'Ofosuaa, you dis appoint me,' he said in a raspy voice. 'I don't believe a headache makes a girl dumb before her father.' He advanced on her. Ofosuaa quickly moved away from the window to the door.

'I don't think it's what you imagine.' She knotted her girdle to keep her under cloth properly in place. 'She doesn't in the least breath like –'

'Like your mother's cu –' he snapped his fingers, his teeth clenched as though he were in excruciating pain. His whole body shook. And as if to prevent his huge frame from coming apart, he wound his arms around himself in a strong embrace of his own body. Suddenly, the tension

96

in his body loosened and he stood breathing heavily. His cloth slipped down his shoulder, but he did not pick it up. He just slumped on to the bed, sitting at the edge. 'I'm terribly sorry,' he said about the obscenity that he had almost let out of his mouth against his wife.

'O, my man.' Ofosuaa went to him. She ran her hand over his chest. 'You don't have to be angry. You don't have to worry. What can frighten you?'

'I'm not sure. I only know I'm afraid. The hawk and the hen incident. The dream, that dream, my woman. I must have bitten into something too tough for me to eat or chew..' He beat the bed with his fisted hand. 'Please, ask my daughter to come here.'

'She isn't in the house.'

'Can you please ask her again what bothers her? She's hiding something from me.' He stood up and donned his cloth well. 'Let me know what the problem is with her on my return.' He walked to the window and stared outside, not even turning to look at his wife as she left the room.

The splatter of many years torrential rain had robbed the buildings of their grace, changing their white or cream tones into dull yellow or mustard brown. In the bright sun of the morning, they gave off a vague odour of spent limestone. As faint as the smell was, it reinforced Ayowa's indignation at things wasted, like the red ochre batter used to polish the tripod clay hearth each morning only to be vitiated again by another use. Of what use was it then? Once when Ayowa was upset with herself for breaking Obaa Panyin's reading glasses left on a chair, which Ayowa had not noticed before sitting on that chair, Obaa Panyin asked Ayowa not to be perturbed because everything happened for a purpose. Ayowa thought that comment was inane; what good could come out of things broken through sheer carelessness? Or what noble compensation could there be for a virgin stripped of her honour in a wanton sexual assault by a depraved man?

Suddenly, she began to feel light and happy, as if she

did not have to worry about anything else but her determination to go on in life. No matter what happened to her, in the process of human growth, in the search for meaning, her determination was the only thing that mattered. All the world was a prop for life to go on. Make overs ensured a continuity; they translated the foibles out of innocence and the weals of experience in to modes of maturity. When she had tripped and fallen, she picked herself up to go on. She had put the injured chick behind the pitcher, just for it to get well and go on. The clay hearth had to be polished fresh with red ochre each morning for a new fire to be made in it. The houses splattered by years of torrential rain could be given a fresh coat of paint to look new... And she found her under standing of it so profound that she wondered how she could have come up with it in her moment of great agitation.

Like some other houses at Nkonsia, Benoa's was of the simple *Atakpame* architecture, constructed in layers of mud. The building had stucco only on the inside walls of the rooms. The house stood in an L shape, a split bamboo fence enclosing the rest of the compound to form a small patio. The bamboo had gone pale, but some of the dracaena poles to which they had been fixed for upright support, fed by water from the bathing place, had sprouted leaves. Ayowa drew up her long skirt-like cloth and hopped across the waste from the bathing place that seeped out under the fence. With casual effort, she pushed in the little gate nailed together from hewn pieces of *Wawa* and entered the house.

In dark brown khaki shorts stained so much with resin, Benoa was standing on the last but highest rung of a raffia ladder and covering with palm fronds the mud walls of a section of his house that had no roof over it. Rain had washed the top layer down to half its original height.

'Good morning,' Ayowa greeted Benoa, smiling and trying to sound cheerful as she paused and looked up at her uncle.

'Yea, it looks like a nice one.' He looked down at Ayowa

from his height. His haggard looks made him appear much older than the middle aged he was. 'What is keeping your father inside his house? I just came back from the palm wine bar. I waited so long for him. Had he left for Nna Asaa's when you set out?'

'He was about to,' Ayowa said. 'Is Mansa here?'

'In the kitchen.' Benoa hurried with his work.

Mansa had heard Ayowa. She hastened to turban with a white rag, the bristle end of the pestle she had just cleaned, and leaned it against the inner corner of the wall. She fetched a towel hanging from the kitchen door, flung it around her neck and took a bucket with a small calabash in it and went outside with Ayowa. Mansa had been born a few hours ahead of Ayowa, and because of that they addressed each other sister. Along the lanes, Mansa had to quicken her pace to catch up with her taller cousin. The path into the bush at the fringes of the town was broader and so Mansa walked beside Ayowa, both of them involuntarily increasing their pace down a steep slope near the refuse dump where two vultures were foraging on trash close to the path. They leaped away on to the garbage heap proper as Ayowa and Mansa got closer.

'You don't look happy this morning,' Mansa said.

'I just needed to get away from the house.'

'Lick your elbows if you aren't hiding something from me,' Mansa teased. Ayowa managed a smile. 'For the first time, you missed Odenchey dance last night. Many people were disappointed. They left early because you weren't there,' Mansa said. Anytime it had been Ayowa's turn to lead the singing at Odenchey, the crowd became larger and taller as people craned their necks to see her in action in the open space.

'Who is the man?' Mansa popped the question.

'What?' Ayowa asked, shocked.

'Don't play me for a fool,' Mansa insisted. 'You know what I'm talking about. When a girl stops attending Odenchey dance sessions, we all know what it means. Who is the suitor?'

Ayowa could not resist the funny look on her cousin's face; she burst out laughing in spite of herself. 'I'm sorry if I disappointed anyone yesterday,' she said. 'As far as a man is concerned, you'll always be one of the first to know if there's somebody. I just don't like it when people shout my name in the dark during Odenchey. Who knows which devil gets to know me? Now I feel lost.'

'Your charm alone dispels any evil force, so don't lie to me,' Mansa said. 'Whatever it is that you're hiding from me shows on your face. I'm not only your cousin, but a friend too, and a sincere one. I'm there to help.' Close by them a white and black finch twittered. The two girls looked and saw the finch toss itself from a wild cassava branch into a glob of water in the saddle of a large cocoyam leaf, where it cavorted for a moment, then flew back to the cassava branch twittering, ruffling its feathers to dry them.

The path was beginning to widen as it went further and further into the bush. Some girls were coming from the opposite direction, chattering. Ayowa placed her finger on her mouth to indicate silence to Mansa, who dropped behind for the other girls to pass. Their buckets and sunflower tins balanced on their heads, they greeted the two cousins as they passed them and resumed their conversation about a drunk who had mistaken kerosine for liquor. Mansa caught up and walked abreast with Ayowa. They went on in silence until they reached a section of the stream called *women's pool*. Men were not allowed in it on Thursday. Some girls had already done their washing. Having spread the items out on the low bushes around to dry, the girls were in the pool playing water hide-and-seek. One of them popped out and hurled an invitation to the two cousins, asking whether they were coming to join the others in the water. As quickly as she had come out, she disappeared under the water again.

'Do we need to go to the head pool?' Mansa asked.

'There's something I want us to discuss.' Ayowa glanced at the pool, nostalgic of the freedom of the girls swimming. As they passed the pool area, she lied to

Mansa. 'My mother told me last night that girls have to discuss certain things among themselves.'

'My mother tells me such are the signs of maturity,' Mansa said. 'We only go to them for advice when the matter is bigger than our age. Or when a bad friend is trying to poison our minds.'

'My mother says it's always convenient for a young woman to know certain secrets a man won't think of,' Ayowa said. 'Our world is completely different from theirs. They don't have to go through the cycle of monthly period.'

The footpath became narrower here. Long masses of grass almost crossed over it, and the two girls literally had to wade through. They soon came to the head pool of the stream. They put their containers upside down beneath the kola tree and sat on them. It was quiet all round, except an occasional chirp of a bird that rose above the muffled shrill of cicada in the bushes in the background. Ayowa checked for the stinkhorn she had seen some days before but it was gone. Completely disintegrated, she found no traces of it at all. Instead, the Blood lily close by had bloomed. Atop its lonely stalk shielded near the base by a bract of lush lance-like leaves, the scarlet ball of long anthers glowed like a star among the low green underbrush.

'Is it always true a young woman may be pregnant if she doesn't see her period at the end of the moon? Is it also true that a woman can destroy her belly?' Ayowa asked. Mansa stared at her, an expression of horror on her face. Then she turned away from Ayowa to avoid the look in her eyes suggesting that Mansa ought to know since she was acquainted with some of the older girls in town referred to as *hard*.

She carried the buckets to the stream and began to fill them, using the calabash. Ayowa went and stood beside her, watching the whirligigs. Having been agitated by the presence of the two girls in the water, the whirligigs had broken their serene swim in circles. They now skittered in wild loops on the pool. Ayowa flung her hand at a dragonfly that had flown almost into her nostril. The insect darted back. Its big glassy eyes on her, it hovered in a momentary tease, then dashed away into the forest of water-canna.

'Did you hear my questions?' Ayowa asked Mansa.

Mansa looked to the right, and then to the left. 'There are certain things that we can only talk about within the four walls of a room,' she said. 'Adia has done it before, but I need to be sure about it from her. We don't want to talk about the things you're asking while we're standing in a stream, especially on Thursday. A stream is a god. And today is their day, you know. The spirits are abroad, you know.'

Ayowa nodded in agreement, her lips drawn tight. They both made circular pads from the towels, placed them on their heads and then balanced the buckets of water on them. They headed home, hardly saying a word between them.

The bright and warm morning sun, coupled with the chirrup of the weaver birds in the royal palms and the accacias at the market area, charged the atmosphere with the prospects of holiday full of leisure and relaxation, but Kani knew that for him, it was going to be a long uncomfortable day. Already, he could hear faint metallic snaps in the air; they only lacked the sharpness and intense rapidity with which the corrugated iron roofing sheets crackled from high noon heat. He hung his head as he went along the lanes on his way to Nna Asaa's palm wine bar.

Not even once did he raise his head to greet or respond to the salutations of the people he met. Through the corners of his eyes, he could see the women cleaning their neighbourhoods pause and stare at him, obviously amazed that he was not his usual vocal and amiable and generous self that morning. In normal times, he would go beyond the etiquette of mere street greetings; he would enquire about the welfare of a household. And, if there

102

was the slightest hint of a family's uncertainties about the day's meals, he definitely would part with something. There was a song by the Adenkum group of women which said that anybody Kani met on his morning trip to the palm wine shanty never went to bed hungry. This morning, however, all his preoccupation was with his fears that Ayowa had let some man deceive her.

The palm wine shanty was already filled with men when he arrived there. Roofed with raffia thatch and enclosed within a plaided palm frond fence, it was a penthouse set against the north end wall of Nna Asaa the seller's house. As soon as Kani entered it, Addo-the-tapper and all the young men rose and offered him places to sit on the coconut palm boles that lined the lengths of the shanty. He casually waved his hand in a gesture of salutation to the men and Nna Asaa. Sitting near the entrance on a high stool, she was behind a large black earthenware pot set on a small padded wicker basket. She appeared to have braced the pot with her thin legs, the cloth covering them drawn up to her knees and thus exposing her shins.

'You look like a member of a royal entourage,' Nna Asaa said. 'What is cooking at the Paramount chief's palace today?'

'Nothing that I know of. I'm going to see Owiredu.' Kani sat near Benoa. Beside his brother-in-law, Benoa suddenly looked like an old man on a misguided diet course.

'I hear his illness isn't of this land,' Benoa said.

'May God give him back his strength as –'

Kani interrupted Nna Asaa. 'He must go to a big hospital in Accra, instead of sitting around, waiting for miraculous cure from the air.' He looked at the large calabash before Benoa, almost empty of palm wine. 'What is that doing before you? Or you just are enjoying the theatre of the flies flying in and out of it?'

'If you had delayed a little more in coming, all the palm wine would have got finished.' Benoa tagged lightly at the wrinkled skin clinging to his chin like a small empty wineskin. 'All that is left of the white stuff is this before me here. You're welcome to share it with us.' He stretched his arm to indicate the large calabash before him. Like the Raven and the Vulture, Kani understood his brother-in-law's proverbial invitation to fill the calabash before him with palm wine. Kani laughed aloud, hoping that could diffuse his inner apprehension about Ayowa.

'Can Nna Asaa let me go for a day without a taste of her good palm wine?' Kani picked up the large calabash and handed it to Nna Asaa. 'Fill it up for us,' he said.

She placed the calabash on her lap and proceeded to fill it. 'How can I let the day's drink of life get finished without my nobleman's having had some?' Nna Asaa asked in her tremulous voice. Her hand trembled under the weight of a smaller calabash fixed to a long stick as a dipper to scoop the wine from the large black earthenware. When the big calabash was full, she placed a smaller one on the drink. Addo-the-tapper got up and took it from her offering hands. He placed it in a dent in the cement floor before Kani, who gave a hundred cedi bill to Nna Asaa. She shoved the money down her big *kaba* blouse. Clinking coins, she fished for change in a small sack in her groin area and brought out the exact amount in smaller bills and coins.

'Keep the change for now.' Kani's eyes rested on a soup crock simmering on a coal-pot beside the earthenware. 'Some soup will be in order.'

'That's a man of my heart.' Nna Asaa dropped the change in the sack inside her *kaba*. 'I keep saying no one should ever drink on empty stomach, but people don't listen to me.' She drove a ladle through the soup on the coal-pot. Kani sat silently, his gaze on the wine pot as though he was contemplating the dry trails of palm wine and the flies scudding around the pot. Benoa waved his hand over the calabash of wine before Kani to drive away flies.

'But why were you so late in coming here after my message?' Benoa asked. Kani sighed, thinking for a moment.

'Sanyo had to do one or two things on my car. I had to stay and watch him finish the work.' He dabbed the tip of his broad nose with his satin kerchief; he could never bring into the open his observation that Ayowa was concealing something from him. 'You may take the head of the palm wine,' he said.

Benoa drew up his cloth to cover his clavicles and shoulders, the joints of which stood out in shiny little knots. He fetched some of the wine with the small calabash, picked out some brown stuff in it with his right index finger, and then began a libation. '*Nananom* our ancestors, here is a drink for you.' He poured some of the wine into a small hole that showed the earth in the cement floor. The drink quickly sank into the ground.

'Spirits of the land, come and share with us this drink. Your own son noble Kani, the mighty hawk and Victor, has bought it for us.' Benoa poured out some more drink. This time, however, the quantity was quite great, and all of it did not sink immediately. It formed a head that began to flow away into one of the drainage grooves incised in the cement floor like a huge skeletal remains of a palm frond.

'If it were you who bought it, would you pour so much away?' Addo-the-tapper said. 'After all, if you give the spirits too much, they'll become drunk and forget to hear our supplications.'

'Shut up!' Benoa said, the tiny folds of flesh under his chin quivering. 'The drink comes from the spirits. If we don't give back to them what they've so benevolently given us in abundance, do you think they'll put some more into the trees for you to tap?'

'What do you have in abundance?' Addo snapped at him.

'Will you let him finish with the prayers?' Nna Asaa said above the murmurs that rose from the other young men. Benoa only shook his head in disdain at Addo-the-tapper.

'*Nananom Nsamanfo,*' he concluded the pouring of the libation, 'please, listen to us any time we call you.' He poured a few more drops down, then put the remainder of it in the small calabash into the bigger one. He fetched another calabash full. As he gulped it down, Addo angrily watched Benoa's sunken cheeks bulge and shrink as he swallowed the drink with muffled chugs.

'Asomorodwe-the-beetle. It buys no drinks but gets drunk all the same,' Addo said. Benoa wiped his mouth dry with the back of his hand, then turned to his brother-in-law. Kani was still looking at the floor.

'You're unusually quiet,' Benoa said. 'Owiredu is going to be well. He only needs to see one of these doctors with a name.'

'I wish it were that simple.' Kani sighed.

Suddenly, in a frantic gesture, he sat up and fetched some of the wine. Staring at a black speck bobbing with the drink, he let out a guffaw, looking around at the faces of the men, as if hoping to infect someone with his morbid hilarity. 'When one is bigger than his adversary, one swallows him in a drink,' he said. The men laughed as Kani set the calabash to his mouth and drank it all. 'I don't want to become deaf. Please, bring us the meat. I wonder why these men will drink without eating meat.'

'Benoa complained the soup had too much salt in it,' Addo said. 'But he hadn't even tasted it.'

'Let the young men complain, and not you who need some inducement to enable you to climb into bed with your wife,' Kani said and everybody in there laughed. 'Give us fifty cedis worth, Nna Asaa.' Standing up to get more money from his shorts, he bumped his head against the raffia thatch and so had to bow his body halfway.

'A man among men,' Addo insinuated. 'When one doesn't have money, one believes in the power of the herb.'

'It's the other way round,' Benoa said and dipped his hand under his cloth. He rummaged in his pocket for a crumpled packet of Durbars, and took out a cigarette already smoked to a third of its length. He tore off the light aluminium foil lining the packet and clipped it around the unsmoked tip end. As he set it to his mouth,

Addo proffered a plastic lighter already lit. Benoa studied his face incredulously.

'I fight my enemies face to face,' Addo said. 'What do I gain burning your grizzly hair dyed with soot from the bottom of soup crock?' He lit Benoa's piece for him.

'I know that sometimes you're a good man from deep within.' Clouds of smoke issued from Benoa's mouth and nostrils. 'Well, see what Nna Asaa has in that clay bowl for us.'

'It's porcupine meat today,' Nna Asaa said as Addo took the bowl of soup with chunks of meat in it. He placed the vapouring bowl before Kani. Pressing the tips of his thumb and index finger to a corn husk string wound around the meat, Kani lifted a piece. He untied the band to keep the piece intact while it cooked, and ate it.

'I should admit it,' he said, blowing his mouth. 'The soup tasted good, but it's so spicy hot as to give heart palpitation.'

'Your systems need something medicinal everyday,' Nna Asaa said. 'I added ginger and black pepper.'

Addo fetched himself some of the wine and drank it. He then squatted before the bowl of soup, waved away some flies and took a piece of meat. His mouth full, he gabbled, 'Only someone with no sense of taste or smell will say this soup doesn't taste nice.' A wee morsel of food flew out of his mouth and landed on the floor, close to the bowl of soup. Benoa pushed him back from the soup and Addo landed on his haunches.

'We don't need your sputum to flavour it any further,' Benoa said, mouthing a big chunk himself.

'Mistletoe.' Addo pointed at Benoa, who fetched some more wine and pushed down the food in his mouth with it. He knew that Addo's words could be more sarcastic, sharp and cutting like the knife he used in tapping oil palm trees. The next reference he was sure Addo would make would be to the allegation that Benoa took a bribe of three hundred cedis two years ago so that his oldest son Ayerakwa could become a carver's apprentice in another town, instead of his sending him to secondary school.

From somewhere along the lane, the men heard a running engine. As the fluid sound got closer, Addo went and stood at the entrance of the shanty, watching. 'Your car is here, Nana,' he announced as the Mercedes parked to the side of the lane.

'I've got to leave you now, folks.' Half stooping, Kani walked out of the shanty and donned his cloth well.

'Tell Owiredu God will heal him,' Nna Asaa said.

'He needs a doctor, not God,' Kani said back.

'There's a white man who teaches at the Abuakwaman School at Kibi,' Addo said. 'He drinks palm wine. He says it's the drink of God. It gives him strength. He says he feels closer to God in this land.'

'That one is an indigent white man,' Kani said. The men inside broke into laughter. Benoa laughed so much that he began to cough violently, making noises like dry paper being crumpled. Addo still stood at the entrance. He saw Entea come out of the front seat of Kani's car and bang the door shut. He had a short black stick which he was swinging like a band leader. After he held a brief conversation with Kani, the nobleman pulled out a wad of cedis and passed some to Entea, who then strutted to the shanty.

Addo spat on the ground. 'If I don't quit tapping, I may be compelled to commit murder with my tapper's knife,' he said. Nna Asaa shot him a hard look, and Addo quickly made himself clear. 'I can't believe Entea is riding in the nobleman's car.'

'You haven't seen anything yet.' Entea pushed Addo aside and entered the shanty. 'Wait till you see me in the sun, riding beside Kani in the back seat of his car and waving at you empty barrels.' He had a bunch of ground cherries in one hand which he began to crush in his palm with the black stick. They emitted little explosive noises as they burst.

'You desecrate Kani's name and his family,' Benoa said.

'I'm a friend of his family's,' Entea said. He fetched some of the wine. In silence, the men watched him gulp it down at a stretch. His eyes were popping when he inished. Patting his belly, he belched. Then he placed the small calabash in the big one containing the wine, deftly swivelling it. For some moments, the small calabash went on turning round and round, casting small ripples on the surface of the palm wine in the big calabash. When it finally stopped, he rattled a conventional drinking slogan in appreciation of his own effort. '*Ekpele kpeledzi, anante anangbe.*'

Addo shook his head.

'You all strike your chest to claim you're men. Don't you know that implies retreat?' Entea demonstrated it, knocking his chest with light blows in quick succession and walking backward. 'Where I have been, men strike their back. That implies forward ever into action.' He struck his back at his nape, moving forward to the bowl of soup. He dipped his hand into it and fetched a big chunk of meat. Without taking off the corn shuck string, he wolfed it down at once.

'Look here, young man,' Nna Asaa addressed Entea. 'It isn't good for people to be afraid of you. It is a virtue if people respect you. Some people may fear you, but I'll skin your so-called manhood from you if you bring your insolence here. I've had enough with you.'

Entea looked at her, shocked. He had not expected such an affront from Nna Asaa. 'I'm sorry, good woman,' he said. 'You're the woman whose fingers were destined for delicacies. When you cook soup with rat and crab, it tastes like beef –'

'Don't you patronize me!' Nna Asaa said.

'I never intended to. I came to this shanty to have a good time,' Entea said. 'But as you can see, it's these young men who don't like me. So, I do what I do as a defence mechanism, like the skunk, you know. But I'm not nasty at all. Good day to you all.' He left the shanty.

The men started chattering as they drank and ate. Soon, they heard the drums summoning them to attend communal labour on the construction of a new middle-school building. They all went away a short while later.

# Chapter 7

Earlier in the evening, it had drizzled. It was the type of rain children described as a sign that the leopard was washing its baby; the sun had shone as the light rain came down. Now, fog rose from the Atewa hills to merge with the still overcast sky. Though thunder rumbled faintly in the distant east, Kani's children were eager to go out for the Odenchey dance before their father returned. They had very little time for recreational activity any time Kani was around. Impatiently, they watched as Ofosuaa carefully ladled out soup on the bowls of *foo-foo* that they were about to eat.

After the morning fracas with her husband, Ofosuaa had maintained a pleasant disposition to the astonishment of Ayowa. It was as if whatever happened in the morning did not relate to Ayowa in any way; Ofosuaa had not asked her anything with regards to it. Ofosuaa had reassured herself that there was no problem with her daughter; having studied Ayowa closely, Ofosuaa had determined that Ayowa was not pregnant; the flesh around her eyes did not appear baggy; her complexion did not seem to have changed in any way. Ofosuaa believed that Ayowa still had to overcome the trauma of her experience with the young man who had pressed her breasts at an Odenchey dance.

While they ate, Ayowa brought up a conversation about the chick that had been hurt in the morning. It had recovered. Ofosuaa explained that she did not know what secret lay behind the healing powers of pitchers set against the inner corners of kitchens, but it was an ancient nowledge passed from generation to generation. And as far as she could remember, the magic of pitchers in kitchen corners had never failed. Ayowa told her brothers that she would light all the lamps in the house so that Misa could go with the others to watch the start of the Odenchey dance. Ayowa said that she wanted to chat more with her mother after meals in the evening and so she stayed at home. Even when she heard the engine of her father's car, she did not become frightened. It was a relief for her, however, when her mother asked her to go and warm her father's soup. Thus when Kani entered the open porch, he did not see her. She was in the kitchen.

'Good evening, my woman,' Kani greeted Ofosuaa. 'It's been an exciting day with Owiredu even if he didn't look good. My woman, illness can change a person within a short time.'

'Welcome back, my man. As it's said, the only thing that gives one's enemy an undue advantage over one is a debilitating illness.' She followed Kani into his room, where he took off his cloth and threw it in a heap on the bed. Ofosuaa collected it and began to fold it. Kani sat down at the edge of the bed and held his head between his hands, his eyes on the red Persian rug, his gold chain dangling before him. Ofosuaa continued talking: 'Did you talk him into going to Korle Bu hospital?'

'He's going next week,' Kani said. 'But we talked mostly about my daughter.' He stood up to his full height and stretched himself, yawning. He took off the gold chain and put it on the chest of drawers near the bedhead and reached for his bottle of schnapps in which were roots and spices, and shook it. He poured himself half a glass full while Ofosuaa still worked the cloth. She hung it folded on the far side of the canopy frame of the brass bed. 'You must be tired. Will you wash yourself before you eat?'

'Yes, with lukewarm water.' Kani drank his schnapps, then sat down on the bed again. 'Did you ask Ayowa what the problem with her is? I want a detailed description of everything.'

Ofosuaa thought quickly and made up an answer. 'She complained of abdominal pains,' she said. Kani fixed her with his big eyes in an upward glance and she realized immediately her folly in lying to him. 'But she's scared you might beat her up because a man touched her breasts at Odenchey.'

'Beat her? Whenever have I laid a finger on her?' For some moments, Kani shook his head from side to side slowly in disappointment. 'Woman, you shame me. So you can't tell what could be wrong with your daughter when she tells you yesterday she has headache, and today she has stomach troubles?' His eyes were calm as they gazed at Ofosuaa.

'I know what you mean, my man. But it's nothing of that sort.' She went closer and put her hand on his shoulder to reassure him. 'I have studied her closely.'

'Are you only refusing to admit it because you can't imagine our shame?' His voice was edgy. His nostrils dilated as he breathed heavily. He pushed Ofosuaa's hand away. 'Do you know what I'm feeling within me now? Did you find out whoever it was that pressed her breasts? Did you inspect her?'

'Inspect her how? What do you know about women?'

'Enough to recognize it when my daughter is hiding something from me. Where is she? Call her here. Bring her here with you.'

'Please, eat something first.' Ofosuaa placed the back of her right hand in her left palm in a pleading gesture. 'At least, drink some soup. I don't believe you've eaten anything the whole day. It obviously was a tiring day. Eat and rest awhile first.'

'I don't feel for food any more.' He stood up and swathed his evening cloth around him. 'I'll let you know when I need food, my woman. Meanwhile, ask Ayowa to come here with you.' His voice was soft but firm. He followed her to the open porch.

The radio was talking softly. He turned it off, went and sat in his hammock chair, placing his pipe on one of the

112

Windsor chairs closer to him. Nothing seemed pleasant to him; he only wished to smoke to quell some indefinite rumbling deep inside him. He opened his tobacco pouch and took out a piece. Concentrating on stuffing the tobacco piece into his pipe, he did not seem to be aware that Ofosuaa and Ayowa had come into the open porch. He lit his pipe, puffed at it many times and then put it aside on the Windsor chair. Though he sat relaxed, he knew that his fingers were trembling. The anxiety he had had in the morning had persisted all day. Clearing his throat, he spoke. 'I brought you some nice gifts, my princess,' he said to Ayowa in a seemingly well composed manner, not looking directly at her. 'Have you had something to eat yet? Your mother tells me you don't eat much these days, and that something is worrying you. What is it?'

Ayowa just stood, looking down at her feet. Kani moved his eyes from mother to daughter and marvelled at the likeness of Ayowa to Ofosuaa. He thought that anybody who did not know them might take them for twins in a distance, were it not for the difference in their heights. Ayowa stood a couple of inches shorter than her mother. For a moment, however, Kani lost sight of Ayowa from the blinding flash of lightning that rent the sky. Thunder clapped and roared, bringing down a flurry of rain which presently beat a tattoo over the galvanized iron sheets in the distance as it receded. Ayowa moved closer to her mother when the gusty wind sprayed her with cold water.

'My princess,' Kani called her. Ayowa raised her eyes to look at him briefly. 'It isn't appropriate to say it before you. But I suppose it doesn't make any difference. You know that I love and like you best among all my children. I'm ready to put down my life now. To save you from any trouble. But I can't do that if you don't tell me what troubles you.'

'I told you it was too late, but you weren't listening.'

'What is too late?' Kani asked Ayowa. She raised her head to speak again, but her brothers' noisy entry into the house interrupted her. Describing the exciting dance that the rain threatened to disrupt, they rushed into the open porch. 'Get away from here and go to study!' Kani shouted at them. 'Don't you think about anything else apart from play and games?'

'Yes, go on from here,' Ofosuaa said to the boys, hurrying them away. 'You can talk about the dance some other time.' The boys walked away silently in a file to their room. Soon, they began reciting loudly:

> . . . Suffer the little children
> To come unto me
> And forbid them not
> For of such is
> The Kingdom of God.
> St. M-a-r-k, Chapter 10, verse 14.

Believing the children were alluding to him, Kani stood up and went down the stoop, intending to go and beat them up. But a violent peal of thunder lashed a sheet of rain at him, and he turned and ran back to his seat. He felt defeated and angry about himself. He knew that Ayowa was his irritation, but he also knew that he could never lay a hand on her. But why had he never been able to punish Ayowa even when it was she who upset him? He shifted in his seat to make a pocket on his pair of velvet shorts accessible to him. The movement, however, scared Ayowa, who jumped closer to her mother.

Kani dried his face with his cloth, then searched through his pockets as though he were looking for something small but essential. Pulling out his hand, he addressed Ayowa. 'This is for you, my princess, if you'll tell me what bothers you,' he said. 'You may not know it, but you've been causing me a great deal of worry by your silent attitude.' He stretched his arm toward Ayowa. She saw that it held a wad of cedi bills.

'Father, it isn't money that I want.' She sniffled.

'What makes you sad?' Kani asked as Ofosuaa dabbed her

114

daughter's face with the hem of her cloth. 'Please, don't cry. I'll give the money to your mom to keep for you. I'll do everything in my power to make you happy. Just let me know what the trouble is. That's why I'm your father. Tell me what disturbs you. I promise you, I won't be angry with you.'

'I'm afraid, father.' Ayowa broke out crying.

'Afraid of what?' Kani asked. He could see the fear buried deep somewhere inside him surging to the surface. What would he do if Ayowa was pregnant? 'You needn't fear anything. I'm always with you. The whole of this town shudders when I speak.' He sat up and struck his massive chest. 'I'm a friend of kings. Tell me, my princess.'

'I'm afraid to say it here.' Ayowa shook with the spasm of her crying. She clutched to her mother for support. 'Help me, mother. It's so painful. No other injury could be so painful.'

'What injury are you talking about?' Kani asked. 'Yes, maybe you want to confide in your mother. Maybe, it's women's problem now. My woman, please take my daughter into my room.' He hurried them away with his hand as Ofosuaa put her arm around Ayowa's shoulders and went with her into the room. 'Yes, take her into my room, my woman. And tell your mom everything, my daughter.' Breathing heavily, Kani sank deep into his hammock chair, as if the canvas could form a shell of protection for him against some unknown terror he knew could tear him apart.

He could hear Ayowa's muffled cry occasionally interrupted by whispers inside the room. As he sat there, he felt his heart pounding, in his head and hands and feet. The darkness out there was like a flood, a deluge rushing to engulf him. All his life, he had desired to live in peace, rejecting troubles. Maybe, there was some benevolent force out there after all, which might have been too good to him, giving him so much that he might have taken certain things for granted. 'O, God Omnipotent, if you're there as they say, please help me this once more,' he said under his breath. As far as his past life was concerned, he

could really not remember when he had had to wake up
in the deep of night and go anywhere in search of a
hospital for any of his seven children. Not even once had
he spent a sleepless night or minute to think about what
his family would eat the next day or how he would pay the
tuition fees of his sons in secondary school or overseas.
Never had he wondered what it was like to go out seeking
a loan early in the morning. The only person he had ever
felt more concerned about was Ayowa... He suddenly lost
track of his thoughts as Ofosuaa rushed out into the porch
and knelt down before him.

'What is it?' Kani exploded in a fit of anger as if that
alone could alter what his wife had to tell him. Deep
silence fell on the house. The children had stopped their
studying. They had come out on to the cloistral veranda to
watch and listen to what was going on in the open porch.
'Get back inside your room,' Kani yelled at them across
the patio. 'What is it, Ofosuaa?' He bawled again. Then in
a low tone, he said: 'Whatever it is, please say it softly.
Softly, please.' He tapped Ofosuaa on her shoulder as a
child would do to his mother for attention.

Ofosuaa stood up, slowly and silently. For the first time
ever since she had known him, she heard a subterranean
tremulous quality in Kani's voice, as though a part of him
somewhere deep inside him, was squeaking. And he
appeared small, shrivelled in the hammock chair. 'O, my
man. Ayowa was raped six weeks ago. At Ntanoa farm. And
she hasn't seen her period since then. And he threatened
her with death if she said anything about it.'

Kani braced the arm rests of the hammock chair with his
hands and stiffened. His body shook violently and the hairs
on it rose erect. He managed to ask: 'Who was the beast?'

'Our daughter has been suffering silently all these days.
Crippled by the sting of a scorpion.' Her eyes brimmed
with tears. She sprawled on the floor and wound her arms
around Kani's feet, looking up into his grim face. 'It's
abominable. The man. I fear to mention his name –
Entea!'

116

Kani felt the muscles around his bottom contract and taughten, giving him an unbearable sting that left an uncomfortable hard knot in his anus. A hot feeling then rose through his spine and exploded with a painful jab in his head. When it all ceased, he was wet at his bottom, and all the pent up anxiety of the day within him found expression in a feeble utterance of 'Ao!' He felt tired suddenly, and weak at his joints. He immediately craved for schnapps made more hot with plenty of pepper and other hot spices and roots. From the doorway, Ayowa's quiet cries reached him. He tried to rise from his chair, but he could not. He asked huskily: 'Why didn't you tell me, Ayowa? Entea can't kill you.'

'He has already murdered my soul,' Ayowa whimpered.

'O, my heart. Now, I know what you meant by it was too late.'

'What shall we do?' Ofosuaa wept loudly. 'Why should this happen to us? And at this time? Let's take her to the hospital. The doctor will determine if she's indeed pregnant or not.'

'What? Are you out of your mind? Do you want everybody to hear about it? Take her with you to go and sleep. This isn't a problem for women any more. Remember to give her the money.' Kani only looked straight ahead into the dark void. Ofosuaa took Ayowa's hand and, together, they went down the stoop into their room.

'I'm scared to death, mother,' Ayowa said. 'I can't wait to get rid of this belly. There isn't any worse evil than what has happened to me already.'

'Don't think like that.' Ofosuaa sat beside Ayowa on the bed. 'Right now, I don't know what we are going to do. But I know for sure that everything is going to be all right. Your father is a powerful man. He'll solve this problem by tomorrow morning. If he says he'll put his life down to save you from any trouble, then he means it. Cheer up. Think about nice things and have pleasant dreams.'

They both prepared themselves to go to bed.

* * *

Kani sat for a long time in his hammock chair. His mind remained virtually blank and he looked into the darkness outside the open porch. The heavy downpour had made more dense the silence that had settled over the house. The sky was clear, and the half moon, about to set, had gone behind the Ajapomaa hills which, set against the glowing sky, looked like the silhouette of a huge predatory animal gone to sleep. Kani felt as though there were many pins pricking him at his buttocks.

He rose, dimmed the aladdin, then went into his room. Changing his velvet loose shorts and underwear, he reached for the bottle of liquor. He shook it and drank two full glasses. They failed to intoxicate him. Instead, he felt hot all over his body, with a strong pounding feeling in his head. He wandered outside to the open porch. For some moments he watched the sky and bit his lower lip. He went down the stoop. He raised his head and looked at the tympanum, at the image of the hawk and shook his head from side to side slowly. Then he went back to the open porch. He sat down in a Windsor chair and threw his head back. As he did so, he felt dizzy and nauseous. Jumping up, he hurriedly went down the stoop and crossed the patio to the bathing place. He slopped down on the concrete block on which he sat to wash himself and vomited painfully on the cement floor. His head felt clear, but he remained weak and trembled a little. He thought it was because of the cold weather.

Pacing slowly and thoughtfully to his room, he lay down on his back. His hands clasped together beneath his head on his pillows, he stared up at the ceiling and began to think, wondering, talking to himself sometimes... Indeed, the sage of the elders is true; what one dreads most is what always stalks one. What did he do wrong, he who had always wanted to help everyone? How could he have known that Entea was the personification of the devil, as Benoa had been saying? He let his eyes wander about the canopy frame of the four-poster, wondering if God knew about what was happening to him, and if He was aware of he different shapes Kani's pieces of cloth had formed as they hung on the bed. A whole lot of things, even those that he would usually consider trivial, assumed significant importance for him.

'By merely associating myself with Entea, I made myself the bole-bridge over which the devil crossed the abysmal distance between us to become my bedfellow. How would I have known he was out to destroy me? Why should he seek to destroy something good and beautiful we all have taken so much time to nurture so we all can enjoy? Like the proverbial communal clay bath pot of Kibi, why should one person lay claim to it and prevent others from sharing in its pleasures?'

Kani turned on his side to relieve the pressure mounting on his back. What would he do about the stigma that would be attached to Ayowa's defilement? What about the embarrassment that he would carry with him in the wake of the discovery of the scandal by the town? It would be broadcast everywhere that he wanted to cheat his own sick friend Owiredu by asking his son to marry a woman pregnant from a rape in the bush by her own kinsman. What sane man would want to have as his own a belly impregnated by Entea, who thought he could usurp power because he had been loaned a firearm? How would Kani present the case to the elders of Nkonsia? And would they say his is a man of means and so his case must be handled differently? No, the customs of the land did not respect status.

Kani must not permit himself to become the chewing stick of the townsfolk. What would the women insinuate in their gossiping at the market area, on the paths and bush tracks to their farms or the stream side? Or should he just eat the rump of a hen, as it was said, and turn deaf ears to what people would say? A man as he, whom even the King of the Abuakwa State treated with great respect, why should he allow himself to go through any humiliating exercises? In light of all that, would he be able to walk about like the respected person he was and respond to the greetings of people in a dignified manner? Would people continue to bow a little before him as they greeted him. No, he could never stand the shame and the embarrassment in the town.

He had made so much noise about his marrying Ayowa to Owiredu's son. And now, how would he back away from it? He rolled over and faced the wall near his bed. He wished there were some crack in it through which he could see whether Ofosuaa and Ayowa were asleep or awake, thinking, too. 'If only sleep will come to me, my pillows may give me some idea about what to do by morning,' he said and pulled up his legs to lie in a crouch position, staring at the white blank wall. And he stared silently for so long that there appeared to be nothing in front of him. And he could not tell if he was awake or asleep; but he believed that he was awake, facing a vast void in the blank wall.

And he stood at its edge, on a precipice, all alone looking. And he saw Obaa Panyin floating above the void and she beckoned him to come to her. And because of the great void he could not and so he felt afraid. And then, he saw Master Darko and Sanyo and the dead previous priestess of the Twafoor fetish closer to him than Obaa Panyin but below him, repairing in their hammocks hanging down in the void along the wall of the precipice all of them in a fiendish grin at him. And he wondered why they were there to frighten him even the more. And he wished that he could get away from them and reach Obaa Panyin, for it was she that he had ever wanted to be with. But he could not; he lacked the necessary strength to jump across the void. And Master Darko and Sanyo and the dead fetish priestess extended their hands to him asking him to stay with them, urging him to take their hands. And he took them. And he found their invitation quite agreeable, for there was no void between them and him. And he found his union with them pleasurable and full of ease and almost blissful. And he wondered why it had to be so, for it was as if they led a precarious life hanging out there thinking and believing that was living

And immediately, he felt an intense pressure on himself from all sides. And it was awfully painful and he thought he would explode. And he had a strange sensation that he had wasted his life creating monuments of little value, the essence of which could not give him what he desired most the moment he needed it, which was to be flying with Obaa Panyin over the void. And he felt greatly disappointed about everything else and repugnant about himself. And he wished that the nightmare would be over, and so he pinched himself and the nightmare stopped immediately, but the void remained. And so he stretched out his hand to feel the wall to reassure himself, but there was no wall. And his fears intensified. And just as he was about to scream, his hand hit the wall.

He found the wall to be hard and cold. It felt solid and unyielding. Where could it have gone only a moment ago? What did it all mean? How could he go to the elders and ask them to leave him alone because the things they spent so much time over meant nothing at all? On the other hand, why should he go to them at all? The so-called rites of absolution, who did they pacify?

In the past, nothing other than absolute destruction had been the lot of rich fathers who had been the victims of similar incidents. Anante of Bunso had been sincere and chosen to go public after he discovered his daughter was pregnant just when she was about to be married to a rich suitor. What was the result? His daughter's rich suitor sued Anante before the State Council, claiming that Anante, by attempting to marry off his pregnant daughter, was implying that the rich suitor's blood was mixed with hot water; he was not a man enough to father his own children. Not only did Anante lose a great deal of money, but also the incident had been relayed around. Anante's daughter never found another suitor. Anante drank himself to death.

What was the essence of the rites, then, if they did not wipe away the degradation? Or was there some element of insanity in the humiliation itself? Was there something secretly involved in the absolution that compelled a man

to step at the heels of his ancestors? Anante would neve
have destroyed himself merely because of the disgrace
Dishonour, like wounds, healed with time. Kani must b
all means avoid declaring the case public. Entea's being
clan's man to Ayowa made him a blood relation; therefor
the crime of incest, which used to be punished by death i
the old days, had been committed. Worse still, it had bee
a forceful defilement in the bush on the naked earth an
under the open eyes of the so-called spirits, making it no
only a gross offence against the laws and customs of th
land, but also an act of grave irreverence to the soul an
spirit of Ayowa and womanhood.

Indeed, if Kani were to report it, Entea would b
punished severely. In the days of old, he would be kille
or banished. But what would be the use? It would onl
reveal that Ayowa had been defiled by a blood relation
and that she was going to have a baby. And this was don
by no other person but Entea. What profanity! There wa
only one solution: quick marriage, but Owiredu, in all hi
pain and suffering, would not be so stupid as to allow hi
son to marry Ayowa when she was heavy with anothe
man's child. What must Kani do? There surely must be ;
way out. There had been similar situations, no doubt, tha
the victims had turned to their advantage.

Wondering what time of night it was, Kani turned round
on his side on the brass bed to look at his clock. It was pas
two. How quickly time flew in moments of crisis. It sur
prised him that for the first time in his adult life, he had
stayed up so late. For no apparent reason, he began won
dering if Benoa was up already looking out for the return
of the palm wine tappers. He laughed. How strange it was
that the mind, failing to find a quick solution to a burning
issue, usually wandered around, giving substance to things
that in normal times were not considered important. He
sat up on the bed, in the middle, so that his long and stout
legs did not touch the floor. He reached for his pipe, lit it
and slid to the edge of the bed, propping himself with his
hands to be able to stand up.

He paced slowly outside to the stoop. Because the laddin still emanated low light from the porch, the patio emained lit up. The sky, however, looked like the inside f a huge black dome of a pall, littered with many sharp oints descending to bury him under. He felt frightened nd so lowered his head to the Ajapomaa hills, thinking loud but softly: 'Grandchild of the Buffalo, Great sire of he Hawk, I am in flooded waters. I cannot free myself. Vho will rescue me?'

Yonder the hills, the sky flickered faintly.

He puffed at his pipe. For how long could he keep this uiet? If it were not the baby growing in Ayowa's womb, ie would just pacify her insulted soul with eggs and a heep and let things be. But pregnancy was not like lies; it ould not be hidden for long. Soon, his daughter's belly vould start showing. And those elders whose appetite for nutton and schnapps was insatiable would begin asking iim through their pretentious smiles indicative of their nowledge in the matter; 'Nobleman, we didn't hear of our daughter's wedding to Owiredu's son; what disease is his that makes her belly swollen but doesn't make her vrithe in pain?' Yes, lies could be hidden for a long time, ut not pregnancy. But who would help him hide a lie?

As he watched the smoke from his pipe twiddle and rise o diffuse in the cool air, his mind stumbled over quick narriage again, and an idea occurred to him. It was not lefinite at first, but even the mere hint of it brought him a leasant feeling of hope. He puffed harder and quicker so hat he could watch the billowing smoke rise while his nind fought gainly to hold on to the thought. The more ie smoked, the better the idea took shape. He took the ipe from his mouth, held it in his hand, and just watched he smoke go up and up. And he looked at it rise and rise intil he could not see any more smoke but the sky itself. This time, he did not feel frightened at the myriad of glittering stars spread over the expanse of God's velvet. It vas a sight of assurance and comfort.

# Chapter 8

At first cock crow, Kani took his electric torch and walke
out of his house into the cold dark night. His min
remained preoccupied with fears of rejection, and ult
mate degradation. He could smell fermented food an
liquor mixed with burnt tobacco on himself, but h
thought it only persisted in his nostrils. He walke
cautiously, making sure that his sandals did not mak
much noise. Even so, he heard the echoes of his ow
footfalls somewhere at the end of the straight lanes. Th
rows of houses along the streets appeared in the dark lik
vague shadows of huge buffaloes gone to rest on thei
bellies after a wild chase by some predator. They seeme
to engage in a whispering conference about somethin
from which Kani alone was excluded.

A few feet away from the entrance into Benoa's house,
door slammed somewhere and he found himself caugh
in the yellowish glow of a lantern from a nearby house
Instinctively, he jumped back, his intent being to see
cover near the fence around Benoa's house. What woul
that person think on seeing him there at that time of th
night? Would he shout thief! thief! and arouse th
neighbourhood? Then, the people would come up witl
another explanation for his wealth; Kani was a nigh
prowler! His thoughts were painfully interrupted by th
futility in the attempted escape itself as he felt cold wate
welling around his feet. Slowly, he bowed down his head
and looked at his feet squished in dung mud. He had
landed in the seepage behind Benoa's bathing place.

'O, great Anorchey!' he mumbled the name of th

legendary genius of a fetish priest. 'I've lost even before the battle has begun.' His personal taboo was never to cross the wasted water from somebody's bathing place, let alone squat in it. Worse still, he realized that he was a huge dark figure crouching before the pale array of bamboo stakes faintly illuminated by the receding lantern whose carrier might also have been aroused by a similar urgent need in Kani's bowels now, growling for relief. He struggled to his feet and tottered away from the stench of rotten organic mud, conscious of the reluctant drag of his cloth's end behind him. It had soaked dung mud. By the impact of his body, the little gate admitted him, swinging back stiffly on its cut-out tyre hinges.

He went past the dry palm frond penthouse in which Benoa's wife cracked palm kernels and tapped Benoa's door. His ear glued to the crude Odum door, Kani listened attentively. There came no answer from within, so he knocked again, much harder this time. He flashed on his electric torch to be sure it was the dracaena palm leaves that looked like a man with a hat of long ears watching him from the bathing place. He proceeded to inspect the small yard, moving the light beam slowly from the bathing place constructed from rusted roofing sheets and tacked inside the corner of the bamboo fence, to the small platform of firewood sheltered from the weather by plaited raffia fronds. The beam caught the glare of small reddish eyes on the firewood platform, and the cocks roosting there beside the crowded small coop began to cluck loudly. One crowed.

Kani snapped out the electric torch.

'Who is there?' Benoa shouted from his room. Kani heard the sharp metallic sound made when a machete was drawn across cement floor. He quickly stepped back from the door.

'It's me, Brother-of-man,' he said.

'At this time of the night?' Benoa cleared his throat, but the edge in his voice had betrayed his being annoyed for having been awakened at that time of the night. He opened the door. 'What is it?'

'I need your help, Brother-of-man,' Kani said softly.

Benoa drew back, blocking his nose as some stench assaulted him. He left the door ajar, went and turned on the wick of the oil lamp on the window-sill to brighten the room, but it gave off more soot than brilliance. Benoa gesticulated toward a short kitchen stool in one corner of the room, and went back to his bed. Perching gingerly at the edge of the quilted reed mattress, he cautiously shuffled his buttocks to get into a better sitting posture without disturbing his wife. The effort, however, proved fruitless. The wooden bed creaked terribly and the sleeping woman twisted and turned on her side, mumbling as she discarded part of the cloth covering her thighs. Benoa rose and dragged it over her. He sat on the bed again and propped his head up in his hands, looking at Kani.

Where Kani sat, the mud walls had been washed at the top by rain water leaks through the wood shingles. The liquid mud had made serpentine trails down the cream walls, and in the background, they made him look fiendish, his bald head emanated shimmering heatwaves that rose to the roof. Benoa rubbed his eyes and looked again, shocked at the frowzy appearance of his brother-in-law in the dim corner of the room.

'You look terrible,' he said.

'I'm terrified, Brother-of-man.' Kani stared up at the roof beams as though he was contemplating the tangles of long cobwebs made thicker over the years by soot from the oil lamp. His massive chest kept rising and falling quite visibly as though such outward display was absolutely necessary for his chest to have the ability to contain whatever it held inside it. He said: 'The bag of virtue has failed. The sack of evil charms has won. The wealthy noble has led his house to its doom. I need your help.' He hung his head. The cold cement floor had come loose in places, looking like a weak floor stomped with steel boots.

'It must be a heavy thing. I can see it in your face.' Benoa leaned forward, wrapped himself fully in his cloth

126

to keep warm. Like the raven and vulture, he had understood the rich man proverbially. 'Shall we look at the contents of the evil sack?'

Kani nodded his head eagerly. He looked up suddenly past his skinny brother-in-law, making desperate signs with his head and big eyes toward Buaa still asleep on the wooden bed. Turning to look at his wife, Benoa asked: 'You want us to talk in private?'

'That will be most welcome.' Kani's stomach gave a loud and long rumble. It subsided only when he stood up. 'I didn't eat anything last evening,' he said. The smell of burning fuel in the room irritated him and he began to cough. Buaa turned on her side, mumbling something. Benoa quickly searched for a spent matchstick from the floor, kindled it by the oil lamp on the window sill, and lit a lantern. Both men went outside, Benoa in the lead, and headed toward the penthouse. As he waved aside the raffia rind mat which served as a door and entered it, Kani remained behind.

'Aren't the children in the next room?' he asked.

'The roof leaks like a colander,' Benoa answered. 'When it rains, the children sometimes go to sleep at their uncle's. Those who have uncles aren't like us; they're lucky.' Both men laughed – an uneasy chuckle full of anxiety. Kani bowed low to enter the penthouse. The two men then sat down on short kitchen stools in the centre of the hut, facing each other, the dying fire to their side. 'It's cold this night.' Benoa poked the fire.

'It was a heavy rain last evening.' Kani looked at the lantern. Placed on the levelled-off top of a heap of cracked palm kernels – one the items Buaa used in soap manufacture – its glow seemed to frighten him, and so he stretched his hand and turned down the wick. Benoa looked at him, surprised that a mere glow of a lamp should make him feel that insecure. Benoa proceeded to put more wood on the fire. Only a few embers remained in it from the past evening. When the smoke thickened, he blew air into it until it burst into flames.

'This will warm us while we talk,' Benoa said.

'Yes, it feels comfortable now.' Kani drew his seat closer to Benoa, as though that ensured his safety from some unknown attack from outside. A pungent odour like the smell of fermented palm wine mixed with rotten food engulfed Benoa. He moved his head back from Kani and tried to draw his cloth up to cover his nose. But at a mere tug, the frail cloth tore up under tension from his parted legs. Embarrassed, he quickly tied the ripped ends together.

'As much as they cost now, you'd think they'll make cloths as good as they used to in the old days,' Benoa said. 'This piece is only three years old.'

'I could buy you a new one at daybreak.' Kani offered eagerly, looking at Benoa's face with expectation. The dark hollows of his sunken cheeks in the dim of the penthouse made his face appear more solemn. He rested his elbows on his knees and clasped his hands together before him, leaning forward a little, his nose shied away from his rich brother-in-law.

'So far, it's been peaceful here except that I haven't been able to sleep well at all,' Benoa said. 'There seems to be some lump in my bed. It keeps nudging me despite how I turn or lie down –'

'The bed you sleep on every night? Very strange indeed.' Kani shook his head sadly. 'We're both caught in the same snare. It's your niece, Ayowa. Her precious guinea beads have been used by the devil to crack nuts. I came to you for a great help.'

'I'll do all I can to help, provided it's within my capabilities,' Benoa said. Kani sat up and stared at him. Perspiration had formed on his receding forehead and at the tip of his broad nose. Many times the vital issue came to the tip of his tongue, pricking him to say it, but he did not have the courage to let it out; he only kept making faces in the dim light of the room. Not understanding them and not knowing what was going on, Benoa stared back at Kani, a frightened look on his gaunt face.

'What is the matter?' Benoa asked.

'It's within your powers to help me.' Kani evaded the question.

'Brother-of-man, we don't beat the sides of a drum when its face is right before us. We can't sit here all night.' Benoa said. Kani took in a deep breath, looking Benoa straight in the face again. He felt a lump in his throat, and he knew he had to talk.

'I've just discovered Ayowa is pregnant,' he said. 'She was defiled in the bush by Entea. And her belly is a month old, if my calculations are correct.' Now, he felt some relief in his chest and so he breathed slowly. All that he had been afraid to say since he got together with Benoa was out, and now it was the turn of the other man to talk. Benoa, however, drew back from Kani slowly. It was all silence between the two men for a long time, a silence mitigated only by the croak of a toad somewhere in the lane outside. With the fire burning to their side, they just sat, conscious of the stench in the penthouse, their terrified eyes on each other as though they were at a game of checkers and either one had to study the other one closely before any new move was made. Then, Benoa spoke.

'*Beautiful Boadu of Sagyimase,* the enclave of the Wise and the Beautiful and the Benevolent,' he said all of Ayowa's appellation. 'The great *Bridal Food Bowl.* What has happened to you, and so children can't find anything sumptuous from you to eat this day?' Benoa shook his head.

Kani looked at the ground. In the flush of the fire, his bald head appeared as if it had been smeared with red oil. Benoa rose like a tired man and went outside. Soon, the splatter of his urine on the gravel at the bathing place filled the house. He stayed outside for some time, pacing the length of the small yard before he went back to the penthouse. He stared at Kani with a look that definitely implied *I told you so.*

'What shall we do?' Benoa asked in disappointment as

his only niece – the parent sucker that would give birth to the ratoons – had been destroyed. 'Are we going to sit down and watch Ayowa consumed by this dreadful thing? Speak, man, speak. And I'm listening.'

'That's why I'm here.' Kani drew closer to Benoa. He placed his big hairy hands on Benoa's knees, a look of frightened guilt on his face. 'I came to ask you to make Ayerakwa marry her.'

Benoa sat still for a long time, contemplating the leaping flames sending flickers even to the thatched roof as though they wanted to set it ablaze. In no minced words, Kani was asking him to take responsibility for such great profanity. What did Kani think of him? He began nodding his small head, his greying hairline red from the fire. Then he laughed – a curious type of laughter only the poor enjoyed when bemused by something simple yet incomprehensible. He laughed so hard that his hollow cheeks and the tiny dewlaps under his chin trembled freely. Like the raven, Kani knew what the unusual mirth implied; Benoa was not a fool to put his finger in the hungry cobra's mouth, for what they were discussing was not a laughing matter.

'But Brother-of-man,' Benoa said in a deliberate slow voice. 'You know yourself that this is impossible. No sane person will do what you ask, especially when you brought the problem upon yourself.'

'I'm not the problem.'

'You brought it on Ayowa.'

'That makes it your problem too.'

'How am I capable of helping? I don't have a solution.'

'I wouldn't be here if you didn't, Brother-of-man.' Kani pressed the thin thighs of Benoa with his massive hands. 'It's only a matter of your consenting to save me, and my house from humiliation. Some animals walk in pairs so that when one has got something on its eye, the other can blow it off for it. Consider how intimate your family is with mine. Consider you and me. Ofosuaa and Buaa. Ayowa

130

and Mansa. Misa and Opia. Ayerakwa practically grew up in my house, with my sons. He used to teach Ayowa and the other boys how to do their homework. You and I eat from the same bowl most of the time, and your wife and my wife exchange a bowl each of their food every evening. You and I drink palm wine with the same calabash. You send Opia to me. I send Misa to you. We understand our own language. You're the maternal uncle of my children. Who will question our integrity? Who will question the plans we make for our children?'

'Remember, it isn't only dishonour that is involved here.' Benoa took Kani's hands off his thighs. 'The soul of Ayowa, and the spirits of the land and the skies have been insulted. They must be pacified.'

'Where were these spirits when an innocent young woman was being sexually assaulted?' Kani spat on the ground. 'Anyway, think about what happened to all those who had been through similar experiences and decided to go public with it. Where are they now? What was the result after their bold deeds? You must be the first person to admit the importance of why I want to avoid performing any rites in public.' Tiny white froth had formed at the corners of his mouth.

Benoa looked at the big man whose shadow, thrown on the rough mudcast wall of the main building behind him, moved about in a weird dance with the leaping flames. Each move by the shadow seemed to him like an unwarranted attack against him. For the first time in his relationship with Kani, Benoa saw him a vicious selfish man; he was not thinking of Ayowa's ordeal but his own humiliation that he wanted to avoid.

'Whatever you do, you must know that the spirits are more important than the human aspect you're concerned about.' He clasped his hands before him in a thoughtful mood. 'You fear disgrace and dishonour, but what about Ayowa?' Benoa had his finger pointed and almost in the face of his brother-in-law, who sat leaning forward on his kitchen stool. Kani remained silent for a while, then he

131

drew his stool closer to Benoa and spoke in a whispering tone.

'Ayowa is no problem. Your agreeing to help me is the most important matter here. So long as we two reach a consensus to keep this quiet, everything will be peaceful. All that I want is to prevent Ayowa from giving birth to a bastard. You know that I can never mention the name of Entea as the father of my grandchild.'

'What about the spirits of the earth and the sky? What about the benevolent tutelar ghosts who will be aware each day that Ayowa is walking about under defilement?' Benoa struck his left palm with a right hand finger to stress his points, his eyes riveted on Kani. 'And remember, it isn't they alone who have been subjected to immense humiliation.'

'If these are all your fears, I'll provide cartons of schnapps – E.K. brand – and hundreds of fat, unblemished sheep for surreptitious oblations to pacify them.' Kani went on his knees. 'Everything will be all right, Brother-of-man. I promise you. I've thought carefully about it all. Sometimes, certain things happen and we lament they're bad. However, if we consider them carefully, we realize they have their good sides.' He crawled past the fire to place his big hands on those of the poor thin man, bowing his head till it touched Benoa's lap. 'Please, help me,' Kani whispered.

Looking at his head, Benoa felt he could crack it with one blow from his small fist. 'Was that why you offered to buy me cloth?' he yelled. 'And what about the elders? They also are important in such matters.'

Still on his knees, Kani raised his head and looked into the emaciated face of Benoa with a pained expression. 'Brother-of-man, our own secret prayers will be sufficient without the prying eyes of corrupt fornicators and adulterers whose main interest will be to forage on the sheep and drinks I'll offer.' Kani rambled on slowly and softly, the wet sounds of his lips punctuating each word he said. 'Everything will be all right. Every prayer must be a prayer. And the gods will be pleased about it that way.'

'What do you believe about the gods? And what do you know about the spirits? Since you became your own god, you've even forgotten you lived under a sky. And what about Ayowa?' Benoa poked the fire. He wanted to get away from the rich man, who rose and sat down on his stool. 'She's my niece. I'll not be silent over the humiliation and disgrace she's been forced to take.'

'We could absolve our two children, Ayowa and Ayerakwa, secretly. We'll then decide to keep it quiet between ourselves.'

'It's no more a secret once you've told me.' Benoa held a brand up, as if to strike Kani, who drew back suddenly. 'You don't know who is eavesdropping now. Remember that walls have ears, especially at this time of the day.'

'Brother-of-man, your voice,' Kani said feebly.

'What about my voice?' Benoa yelled back.

'Can you lower it a little? It's quiet and still early.' He scooped up his cloth and buried his head in it to rub his face dry. Both men remained silent, as if completely exhausted by the argument. Only the fire crackled, sending sparks into the air as it burst into flames. And the shadow of Kani kept dancing to the movements of the leaping flames, as if it had already anticipated every move and beat of the flames even before they flared.

'Everything is in our minds, Brother-of-man,' Kani said. 'If we think positively, the spirits will rain blessings on it. But if we think evil, the outcome has to be disastrous. There is no matter that has exceeded man in size. It's man who makes all troubles. And it's man who, with patience, dismantles all troubles.'

'I'm sorry I can't do what you request of me.' Benoa stood up. 'I must go back to bed. You don't think me a fool because I'm poor. I respected you greatly. That was why I sat here, listening to all that. Good morning. I'm off to bed again, to be with my wife.'

'Are you ridiculing me or what? Stay!' In an instant,

Kani was up and blocking the way out of the penthouse with his huge frame, the thatch roof virtually resting on the back of his thick neck. Benoa tried to force his way out, but Kani lifted him bodily off the ground and carried him back to the seat which Kani had been on. Benoa stopped breathing; the smell on Kani's breath was unbearable.

'You're causing me great discomfort.' He gasped, swallowing a mouthful of the stench, then struggled to free himself. 'Brother-of-man, I don't think I like this. Maybe you don't understand. What I'm saying is if we don't take off the scab from the wound before applying medicine to it, it'll inflame and turn worse.'

'Sit down and let's talk!' Kani pressed him down on the shoulders. Benoa resisted for a while, then gave in, flopping on to the hard stool. Kani continued to address him: 'I understand you all right. We've been speaking the same language. I think it's you who don't understand. We don't have time. And I'm assuring you that I'll do everything in my power to forestall anything bad that may be in the wake of it all. It's as simple as that.' Kani loomed over him and struck his massive chest.

Benoa held his head between his hands and looked down. He feared that if he tried to do anything Kani disliked, the big rich man could crush him to death. Benoa had never seen him this desperate before. He looked up at Kani, smiling enigmatically. 'Well, I see your point after all,' he said. 'Let me go and sleep over it. Our pillows have always served us wisely.'

'Brother-of-man,' Kani chuckled. He dealt a few knocks to Benoa's head with his index finger hooked. 'All your senses are here with you. I came out with you from that room. As we came out, you didn't leave any part of them back there.' He sat down on Benoa's stool so that he was close to the exit way.

'Yes, yes, but as our elders say, pillows contain wisdom. Moreover, I can't decide for my son. Ayerakwa isn't here, you know.' Benoa looked up at Kani again. Kani had his popping eyes fixed on him. They were red and reflected the firelight. Then, the two men stood up simultaneously. Kani dipped his hand under his cloth, into the deep pocket of his loose pair of shorts. When he brought it out, it held something.

'This is for you.' He stretched out his hand until it came close to Benoa's face, not far from his nose so he could smell it. The odour was not definite. It was something milder than the fetid smell in the penthouse, yet it was potent in its own way. It was confusing though, of fresh paper and tobacco and new cloth, and above all, the rotten sputum of man. It intrigued him and so he breathed in harder as he lowered his eyes to have a real look at what Kani held before his nostrils.

In the firelight, he caught the fuzzy outline of designs on cedi bills – a wad of them. Money! Mere sheets of paper, yet each one was worth a hundred cedis. An extremely cold sensation started under his left foot and gradually spread numbness over his body. He managed to scratch his head, but not being able to think, he stared at the bills as if mesmerized.

'Don't be a fool, Brother-of-man,' Kani rasped, chuckling. 'This is money – the spirit of man. I don't know how much is in there. And I don't care. It's all for you. All of it, I say. And more, much more will be coming.'

Benoa tried to speak, but no word would come out of his mouth. Some shrilling sound had begun in his head. Soft and slow at first, it intensified the more he listened to it as he stared at the cedi bills. In his amazement he wondered if this was how he had felt when he had collected his compensation money for his first building pulled down to make way for the highway. Kani, on the other hand, waited for the poor man to take the money. As he made no effort to take it, Kani shoved it all under Benoa's cloth near his chest.

'Bro-brother-of-of-ma-a-man,' Benoa stuttered. He thought of removing the money from where Kani had pushed it, but he could not move his hand. 'In fact, you're forcing down my throat something very bitter. I need time to-to think.'

'Every good medicine is bitter. After the discomfort in swallowing it, you get better. You then enjoy life as never before.' Kani grinned, patting Benoa on his left shoulder. 'And remember, there isn't any time to waste. I'll organize the biggest traditional wedding ever held in this part of the country. Just to honour your family and my family. Just to draw a difference between us and the other people. Just to show how special we are. Just to show we made the right decision and that we both together with our wives like the arrangements. Money should be put to work, instead of our suffering humiliation. I promise you, I'll honour you.' He struck his chest.

'But...but,' Benoa struggled with the words. 'I can't decide for Ayerakwa. He isn't here, you know –'

The violent torrent of words that came out of Kani shook Benoa out of his confusion. 'You have grey in your hair. Don't act like a child. Don't act like a fool,' Kani thundered. Then, in a much lower tone, he said: 'See all your shingles are tumbling down. One may hit somebody one day and you'll be in trouble. Your cloth rips apart in public. Your children sleep somewhere when it rains. Think about what I've promised you. And remember, it's your own, one and only niece Ayowa, involved in this.'

'Yes, yes, Brother-of-man,' Benoa chuckled. 'The mud dauber- wasp hums when it's building its mud-nest high in the corner of someone's room. What it implies by its humming to human beings is *a true relative is the one who has been generous and good to his kinsman.* When is the wedding?'

'In four weeks, if you wish. But we can't delay,' Kani said, elated. 'Lest the belly betray us. In fact, there is no time left.'

'I see what you mean.' Benoa took out the money and held it before his eyes. 'It's beautiful, so beautiful that I can't take my eyes away from it. You did the right thing by coming to me.'

Kani nodded his head in agreement. 'Day is fast approaching. I think I'll take leave of you now.' He wrapped his cloth around him well. 'We'll start talking about detail plans soon.'

'Indeed. Go with the coolness of the morning. And give my greetings to my sister, and my niece,' Benoa said. The two men shook hands – the thin poor man's hand lost in the grip of the massive hand of the big rich man. They both stared at each other, their faces beaming with smiles characteristic of men who had successfully accomplished a conspiracy. As Kani stepped out of the penthouse, a cock crowed loudly from the firewood platform near the bathing place. He just looked ahead of him. Far away behind the Ajapomaa hills, the sky was turning grey with the coming of a new day.

# Chapter 9

Benoa had lapsed into unconsciousness inside the penthouse. When he came to, the sun was already up, and daylight had consumed the glow of the lantern on the small heap of palm kernels. It burned with a low sickly yellow flame. The fire too was almost spent, except for a few pieces of wood. They gave off thin twirls of smoke that hovered above the ground in meandering loops before escaping outside through the slits in the raffia rind mat door. He looked around him, as if to be sure of his surroundings. The old thin layer of red-ochre coating of the earthen floor, neglected for many weeks, had cracked and pushed up in several places, looking like scabrous skin.

He rubbed his eyes and looked right before him. There lay eight hundred cedi bills, crumpled up. As he watched the money, the buzz in his head returned, increasing the speed of his heartbeat as it thumped harder and louder. The chirping of the weaver birds outside in the coconut palms and acacia trees added to the buzz in his head and so he closed his eyes tight, hoping that would alleviate the headache he was beginning to have. And he saw shadowy things jump before his eyes in circles, as if they were in a ritual dance celebrating the *abusua* – the season of family cohesiveness. It was interesting for him to notice that he was one of the images in the dance, and in fact, it was he who sustained it, so that when he stopped, all the other images disintegrated and vanished into thin air. He opened his eyes and collected the bills from the ground, straightening them one after the other carefully. Dazed still, he staggered to his feet and waddled toward his room. He paused in the doorway for some time, limp against the jamb. He contemplated Buaa, his wife, who was awake and dressing up.

She was of medium height, but her skinny figure made her look tall in a distance. As she worked to tie a faded scarf on her head, Benoa could see every movement of her shoulder blades under her dry skin. It showed white in certain areas where she had scratched in her sleep. She turned round and saw her husband. 'Where are you coming from this time of day so drunk?' she asked. She had tied a piece of cloth around her so that half her flabby breasts showed. As Benoa kept staring at her, she asked again. 'Are you sick or something?'

Benoa showed her the bills.

Buaa gaped at the wonder in her husband's hand, her mouth bare of her two lower front teeth. She had lost them in a fight over Benoa with another woman at the stream-side fifteen years ago. At that time, Benoa had pawned his cocoa farms for three hundred cedis to pay off some debts. Some of the money had been left over and for a few months, he had been a man about town with an accolade of *Master extravagant who would shoot himself dead if he had only ten cedis on him at any time.* Unfortunately for Buaa, when her husband's propitious moments were petering out, she engaged in that fight with a much bigger woman whom she had suspected of having an affair with Benoa. The woman beat her up mercilessly and the money that could have gone to fix her teeth went to pacify her alleged rival.

Still agape and her eyes fixed on the cedis in Benoa's hand, she walked slowly toward him, as if for the first time in her life, she had realized that a cautious approach to her husband was a necessity. When she was an arm's distance away from him, she stopped. She stretched her hand and with her thumb and her index finger, she gingerly felt the pieces of paper which were cash, as though she was afraid of them. 'Money! It's money. And so much of it,' she said. Benoa nodded his head in agreement, his lips closed and pursed in a thoughtful mood. 'God Almighty,' she said huskily. 'Come right inside before the devil whisks it away.' She took her husband's hand by the fingers and pulled him into the room carefully, as though their life depended on that delicate hand-grip. They both sat on the creaking bed. 'From where did you get it?' She whispered, then backed away from him, slowly. 'Or you stole it?'

Benoa watched her walk away to the foot of the bed in a teasing manner. He knew that she wanted to annoy him, but he swore in his head that he would not allow her to upset him that morning. He watched her search through a rattan basket on top of a *chop-box* – a wooden box containing all their precious worldly possessions, and found a *kaba* blouse. She put it on. She might have had the blouse sewn at a time when she was plump. Now, the *kaba* was too big for her and the V cut of the neck hung loosely around her skinny neck, showing the hollows at her clavicles. Benoa watched her still as she took off the cloth wound around her and tied on her skirt-like cloth.

'You know I'm not a thief,' he said quietly.

Buaa sneered at him. In her piping voice which had a sarcastic tone to it, she said: 'Sometime last year, you brought home a game of antelope. You claimed one of your springs at Odadamu caught it. But those traps had been ineffective for over a year.'

Benoa looked hard at her. 'Money is a devil,' he said.

'I can't understand you, Benoa,' came Buaa's whining voice in a reprimand. 'All our lives we've been poor, dragging out a miserable existence. When you pawned your farms for money that could have gone to re-roof your house, it only cost me to lose my teeth. You wear an old russet cloth, as if you're constantly in mourning. When I wash it, you have to remain indoors, so to speak, perched on this creaking bed, looking up as if reckoning the countless leaks in your shingles. Until the russet cloth is dry, you don't go out. What has got into you now that

140

you've got money? Why is it the devil now? I want you to know that I'm tired of this miserable life of impoverishment.'

Benoa stood up slowly. He discarded his sleeping cloth and dumped it on the bed. He reached for a coarse brown cloth that hung on the headboard in a heap and donned it. He sat down again on the bed. To avoid looking into the provocative lean face of Buaa who stood directly before him, he covered his eyes with his hands.

'Yes, you're ashamed of me. But you aren't ashamed that your appellation now is *antobro* – the one who doesn't buy drinks but gets drunk anyway.' Buaa continued her attack. 'Very soon your name may cease to exist. And even children will ask "Have you seen Mr. *A-n-t-o-b-r-o* around?"' Her voice was low but cutting all the same, pronouncing the word as if she were singing a song.

'Have you ever considered that I could divorce you when I become rich?' he asked in a soft tone.

'How ever could you become rich when, with hundred cedi bills in your hands, you're acting like you've taken an overdose of a purgative?' Buaa placed her bony hands on her hips. 'And let me tell you one more thing. Don't you ever think of divorcing me when I've followed you to become this wretched. Which man will want to play with these leather-pouch-breasts of mine again? I'm like the bedbug to you. Even when you've crushed me, my smell will stay on you. And you can't resist me. You'll raise your fingers to your nostrils. And you'll smell me over and over again. Don't you feel ashamed when you compare the taste of my soup to that of Ofosuaa, your own sister?' She walked away to the door and stood there, looking outside. When she turned back to Benoa, she asked, 'Where did you get that money from?'

'Kani gave it to me,' Benoa said, then continued in a firmer voice, his view still on the bills in his hand. 'I've always believed in earning money the earnest way.'

'Kani gave it you? As a loan?'

'What surety do I have to guarantee me a loan?'

'Is it a gift, then?'

'Has Kani ever given me gifts of money before?'

'Whether it comes from Ofosuaa or Kani, it's from the same source. And it goes into the same sack.' She paused and remained silent for some time. 'Let me see it again.' She walked back to Benoa, short quick steps. She took the money from him and counted the bills. 'Eight hundred cedis? That's a lot of money. What for?' Stunned, she sat down beside her husband.

'You should have asked that in the first place.' Benoa kept his eyes on the money his wife held. 'He said more will be coming. If he follows through with what he's promised, I'm sure my days of impoverishment are over for good.'

'Our days. Not yours alone.' She stood up, walked to the door and back to the bed, blinking several times. 'I can't understand why Kani would all of a sudden make such a gesture to us. Eight hundred cedis?' She sat down on the bed again. Benoa took in a deep breath. When he spoke he had his eyes on Buaa.

'Kani wants our son for Ayowa. She's been made pregnant by Entea. Raped in the bush under the open eyes of the skies.'

Buaa dropped the cedis on the bed immediately. Both she and her husband withdrew from them slowly as though the bills were some dangerous objects from which a cautious withdrawal was of paramount importance. Casting fleeting glances at them, she heaved a deep sigh, then stared at the bills for some time. She stretched her hand and touched the bills again, gingerly. They rattled faintly from her trembling hands. 'Now, I understand what you meant by money was a devil. And what did you say to him?' Her piping voice was hushed.

'I said no. But he gave me this money.'

'Yes, this money.' She turned her head and looked at the bills again. 'They're beautiful, but the more I look at them, the more I feel some uneasiness creeping over me. It's like the hunter's tale of *asantrofi*-the-bird. Its flesh

142

makes a sumptuous meal, but the fellow who kills it brings loads of curses on his family.' She touched the bills again. 'It's dangerous. It's contaminated. But I know it can do many things for us. Will you return it?'

Benoa shook his head from side to side. He whispered tensely, fixing his gaze on the floor. 'I just don't know yet what I'm going to do. I guess I have to think. Will you leave me alone for some time?'

'Sure, sure. But don't take too much time.' She stood up. 'I'll go to my chores. Just remember, the money can do many things for us.' She picked up a chewing sponge from the window sill and put it in her mouth as she went out of the room.

Benoa sat on the bed, looking at the floor. Why had he tried being a fool when Kani gave him the money? All his life this was what he had been praying for – to become rich and step in his princeling sandals with pride, like the man he was supposed to be, a man who people respected and listened to with all attention. So far, he knew that he was allowed to talk at meetings because it was his privilege as an elder. His words, however, did not have any impact, like the fruitless efforts of a fish out of water and gasping for life. Now that so much money was coming his way, why should he be frightened?

Yes, Kani said it all. Money was the essence of manhood. With money, Benoa could do anything he wanted. He would command respect all the time. Consider the case of Attah the *Sanaahene* in charge of all the gold and regalia at the King's palace. When it was detected that some gold weights were missing, he resigned his job honourably. He claimed that he was becoming too old to measure gold weights accurately, and that his eyes were turning bad and that his hands trembled when he held the scales and gold dust. But his hands don't shake in public when he has to drink a calabash of palm wine. He never misses a pinch of snuff on the nail of his thumb when he has to snort it, because his hand does not shake.

Later on, when work began on his large new house, rumours went abroad that he was using the money he gained from the sale of those gold items to some white people on the coast. What did the State Council do to him? Nothing! Attah had the power to stuff the elders' cheeks with a few cedis to keep them quiet.

Or the ridiculous case of Anim of Begoro. A poor hunter who spent weeks in the bush gaming, he had heard his wife was having an affair with a rich man in the town. Anim confronted his wife. She denied all knowledge of her relationship with the affluent man. Then, one day, after saying he was going into the bush, the hunter hid under his bed. The fool he was, listening in to the man sweet-talking Anim-the-hunter's wife, and her laughter of acknowledgement spiced with coital mirth, then the intermittent silence only broken by the squeaks of the bed as it bounced up and down. And the bigger fool he still was to describe with such detail the whole incident in public to the council of elders who had met to mediate the matter. In the first place, he was stupid to take the matter before the elders when he could have negotiated privately with the rich man for some money. Why did he think the elders would ask the rich man to pacify him with some money? What happened in the end? The council of elders told him that if he did not trust his wife, the best thing for him to do was break his marriage with her. And the biggest fool in town he really was. He did just that. A week later the rich man married the divorced woman with great fanfare. What did the people say about it? They gossiped everywhere that the woman was too beautiful for a poor hunter like Anim. Yes, money was power.

'No doubt, this is the doing of God Omnipotent,' Benoa thought aloud. 'Would I have believed it if I had awakened to find my room full of money?' That would make God a liar, Benoa reflected, as Obaa Panyin had argued one time about God talking through a table. Of course, God had the power to do anything. And His power was law, and so He would not lie under any circumstance.

144

Because a table did not have the organs designed for speech, it would make God a liar if He chose to talk to men through it. Instead, He would choose some medium that would make God's message plausible. And so He always sent His messengers into the world to guide us. But because of our fears of the unknown, our fears of things untried, we subscribed to the same old notions. We kept to the same ruts, avoiding any new spiritual challenges to find God. 'We refuse Him each day, adhering to creeds and doctrines that have ceased to have meaning for us, expecting God to be of that form or that shape because of what has been drilled into us, and so we miss opportunities each day,' he said aloud.

The mind, as Master Darko had agreed with Obaa Panyin that day, was like the parachute; it worked best only when opened. 'I must consider all aspects of this matter,' he thought aloud. 'Yes, God always chooses some medium that will make His message plausible to us. He's speaking to me now. He's showing me a sign now. Having heard my prayers, He has decided to send me my wishes through Kani. God has therefore arranged this incident.'

With this money, and what Kani had promised, he could recement all the rooms in the house, put stucco on the outside walls and wash them in fresh paint. He could raise new walls and add large new rooms, put a ceiling above all the rooms and re-roof them with shiny corrugated aluminium sheets. He would be able to pay back the securities against his pawned cocoa farms and get them back. He could buy himself three more full pieces of cloth at a stretch, a velvet and *kente* with what Kani had promised later on. And he would put all his children in expensive secondary schools so that they could learn the knowledge of the world too, and go to universities overseas, like Kani's two older boys.

He cleared his throat loudly, looking at the money.

'Please, did you call me?' Buaa broke his thoughts, having rushed into the room at his throat-clearing noise. Benoa turned to her and shook his head negatively. Then he remembered an old song which said 'When a man is rich, his wife will run to him even if he coughs inside his room.'

'You might have overheard me when I thought aloud,' he said.

'Will you return the money?' Buaa stepped into the room.

'I need it.'

'Yes, we need it. But our son?' She sat on the bed.

'He'll be safe,' he said. 'The gods know he's innocent.'

'You're wonderful, my husband.' Buaa hugged him.

'I'll fortify my son's spirit in the Twafoor stream.'

'Yes, this money can do a lot for us, my husband.'

'Things like what?' His voice was harsh.

'I thought you knew,' Buaa piped. 'Things like going to pay back the security and getting back our pawned farms and putting a new roof over this house and plastering the outside walls.'

Benoa nodded his head in agreement.

'Buying yourself some new cloth.'

'I've already thought of that.'

'And buying me some velvet.'

Benoa did not make any response this time, but eyed her with suspicion as she enumerated the items, counting them on her fingers. 'Buying me some jewellery for Christmas this year, giving me some money to attend the final obsequies of Asirifi at Begoro. You remember I couldn't attend his burial because we didn't have money. And I'll need a new pair of princeling sandals –'

Benoa was not listening any more. He reached for a small sack under the quilted reed mattress. In it he kept his money and other valuables. He pushed the eight hundred cedis deep into it and hung it on his shoulder. 'Make water ready for me to wash my face.' He rose from the bed. 'I need to go and send my son a telegram. And remember to keep your big mouth shut about this matter. Or I will sew it up for you. Do you hear me?'

'My mouth is sealed.' She placed her hand over her

146

mouth, bowing her body comically before him. 'But when will the marriage arrangements begin?'

'As soon as my son is here.'

'Say our son.'

He shot her a hard look, then left the room for the bathing place, the small sack containing the eight hundred cedis still slung on his shoulder.

In Kani's house, Ofosuaa was worried. The church bell had struck eight already but her husband had not returned home from wherever he had gone. Seated on a short stool in front of the kitchen, she wondered where Kani could have gone. Better if they had taken the gong and announced to the whole town that Ayowa was pregnant after she had been raped by Entea in the bush; for if Kani had gone to seek advice from someone else, the matter would become public knowledge. While nobody would ask them whether the news in circulation was true, people would look at the family out of the corners of their eyes and say in an undertone, 'That's the family whose daughter had incestuous relationship in the bush.'

That alone would scare people from coming into Kani's house for marriage; no woman might want to marry any of the boys, and Ayowa might never find a husband. The deed alone could make it difficult for her; most men preferred widows to defiled women. Or had Kani gone to take his life? No, he was not a man who retreated in the face of problems. He had said that the matter was a problem for men, so he might have gone alone, looking for a solution.

Her children in their khaki uniforms, were ready for school. They also wondered where their father was. They did not want to ask questions, but they knew that something awful had happened. Otherwise, what was the yelling and shouting the past night all about? Their books and slates on their heads, they ate their roasted plantain and salted tilapia silently as they left the house for school. Ofosuaa walked outside with them and stood in the lane.

She saw Kani coming up the street. Donned in an awkward manner, his cloth appeared to her to be concealing something long underneath the folds in it. She waited until he came close to her. When Kani did not greet her, she followed him into the house. He crossed the patio in his long pensive strides, his bald head bent down. She went with him into his room.

'Where have you been all morning?' she asked.

Kani did not speak. From beneath the folds of his cloth, he brought out the Winchester rifle in its case and slid it under his bed. From Benoa's house, he had gone to Entea's place. Entea was not home. Kani forced the door open and collected his rifle. From there, he went to Sanyo's, washed his face, and then sent one of Sanyo's children to bring him palm wine, which he drank at Sanyo's all alone. Now, in his room, he reached for his bottle of schnapps. He shook it and poured a glass full. Raising the glass above eye level, he contemplated the light brown liquor in which motes of wood and spice bits raced one another in circles. In two gulps, he swallowed it all, winced and blew out the heat through his mouth. He then looked outside through the window. Ofosuaa took his hand and shook it gently to attract his attention.

'I've been worried sick, and wondering, my man,' she said.

'Whoever imagined the tiny ant could kill the mighty elephant?' he said. The flesh beneath his eyes was baggy from lack of sleep, the big orbs themselves red and riveted on a palmette design in the Persian rug. 'Yes, I, the mighty elephant, the grandchild of the Buffalo, am dying. The ant has beaten me, clobbered me –'

'But the ant cheated,' Ofosuaa said. 'It crawled into the elephant's tusk while it was asleep –'

'Yes, yes, and now I'm dying of having banged my head too much against walls to get the ant out. The mighty hawk, the symbol of power itself, I've been conquered by a hen that can't even fly.'

'That won't keep you down forever.' Ofosuaa walked

away from him to the door. She had smelled something awful on him. 'I didn't sleep the whole of the night.'

'How could you with this over our heads?' He sat down on the bed. 'I went to your brother. He's agreed to help.'

'Benoa?' Ofosuaa twisted her face with disappointment. She walked back to him, slow cautious steps. 'What can he do? To what has he agreed? I don't understand.'

'I told you this wasn't a problem for women. Aren't you a sister to Benoa? That makes a perfect match. Sometimes, the solution to certain problems is already there. Even before the problem arises. I wonder why I didn't think of that immediately.'

'A family marriage, my God.' Ofosuaa's face lit up. 'But the arrangements with Owiredu? What do we do about that? Well, I suppose we can let do with walleye instead of total blindness. Every marriage is a marriage. And come to think of it; Ayowa and Ayerakwa grew up together. I think they were made for each other.'

'Benoa is sending him a message to come home soon,' Kani said. 'Now, I can wash myself and rest for some time.'

'Warm water will be excellent for you.' Ofosuaa turned to go away but Kani called her back. Sitting on the bed, he brought out a lump wrapped in a dry plantain leaf from his pocket and gave it to her.

'I passed through Sanyo's,' he said. 'He gave me this medicine. In case Ayowa has some bodily pains. Mix it with her vaseline and ask her to rub a little on her joints every morning when she washes herself.'

'Is there any need for this medicine?' She undid the knot in her girdle holding her skirt-like cloth in place and tied the medicine there. 'I hope you didn't tell him anything else.'

'Sanyo isn't one of the men I discuss my problems with,' he said, irritated. 'And don't hide it there. Go and mix that medicine with her vaseline. Right now. If she isn't in the house now, do it for her when she comes back from wherever she's gone.' His blood-shot eyes pored over his tall wife, who opened her mouth, perhaps to say something. But the flurry of words that followed from Kani nipped her attempt. 'Had you taken good care of her, all these problems wouldn't have arisen. When I say this, you do that. Did you ever go to the farm all alone when you were Ayowa's age? Don't you stand here this morning to spoil the happiness I've had so far? Get out from here.'

But Ofosuaa did not go out. She stood there, silently looking hard at her husband. When she became absolutely convinced that the bad odour in the room was from Kani, she took a step toward him. And they stood toe to toe, almost equal in height. 'What do you mean, Kani?' she asked in a voice hardly her own. 'Where is your pride today, Kani? Remember that it took the two of us to make Ayowa. For nine months, I carried her inside me. I suffered the throes of childbirth to bring her into the world. I'm thankful to God for even the experience of the pain; Ayowa is sheer joy for me. But what about you?' she screamed, her neck stretched out and her face almost in that of Kani. He stepped back, in shock. Ofosuaa stepped forward after him.

'All you know is "Ayowa this and Ayowa that" worshipping her and idolizing her as if she were some trophy of admiration. If she hadn't been afraid of you, she would have told us the very day this tragedy happened. She wouldn't have been tormented needlessly. Look at you now. Why, why? Why do all your children fear you? Aren't you a human being?' Then she stopped, as suddenly as she had begun, breathing hard and staring Kani in the face. Kani had been numbed into silence. And the room was so quiet that the silence began to drain her. She closed her eyes not wanting to see what Kani would do to her. Having spoken to him like that she knew that he would make pulp of her; he would pummel her into submission. She could even imagine the blows coming down on her.

Nothing happened. Instead, she heard sniffles. She opened her eyes slowly as the sniffles developed into muffled cries. She gasped at what she saw. Crouched beside the highboy, Kani was weeping, his body seized by spasms of grief. How could mere words from her tear a man like Kani into shreds? This man whose appellation was 'the warrior who wore a metal smock and ate the red hot metal gong.' How on earth could a woman break him down? The earlier spirit entered her again, and she sought to hurt him more.

'Yes, your own children fear you because you think you're invincible,' she yelled. 'By that you drive them away from you. You make them liars, too. Do you know why Apenten, our oldest son has refused to come home on holidays from abroad? Do you know why Obuobi doesn't come home on holidays from secondary school but goes to Ampatia? It's because they both fear you, like the little ones. The whole town trembles, so you claim, when you speak. And you believe that is a good quality? Today, you whine like a pig when the town speak. There you are, weeping like a child.'

As Kani wept, his tears running down his face freely into the Persian rug, Ofosuaa's heart became soft. She remembered that she was still a woman – a mother, full of affection and love: she nurtured; she did not destroy. She went nearer her husband to comfort, but Kani cringed, covering his bald head with his hands.

'No. No more, my woman,' he said.

Ofosuaa put the medicine Kani had given her from Sanyo on the highboy and squatted to help him up. 'I'm sorry, my man. Wipe away your tears. Please, stand up.' She dabbed his face with her cloth. 'A man doesn't cry.'

'I feel lost, Ofosuaa. I've shared a bad meal with the devil. Now he is out to get me. Some animal has swallowed the Buffalo. I'm no more a man. It's as simple as that. A man is only a man so far as he's in control of situations. A true man stays unshaken, even when the earth beneath him is removed. I'm not that type,' he said, his voice distorted by his crying. 'I'm overwhelmed by things beyond my control. Now I can't place my hand on anything. You should have heard and seen tattered

151

Benoa, leading me by the hand. As if I'm blind. Along ou ancestors' galleries of wisdom. What did I do wrong?' Hi massive frame shook uncontrollably.

'We'll never know why certain things happen the wa they do. My inclination is whatever happens is for the best We don't have to worry about what Benoa said to you s long as he's agreed to help.' Ofosuaa cuddled Kani's hug figure in her arms. 'Forget about what Benoa had to do Forget how you had to persuade him to agree with you The most important thing is his having agreed to help u avoid humiliation.'

'But I'm still frightened, Ofosuaa,' he blubbered staggering toward the bed, but stopping long enough t finish his address. 'There's indeed something out there Subtle yet awesome. Benevolent yet malevolent. It' incomprehensible. I know it, my woman, and I'm afraid It's said that he who goes hunting in the night shouldn' be afraid to wail in the day. The devil has always been in the wake of cheap successes.' He swayed back and forth.

'The spirits know you've acknowledged them. They' take care of everything.' She embraced Kani with her bi body before he could fall down. 'Please, sit down. A mai of stature shouldn't cry as you're doing.'

'I can't hold on any more.' He grabbed a pole of th brass bedstead for support and broke out wailing freel again. 'I don't know I'd been hurting my children so. I'v always loved them a lot. Just that I didn't want them t grow up being soft. But now, it's I who am soft. What is i all for?'

Terribly embarrassed, Ofosuaa cupped her hand ove Kani's mouth to deaden the noise. 'Please, my man. It'l be too bad if somebody outside should hear you crying Think about what might be speculated.'

'Indeed, my woman, I'll stop crying now.' The we sounds of his lips punctuated every word he muttered. He gazed out of glazed red eyes at his wife. 'I love you,' h whimpered, his lips trembling. It was a simple statement yet Ofosuaa felt in it all the genuine qualities of affectior nd love that he had ever had for her. Something soft and ensual touched her insides. She ran her hands over his airy chest and pushed him gently on to the bed, sitting lown beside him.

'Please, no. Not now, my woman,' he protested. But his voice was still filled with love. He reached for the bottle of iquor and shook it. 'I must drink again. In times like this, he best defence is strong schnapps. Do you want to try ome?'

'I have my kitchen chores to perform.' She rose and collected the medicine her husband had given her from he top of the highboy. 'Don't drink too much.'

'I'll drink just a little.' He drank a glass full of the schnapps and bitters. Then he lay down on the bed on his back, clasping his hands together under his head so that his eyes were fixed on the ceiling. 'I wish I could sleep,' he said.

'If you wash yourself, it'll do you some good.' Ofosuaa watched the tremendous heave and collapse of his chest.

'If you can get me food first, I think I'll feel much better.' He paused and turned to his wife, lying on his side. 'Has Ayowa gone to the streamside? Until everything s over, she shouldn't be going out often these days. There are too many eyes around.'

'I'm aware of that.'

'You may go now,' he told her. But he called her back once more. 'I'm just scared of being alone. I hope you'll come with the food soon.' He lay on his back again, trying not to recount the torment he had gone through the past night.

# Chapter 10

For three weeks, Kani and Benoa were the chewing stick of the townsfolk at Nkonsia. On footpaths to farms, on the tracks to the streamside, at the market place or in their bedrooms, the townsfolk talked about Benoa's turning rich overnight. At first, some of the people interpreted Benoa's sudden wealth as having something to do with the deadlock in the case of the Asona and Entea's abominable open statement of going to break the town like a clay bowl. Opong, the Asona clan head, had refused to take responsibility for the absolution rites.

The people's motive for saying this was quite legitimate. Though Kani was not a member of the Asona clan, his wife and children were and, naturally, he had to be concerned about their welfare and protection. The people therefore speculated that Kani had passed on some of his money to his brother-in-law to see to it that the appropriate rites be performed to free the Asona clan from imprecation and evil. Apart from being a member of the Asona clan, Benoa was also the brother of Ofosuaa and therefore the maternal uncle of Kani's children. It would therefore be more in line if he led the open attack to compel Opong to perform the rites of absolution.

And how not so? Kani had failed to attend the latest meeting on Entea. Benoa claimed that Kani was out of town on business and that he was representing the nobleman. Benoa who, after the short period of prosperity in his life earned an infamous appellation as the 'carrier of gold nuggets' to reflect the little knots made to close up the tatters in his cloth, had attended the meeting

154

n Entea at the chief's looking like a man having been
idden from public view for some days to undergo an
ntensive fattening course as a prerequisite to his ascen-
ion to a royal stool. He donned a new full grey piece of
elvet. Voluble at the meeting, he gathered the rich folds
n his velvet and held them just above his waistline on his
eft hand to show how much flesh his bosom and clavicles
ad become filled with, and addressed the elders. All the
ime, he emphasized his points with his hand raised.

'Aren't there men in the Asona clan at Nkonsia? Isn't
here another person of royal blood in the Asona clan
vho can ascend our stool and perform the rites being
equested?' Benoa shouted at the elders. They sat in a
emicircle and listened and watched dumbfounded. Even
he crowd outside, peeping over and through the chinks
n the bamboo palings, were filled with mixed emotions of
istonishment and pride as they watched Benoa.

'How times change,' some of the women whispered.

'Why should we allow one man to hold a clan as a
ansom for the devil? And it's none other than the Asona,
he horde irrepressible, the clan of multitudinous legions,
he clan whose men never desert their cities!' Benoa
tomped the ground in his new princeling sandals, black
ind glossy with the dignity of the affluent. The elders
tared embarrassed by their own lack of initiative, as
Benoa recounted the appellations of the great clan with
uch vigour as could even reach their ancestors buried
ong ago.

'I say I can never understand why we have to waste so
nuch time on Opong, our clan head. Somebody may
nake the argument that it's Entea who should be held
esponsible for this problem, and not Opong. But to those
eople I say it's the person who goes to the streamside to
etch water who accidentally breaks the pitcher. Until
vhat time do we have to hold our patience? Benoa waved
iis raised and fisted right hand in the air at the stunned
elders. 'I want to remind you all. Asona is the lineage of
Heaven's God. No battalions stand before the white-

crested Raven of Asona that feeds on the meat of his compeers. It's abominable for one person to hold it as bait for the devil. Remember, you elders, that Asona is the clan that founded this town. The whole state of Abuakwa was actually founded by the Asona clan.

'I promise you money, Opong,' he addressed the bemused clan head directly, striking his chest. 'I'll give you as much money as you may need to perform the rite of absolution if it's money that's holding you back. On the other hand, I'm ready to bear the cost of your destoolment in order that a new clan head can go ahead with the demands of the townsfolk.' Benoa sat down at last, his eyes still on Opong. One could even have heard the subdued breath of the crestfallen elders and the crowd outside the fence in the silence that followed the impressive speech by Benoa. And so there was no doubt in the minds of the people that Benoa's sudden wealth had something to do with his battle against Opong and Entea's statement that the town was like a clay bowl that he could drop and smash at any time. Kani had given Benoa the money, the people said. What they could not determine was why the money had to be so much, anyway.

Then Benoa's son arrived in town and began regular visits to Kani's home. Ordinarily, Ayerakwa's visits would not have caused any stir among the people. After all, the children of the two families were first cousins. They also had grown up together, Ayerakwa living in Kani's house at a certain stage of his teenage life. But for the first time the people seemed to have really found out why Ayowa had stopped attending the Odenchey dance sessions. However, the people wondered why it had to be Ayerakwa. Why a family marriage at all when there had been so much talk about Owiredu's son? Did it have anything to do with Benoa's sudden wealth and the fast renovation work going on on his house? As the latest gossip gained currency with the speed of a brush fire, the people's curiosity peaked. In fact, Addo-the-tapper reported at the palm wine drinking shanty that he had overheard a bedroom quarrel between Kapre-the-Radio and her husband one night. How he had come by the details, nobody questioned him; but they enjoyed the drama as he acted it out.

'I didn't know Ayerakwa came home to marry,' Radio said.

'So they say,' husband replied.

'But what about his plans with Owiredu?'

'All I know is Owiredu is on his deathbed in a hospital somewhere,' husband said, a note of irritation in his voice. 'And I want you to know Kani and Benoa don't share their secrets with me.'

'Are you implying it's a marriage of convenience?'

'I'm not implying anything, woman.'

'I wonder why Kani would suddenly think of a family marriage.'

'They don't call you Radio for nothing, woman. It's none of my business where Kani takes his daughter. It's late, please let me go to sleep.'

'Well, we'll wait and see what is cooking.'

One Thursday morning, after their usual visit to the palm wine drinking bar, Kani and Benoa went together to the site where the townspeople were constructing a new middle-school block through communal labour. For several years now, the middle school had held classes in the church building and under the shades of the mango trees when the weather permitted it. Last year, however, Master Darko suggested that it was time Nkonsia put up a fitting school block to cater for the growing population of the middle school. The town therefore organized a harvest festival at which Kani donated twenty thousand cedis. Work began on the school block immediately.

Since Benoa had recently donated eight thousand cedis toward the project, he had joined the rank of people who did not have to do any physical work but supervised the masses. Standing near the men who mixed concrete, he motioned his head to the tune from a harmonica a young

157

man played. 'Work and happiness to you all,' Benoa greeted them.

'In work is progress and happiness,' some of the young men said, shovelling concrete into files of buckets and wok-like containers for the women to cart to the masons. 'We feel honoured that rich Benoa is here to see us work,' Radio-the-gossip added.

'The essence of community life is "I wash your back, you wash mine",' Benoa said. He strolled toward the masons working on the building itself. 'If I don't have the strength to do physical work with you, it's fair that my money and mouth should. How are your households today?'

'They're doing fine,' some of the men and women chorused. 'My grandson doesn't have a singlet to use, though,' another woman said. 'And I don't have money to buy him one.'

'Come to see me about that in my house, will you?' Benoa said. He gave a hand to some men working an improvised pulley that carried a bucket of mortar to a builder on a scaffold. The people around clapped their hands. 'I'm so impressed by the work here. I volunteer to buy everybody here palm wine and meat after work,' he said. Someone shouted Benoa's generosity to a few other workers around a big table under the cluster of mango trees. Addo-the-tapper sat there too, marking the names of the workers present.

'We all thank you,' he yelled. 'But some of the women don't drink. Can you do something else for them?'

'Make a list of their names for me and I shall make sure they each get a dose of my hot afternoon porridge,' he said. The people laughed, amused by the amorous raillery in the statement. Benoa had become a completely different man from the quiet and emaciated fellow the townsfolk used to know a few weeks back. With his hair dyed, not with soot from a lantern, but with a hair mixture called *yomo be Ga* which meant 'one can't differentiate an old woman from a young woman in the city,' he appeared

158

a lot younger now. His ebullience even showed in his sleep, Kapre-the-Radio reported to have heard Buaa blabber at the market one afternoon.

After some minutes' chat with the workers, Benoa joined Kani and a few elders behind the table under the mango trees. Some workers still hung around Addo-the-tapper. 'For your big shoulders, this isn't the work you should be doing,' Benoa told Addo.

'If you were literate, you could be doing it so that I mix concrete,' Addo, the temporary clerk, said. He did not bother to raise his eyes from the sheet of paper before him to look at Benoa. 'When is your supposedly big wedding so I can do what I know best, serving palm wine?'

'How strange and fast things discussed in a room get out?' Benoa chuckled. Fanning himself with a new satin kerchief, he pushed down his dumas cloth to bare his chest, and leaned against the backrest of the chair. 'The nobleman hasn't given his consent to my son's marrying Ayowa yet.' As he spoke, the tiny dewlaps under his chin, transformed into rich folds of skin, bobbed with affluent satisfaction.

'Well, what do you say, Nana Kani?' Addo asked.

Kani gazed at the top of the large table variegated by sunbeams that filtered through the foliage of the mango trees. He sighed, as if to convey an impression that it disturbed him to talk about the matter. 'One needs to think seriously about the merits and demerits of such family marriage,' he said. 'I need some more time. What is certain though is that you all will know when I've given my consent to my brother-in-law's request.'

'Are you satisfied now, Mr. One-day-clerk?' Benoa beamed a teasing smile at Addo, who just stayed busy writing and checking against the names on the sheet before him. Benoa then parted his legs a little, just to show part of the designs in his cloth. Dubbed *money doesn't have a master; it flies free like a bird*, the cloth had many grey and brown swans in flight. Then, he spoke slowly at first, addressing no one in particular, but with obvious reference to his nemesis. 'With your insolence to me, I wonder if you'll be allowed to drink some of the wine I'm going to provide these hard-working men with this afternoon.' Benoa patted his bare chest to indicate that the cost of the entertainment would indeed be borne by him.

'How indeed true the saying is that if a person who has never bought a pound of beef before is suddenly capable of buying an ounce of liver, everybody in town gets to know about it,' Addo insinuated as he watched Benoa The people around broke into a hilarious laughter.

'I can beat you to any woman anywhere at any time, Benoa shot back at Addo through clenched teeth. 'I won' be far from right if I say the distance between me and impoverishment is immeasurable. What do you, Addo have? Poverty is your bedfellow. And what woman wil spend her youthful years plodding through the sludge o impoverishment with you?'

'Buaa stuck with you, didn't she? And she gave you beautiful children like Ayerakwa and Mansa. But you shamelessly pawn Ayerakwa for three hundred cedis jus to show misguided women you're a man of substance How right Obaa Panyin is: people waste too much time and energy chasing things of no value, even for the earth. He laughed. Benoa almost got to his feet, but Kani pulled him down.

'I'm not rich,' Addo said, not bothering to take his eye away from his work. 'However, I know that money can do some wonderful things. And I'd like to be rich too. Just show me the source of the powerful charm that transformed you into such a wealthy man within this short period of time Then our competition over women will be fair.'

All the men looked at Addo with cold admonishing eyes. To refer directly to the source of somebody's wealth as being from witchcraft was considered a serious insult.

'It's time you showed some respect to Benoa,' Kan reprimanded Addo. And I wish the two of you would stop arguing between yourselves like little children, especiall in public. Let bygones be bygones.'

Scrunching up his muscled shoulders to imply that he was indifferent to what he had said earlier, Addo blurted: 'If I've stepped on somebody's balls, I'm sorry. I wonder why many people fear facing facts and the truth.'

'Truth is a frightening experience,' Kani said.

'Come to my house this evening,' Benoa scowled at Addo. 'I'll drop some herbal potion in your scaled eyes. They'll become open, then you'll see that cedi bills are posted all around the palm trees you tap every day.'

'Oyiwa!' Addo exclaimed, raising both his hands in the air. 'Be sure to stay home after supper, rich man. I also can do with some help. I've been waiting for some pacification from you. I promise you one thing, though. Even if your wealth elevates you to become a spokesman for the king of Abuakwa state, never hope you and I will ever stop our wrangles if we clash over one woman again. However, if you buy wine, I'll drink some first after you've taken its head.'

'Slothful fool,' Benoa hissed. 'You aren't ashamed to drink my wine. You can go and hang if you don't understand how I became the rich man I'm now. Hard work and planning. And let me tell you one more thing, the amount of money I'm going to spend on my son's wedding alone can care for you all your life. Yes, come to my house this evening. I'll improve your wretched existence for you.'

Though the men thought Benoa had gone too far with his abusive words against Addo, they did not believe that they were empty boast; they knew that some big marriage ceremony was in the wind. As it was said, the amount of effort that went into the preparation of an impending game indicated how good the show itself would be. Reconstruction work was proceeding at great speed on Benoa's house. New walls of cement and cinder blocks were being raised to replace the bamboo paling. Within three days, carpenters working overtime had removed all the shingles over his house and put ceilings above all the rooms and re-roofed the entire house with brand new corrugated aluminium sheets. Its sheen in the sun could even be hurting to the eyes of the astonished towns-folk. Five additional rooms and another set of three with an open porch were being constructed of cement blocks, and the mudcast walls of the existing building were also being plastered and fortified with mortar. By a secret suggestion from Kani, Benoa had built a new bathing place with an underground drainage to the gutters carved outside.

'Brother-of-man,' Benoa called Kani, just to tease Addo with what he was going to say. The mango trees rustled as the wind went through them, sprinkling down a multitude of tiny black mango flowers. Benoa flapped his cloth to rid it of the dead flowers. 'I've been thinking hard about some new business I want to go into. I want to consult you for your advice.'

'Is it something we can talk about here?' Kani rubbed his bald head with his satin kerchief, as if to dry some perspiration there. But only dead mango flowers fell from it to the ground. 'Let's hear it then. It's our elders who say that if someone doesn't have a wise person in his own home, that person must always avail himself with the wisdom of another person in the streets. Get on with it. Maybe some young man here will benefit from my word to you here.'

'I want to buy Ayerakwa a Mercedes Benz bus,' he said. 'He tells me that he's learned how to drive. He could use it to run interurban passenger service in this area. The singing band of the Presbyterian church here could charter it any time they have to travel outside the town to perform.'

Kani tapped his feet in thought, surprised by the urgency in his brother-in-law's voice. Then he said, 'That's a brilliant idea. It's good to put your money to work, but more importantly, I'm highly impressed by your will-ingness to help others. The secret to your going to keep your wealth will be your ability and willingness to give help to those worthy of it. Concerning the details of your new business idea, I think we should talk more about them later on, if you see what I mean.'

'I see what you mean all right –'

'Nkonsia is going to be a model town now that grasshoppers have changed into ants,' Addo said. 'At least, we can be sure of meaningful developments. No more foraging on others' crops; resources will go into adding to the growth of the town. No more mansions in the heat of women's asses.' Turning to Benoa, he said: 'Say, I could become a driver's assistant to Ayerakwa. He's a good friend to me. Come to think of it; maybe you and I come from the same cove from the other world. Otherwise, how could you have taken what was supposed to be mine?'

'Who will supply us palm wine if you become a driver's mate to Ayerakwa?' Benoa asked. The people around laughed.

'Man must always adapt to changing circumstances,' Addo said.

'Well put. Yes, well thought out.' Benoa fetched some water from a basin beneath the table. As he drank it, the men around broke into murmurs which gradually rose into a confused conversation about nothing in particular. While they doubted Benoa's business acumen, they had strong faith in his financial standing. He had been able to buy a rifle, a thing a man needed to be classified as a man of means in the area, and he had hired somebody to hunt with it in the Atewa forests. He had also paid cash to get back all his pawned farms on which he had contracted the services of some men from the Zongo.

As the murmurs died, Benoa reached inside his pocket and brought out a flat silver case. Pressing a small switch on it, he flicked open the case and extracted a cigarette from it. With deliberate slowness, he pressed the lid shut with a thud, then he tapped one end of the cigarette against the lid of the silver case long enough for the men around to notice that it was an imported filter tipped Consulate before he lit it. 'Yes, you said it aptly, Addo.

And for that, I think I'm going to change my attitude toward you. When time changes, a man has got to change with it too.' He blew out streams of smoke through his nostrils in the languid manner of the vain rich, his eyes half closed.

Soon, the talking drums announced work was over. The sun had reached the middle of the sky and the men had great appetite for palm wine to moisten their parched throats. Singing *asafo*, the traditional war songs, they followed Benoa and Kani to Nna Asaa's bar. Benoa treated them to refreshing palm wine and spicy hot meat.

Beneath all the pomp and confidence exuded by Benoa, he, however, remained a perturbed man. He feared enjoying the prospects of a society wedding and amassing great wealth and later on becoming haunted by a curse. He had a foreboding that something evil was bound to happen sooner or later to him or his son. His restlessness grew as the Asona clan elders delayed their decision on Opong and Entea's statement that the whole town was like a clay bowl in his hands and that he could drop and break it at will. For Benoa, there was an obvious link among all the events. It was Entea who had made that abominable statement. It was the same man who had raped Ayowa, whose name translated as a bridal clay bowl. Both Entea and Ayowa were of Asona clan stock. And it was the head of the Asona clan who was refusing to perform the necessary rites of absolution for the clan and the people. To Benoa, these could not be a mere string of coincidences. They were foretelling a tragedy if something was not done presently. While the elders could afford to wait, he swore to forestall any curse his own way.

When he returned home from the palm wine bar that day, he asked his son to come with him into his room. Ayerakwa had been outside, supervising work on the wall being raised around the house. Lanky and medium in height, Ayerakwa had an oval face that seemed to wear a perpetual smile and so he appeared cheerful all the time.

His bushy eyebrows virtually joined where the bridge of his broad and straight nose began. Coupled with his temple hairs, they made him look quite attractive. He had topped his brown gabardine pants with a light yellow jumper the sleeves of which came down to his elbows. His hands in his pockets, he took long pensive strides as he followed Benoa into his room.

Buaa was inside the room. Humming a tune, she was trying on a new *kaba* blouse her seamstress had brought her. She grinned at her husband, showing a complete set of teeth. Her two missing incisors had been fixed, and they were whiter than the rest. She bobbed up her breasts, which looked full like those of a young woman, inside the *kaba* blouse sewn like a bodice to fit her bosom.

'If you would excuse us, I have something important to discuss with Ayerakwa,' Benoa said to his wife. Buaa smiled at him, but she stood her ground. Benoa smiled too, but shook his head negatively. 'I wish you could stay, but this is purely man to man talk. It isn't anything over which we need a family meeting.'

As if in an effort to prevent her *kaba* blouse from coming apart, Buaa took it off carefully over her head. Two cone-shaped rubber foams dropped down from her chest, and she quickly collected them from the floor. Folding her *kaba*, she went to the foot of the huge iron bedstead bought a week ago to replace the rickety wooden one. The new bed was so large that it had taken more than half the space in the small room. Buaa opened the Samsonite suitcase on top of the four new steamer trunks stacked up in a setback manner according to their sizes, and put her *kaba* in it. She then went out of the room. Soon, the two men inside heard her humming another tune in the yard. They both knew the words of that tune: 'I'll have riches before I die.'

Benoa moved two chairs away from the centre of the room and leaned them against the wall. They felt a little tacky and still gave off the pungent odour of Mansion polish. He then drew a stool with a pillow on it closer to his son and sat on it. Ayerakwa sat in a cushioned arm chair. 'Give me that tumbler.' Benoa pointed to a glass sitting upside down near Ayerakwa's seat. Benoa then reached under his bed and brought out a large bottle of cut root pieces and bark around which was schnapps. He shook it, poured himself the glass full and drank it in three gulps.

'Go ahead. Serve yourself,' Benoa told Ayerakwa, breathing heavily and blowing air through his mouth. 'I like the fresh smell of mahogany and cement and polish mixed together in this room.'

'They're the smells of new life.' Ayerakwa took the bottle of liquor and the tumbler from his father, who was now pounding his chest as if to force down the peppermint flavour. He drew up his cloth to cover his shoulders, then looked down at the floor. In times past, the room would be hot and quite uncomfortable, but now, because of the shiny aluminium corrugated sheets that deflected the sun's heat back into the atmosphere, and the ceiling above the room, it felt cold for Benoa. He looked up at Ayerakwa, who was struggling with the liquor, drinking it in sips.

'A man doesn't drink like that,' Benoa said.

'It isn't easy drinking this stuff in one gulp,' Ayerakwa said. He set the tumbler to his mouth and swallowed the rest of the drink in one shot.

'Yes, that shows you're a man enough to take a wife,' Benoa complimented his son. Ayerakwa winced a smile that made his attempt to hide his disgust for the bitter drink only look stupid. He corked the bottle, cupped the tumbler over it, and shoved it under the bed, the tumbler clinking against the neck of the bottle. He sat back in the arm chair. 'I'm listening to you, father,' he said.

Benoa drew his stool much closer to his son. 'Now, you know we have power. So much power that you can afford to absent yourself from communal labour. And you don't have to worry about how much fine you pay to the Town Development Committee. It's all because we have money.

And we have money because I agreed to marry you to your cousin. You know Ayowa is carrying the child of another man. And that isn't easy for you to close your eyes to.'

'I don't blame Ayowa or the baby. They both are innocent. I'll marry Ayowa because I have always loved her. As it's said, what will be, will be. I'll do everything I can to make her happy.' Ayerakwa reclined in the chair, his soft eyes on a crude flower in the slate central to the ceiling while his fingers caressed his temple hairs. 'I was just a servant where I'd gone to learn carving. It was only by the goodwill of the driver of my instructor that I got to know driving. Otherwise, I hadn't even come close to learning about different species of wood used, let alone handle a tool. Under such conditions, only a fool wouldn't like it when he's to lie down on his back for honey to trickle into his mouth. What's best, in this case it happens to be the girl I've always loved and wanted.' Ayerakwa trained his eyes on his father and smiled at how young Benoa had come to look. The drink was however working on Ayerakwa, and he could no more concentrate his eyes on his father. They slipped down to the designs in his father's cloth. One of the birds in the cloth appeared to be flapping its wings indeed.

'I never dreamed I could ever have so much money suddenly.' He dipped his hand into the pocket of his gabardine pants and brought out a wad of bills. He waved them in the air. 'This is me!' he said.

Benoa drew his stool closer still to his son. He patted him on his shoulder, a subtle smile indicative of his son's ignorance about life in general on his face. 'Indeed, we have money and power now.' His voice was soft but firm. 'Yet money, as the name of my cloth implies, has wings and can fly away. And don't forget also that the fool doesn't think about the trickles of honey into his mouth can be so much as to choke him to death.'

Ayerakwa nodded his head in agreement as his father continued talking. 'While we must do everything to protect our money so that none of your brothers and sisters will ever have to plod through the sludge of impoverishment again, we must also do everything to forestall anything ominous that can make the money we've come to possess suffocate us. Kani and I must go and absolve ourselves and our families, especially you and Ayowa, in the Twafoor stream. We'll ask our benevolent tutelar spirits to protect us and our wealth. However, we can only do it when I've heard you say you don't have anything against the arrangements. I know you've already implied that, though.'

'My only problem is I'm not sure if I'm a man as far as decision making is concerned. When is a youth a man?' Ayerakwa looked up at his father.

Benoa chuckled and wiped his mouth with his satin kerchief. 'Of course, you're a man. At twenty-two, and with all the money you've got? Yes, you're a man.' Benoa cleared his throat loudly. 'You'll make most decisions yourself. I only come in to advise. But never strike a woman. Especially the woman who sleeps behind you every night. Even if you walk home to find her in bed with another man, just turn round. Walk away. You're a rich young man. Protect your repu –'

'Yes, my man. I'm here,' Buaa interrupted Benoa.

'No, I didn't call you,' Benoa said to his wife who stood in the doorway. He turned to his son in wonder, expecting some indication that he had actually called his wife.

'I thought I heard my name,' she said, grinning.

'We haven't mentioned your name.' Ayerakwa shook his head, closing and opening his eyes so slowly that his eyelids appeared to be weighed down by some unseen load. 'No one has called you.'

'If you have something to say, please, let's hear it,' Benoa said to Buaa, whose plump cheeks had jutted out in a broad smile and her eyes were looking moist. Benoa thought they held something that went far beyond the reverence and pride her gratuitous smile wanted to convey to him. He also smiled, flooded with painful and bittersweet and promising memories that had pulled him

and her through the hard times of long ago when Buaa
had given Benoa words of assurance of her love and
encouragement in all his endeavours during Odenchey
dance sessions under the 'tree of threepences' singing:

> In spite of his poverty, he's the man
> With whom I'll die out of love
> When I see him on his way to the farm
> It appears to me he has a rifle
> Slung there on his shoulder
> When indeed he's carrying
> A bunch of cassava sticks on his shoulder.

The day she sang that song, Benoa did not even have a
penny on him to stick on her forehead to express how he
appreciated her sincere efforts. Yet they married a year
later. Buaa had to wake up at dawn and go into the bush
to compete with school children in *atowuo* – hunting for
cobs of windfall kola nuts which she sold to cash crop
buyers to augment the little money Benoa provided for
their sustenance. She was heavy with their first child who
died when they were still in the doldrums of poverty. They
knew their son died because they were too poor even to
feed him adequately, let alone clothe him warmly. They
therefore named their second child *Ayerakwa*, meaning
they lost their first son due to circumstances beyond their
control. Of course, they had always believed that Ayerakwa
was their first son returned to make them rich some day.

Benoa pushed his hand under his cloth and into his
pocket. He found a bill. He pulled it out and held it
before Buaa. 'I forgot to tell you how nicely your *kaba*
fitted you. Take this for the cost of its sewing. And keep
the change.'

'Thank you, my man.' Buaa went forward and took a
two hundred cedi bill from Benoa, dropping a curtsy.
'There's another request, if I may make it. It's about the
children. The cocoyams and cassava I use for *foo-foo* stay
very hard even when I boil them long enough to become
soft. The pestles bounce off them in the mortar. I'm afraid

that may affect the delicate sides of the children. We don't want any of them to fall ill.'

'But the food they pound isn't much,' Ayerakwa said.

'Their sides aren't mature enough to take all the strain.' Buaa's voice held a quality that underscored how sincerely she felt concerned about the health of her children. 'They must grow healthy if they're to become the doctors and lawyers and engineers and nurses we want them to become.'

'Son, I understand your mother,' Benoa said rather contemplatively. 'I'll as soon as possible, find some men from the Zongo to do the *foo-foo* pounding each day. So long as it's a real rifle I sling over my shoulder these days, there will be no need for my children to overwork themselves or suffer needlessly.' The three laughed together. Buaa thanked her husband and went away. Presently, father and son overheard her humming another tune in the patio.

'The credit for all this goes to you, son.' Benoa nodded his head at Ayerakwa. 'Before we formally knock on Kani's door, I'd like to go with him to show our gratitude to the spirits of our ancestors. They have made this possible for us. I must also ask the gods of the land and the skies for protection. They must absolve and protect you and your children and all my children from any evil that may be inherent in the marriage. Just because of the circumstances that brought it about. Whatever happens, the gods must help us keep the money and double Kani's for him.'

'That's well said, father,' Ayerakwa agreed with Benoa.

Two days after the private conversation with his son, Benoa went to Kani about a mission he described as special. After eating supper, the two men prepared for a journey they had discussed the previous day at meals. Kani said that the exercise for the special mission was to be performed at night. Benoa was not in agreement. 'Why an oblation in the night?' he asked. 'It isn't the custom. In fact, I have never heard of anything like that before –'

'Anything done differently is special,' Kani said. 'The gods, whatever they are, are omniscient. We don't want people to see us and ask what our mission to the Twafoor is about. We as a people have been performing oblations in the day because our poor senses of perception can't discern the spirit of the materials used for libation at night. But the gods are omniscient; they know everything, even before we get the idea of what we want to do.'

Kani carried an electric torch. Benoa slung on his shoulder a grey baft sack with some items in it. The sun had already set and the grey of dusk was turning into darkness when they set out. Not wishing to be seen by anyone, the two men took the path that skirted Nkonsia and ran off into the bush at the northern side, past the refuse dump. With each step, their apprehension mounted, yet they knew that they got closer to their destination.

Leaving the low-lying bush of outskirt farms behind, they came to a point where the path splayed out to three areas. The outlying paths went to cocoa farms and so were clear. The one in the middle, bushy, ran the long distance to the Twafoor stream. Each year, after the *Akwanbo* festival, when the townsfolk cleared it and went to give homage to the shrine in the stream, the path fell into disuse and so it became overgrown with weeds; the people hardly went to the stream after the festival.

The darkness in the bush was intensified by the glow of myriad fireflies in the low bushes along the path and the serene shrill of nocturnal insects somewhere in the woods. On and on the two men went, hardly talking. After a long walk, they came to the fringes of the virgin forest. The half moon, in its dying days, had come up. Kani stopped, and Benoa stopped behind him.

'You don't want to wait on me while I pass water, do you?' Kani stepped out of the path and gave the electric torch to Benoa. 'Go ahead, I'll be following you. I'll be right behind you.'

'Brother-of-man, you always lead the *Akwanbo* –'

'This is no path-clearing ceremony,' Kani interrupted him. 'And there isn't any need for us to argue now. I've been in the lead since we started this trip. I think it's fair you lead now.'

The night cicadas did not shrill in the virgin forest. It was so deadly quiet that the footfalls of the two men went to deepen the silence in a strange manner. The air felt damp. Now and again, Benoa flashed on the torch to pick the way out of the dark along the low undergrowth. In truth, however, he did so to black out the distance where the tall grey trees in the moonlight, festooned with long ferns and dappled by beams of light, looked like bearded giants with hands joined together in a weird dance. Among the profusion of vines, trunks uprooted or broken from their stumps by a windstorm several years ago lay beneath the high trees. Covered with moss, they looked like huge corpses. Nobody had ever farmed the virgin forest. It was believed to be the enclave of wicked ghosts. Many years ago, it was alleged that traitors and subversives went to take their own lives in it when they were found out.

Both Kani and Benoa remembered one suicide associated with the virgin forest. Counting that year's *Akwanbo* yet to be celebrated, it would be thirteen years since it happened. It involved a man called Senti. Until the scandal that led to his death, no-one knew how he had quickly come by his money and wealth, but for three years, he supplied the elements for the *Akwanbo* festival. Then on the eve of the festival in the year he died, the police picked him up for questioning, only to release him on bail.

At first cockcrow of the path-weeding day, all the men gathered at the outskirt of the town. In Wellington boots into which he had tucked the ends of his pants, Kani went up and down the track inspecting the men. He noticed that Senti was absent. Some of the men said that he had been picked up again at midnight by the police, but Benoa maintained that was not the case; he had been drinking and talking with Senti late into the night. In fact, he almost got into a brawl with Addo-the-tapper for arguing with the other men that the police had not come for Senti a second time. Anyway, since they already had the sheep Senti had sold the men for the sacrifice to the Twafoor shrine, Kani ordered the function to begin.

The men filed along the path, a considerable distance between every two, so that whoever finished weeding his portion, went ahead and restarted another section some yards away from the person who previously had been in the lead. They weeded the path, swinging their machetes to the beat of drums and *Asafo* songs provided by the Nkonsia *Apegya* – the sparkers of fire and lead squadron of warriors in the old times of tribal warfare. When the first light of day came, they had cleared the path to the virgin forest. By that time, Benoa was in the lead, ahead of the other men. At a certain point, he felt something cold touch his bare and sweat-drenched back as he stooped weeding. Raising his head, he was almost petrified by what he saw; Senti was dangling on a sturdy bush rope that hung from the branch of a tree close to the path. It was as if he had deliberately chosen that site to make it easier for his body to be found. His eyes were bloodshot and popping, his tongue bloated and clinging to his mouth by a mere tissue of flesh; it had almost been severed by his clenched teeth. Benoa cut off a piece of the dead man's cloth and burnt it to perform a simple rite of absolution before going to tell Kani. Kani announced it to the rest of the men. They cut down Senti's body and lugged it deep into the tall woods where they buried it like a dead rat.

Though the *Akwanbo* went on, it was more funereal than festive. After the sacrifice, the men squatted near the fire made on the cleared stream banks, or straddled on the boulders around, eating the roasted mutton, drinking and talking in low tones about Senti and why he had killed himself so shamefully. Later on that day in town, they learned that Senti had sold them stolen sheep at three hundred cedis each year for the three years he had been the co-ordinator of the festival.

Suddenly, as if the dead man was around to tease Kani and Benoa, a raucous yelp of some large carnivorous bird rent the dense atmosphere from high up in the virgin forest. Pregnant with fear, Benoa halted in his tracks, his legs wobbling. Kani, too, seized by the shivers, did not watch; he bumped into his brother-in-law who out of spontaneous dread, leapt forward and crashed into a tree. He lost his grasp on the electric torch as he fell helplessly on his back into the bushy footway. The electric torch fell into the bush beside the path. Kani found it, its beam smothered by the weeds. He focused it on Benoa.

'Are you all right?' Kani asked him.

Benoa pointed to a small bump on his forehead. 'It hurts here. My head, Brother-of-man.' He sounded as though he had just emptied all his innards after a strong enema dose.

'Anything good isn't achieved without some sweat and pain.' Kani helped Benoa to his feet. 'Don't worry, we're almost there. Very soon, all our troubles will be over.'

'Yah, the sweetness of the sugar cane isn't thorough, is it?' Benoa said and the two men chuckled, a subdued laughter gravid with apprehension. They went down a small hill, lumbered through a forest of canna and suddenly arrived at a sizeable pool surrounded by flat rocks. They stood silent, their eyes on the tranquil water and a granite boulder that squatted in the middle of it. Even from that distance, they could see its top greasy with several previous oblations, gleam with a spread of diffused moonlight.

They took off their canvas boots and cloths. Wearing only pairs of shorts, they approached the fetish stoup at the shoreline. It was a crock held high in a three-branch-fork fig post. Planted between two large pieces of granite, the fig had sprouted fresh sprigs at the fork, and they reverentially sheltered the earthenware pot. Angry whines flitted around the heads of the men and they felt several smarting stings on their hands as they groped through the leaves to reach the ancient water inside the crock. Hastily, they washed their faces and ears with the water they had scooped.

'O God, this is madness!' Benoa cried.

'We surely will overcome,' Kani said.

Both men desperately kept slapping and rubbing their arms and hands to crush the swarm of mosquitoes on them. Then, carrying the items for oblation in a bag on his shoulder, Kani stepped into the pool behind Benoa. The only noises they heard were the water babbling against their legs as they waded through it to the squatting rock, and the twitter of some bird disturbed in its nest by the presence of the two men. The water reached Kani's calves, but it came higher to Benoa's thighs. Kani brought out all the items in the grey baft sack. They included a full-size bottle of schnapps, three pieces of kola nuts, three eggs, two of which had got broken in Benoa's fall, four old pennies, and a coconut shell cup. They could use glass for the same purpose, but both men had agreed that a coconut shell cup was purer and so was more appealing to the spirits. Kani passed the schnapps on to Benoa who uncorked it, poured some into the cup and raised it in the air. He dropped a drip on the oily top of the rock.

'Almighty God of all the Universes,' he began the libation, pouring more schnapps down in trickles. 'Omnipotent One at whom we shudder when You stir even your finger. You created all the worlds and every-thing in them, including the Twafoor which You appoin-ted for us as Your mediator here.

'We call on You to come and drink with us.'

'The grand one Twafoor, this is a drink for you.' He put down more drops of the drink on the rock. 'It's schnapps, the distinguished E.K. brand from behind the seas in the land of our brothers, the white people.'

'Hear, hear o-o, hear!' Kani responded.

'If we've come to you tonight, we're here to seek protection for our children and households. Your grand-children, Ayowa and Ayerakwa, have agreed to undertake the long journey of responsibility of marriage. You the

Omnipotent and Omniscient One are already in the know of what is behind it all. But we know it's all your doing. You work in ways incomprehensible to us. We ask You to cleanse our children and the marriage of all imprecation.' He punctuated his sentences with more drops of the schnapps on the rock.

'We didn't come to you tonight with empty hands.'

'Wie, o wie!' Kani responded.

'We brought you an egg and kola nuts. We know these are insufficient, but if we live longer, we'll give you more. We therefore ask for life. We ask for good health. Don't let us go blind. We don't want impotency in our families. When our children sleep together, let them have children to carry on our tradition.'

'Well said,' Kani said, moving his head up and down.

'We ask for prosperity for our children. We ask you to guide and protect them. We now present you with the items we brought. If tomorrow comes to meet us, we'll give you more. So, Mighty Creator, Mother of Fertility, we ask You to drink with your servant Twafoor.' And he poured the rest of the schnapps in the shell cup on the rock.

'Well spoken, Brother-of-man,' Kani complimented.

Benoa broke the egg on the boulder. Tossing the kola nuts into the yolk that had begun to slide into the pool, he stuck the four pennies in the tar-like mucus on the rock, according to the four points of the earth.

'It's finished,' Benoa said.

'To good times ahead.' Kani poured himself a drink.

'Henceforth, we walk and talk like the men of means we are.' Benoa also poured himself a drink and drank it in a gulp. Then he emptied the rest of the schnapps in the bottle on the rock. The two men waded back to the shore and began to lace on their canvas boots. Then, from somewhere in the trees in the dark came forth the hoot of the owl. The two men stared at each other as though for the first time in their lives, they had comprehended the lore of the land that said he who went hunting in the night should never feel embarrassed or be afraid to wail openly in the day. Like the Raven and the Vulture, they had understood that in this land, it would never be the custom to pour libation at night, not under any circumstances. They quietly donned their cloths and began the long journey back home. Kani stayed in the lead all through, now and then showing the way with his electric torch. They did not speak a word between them during the whole trip back.

# Chapter 11

A week after the surreptitious oblation in the Twafoor, Benoa and his son went to Kani's house to propose formally to Ayowa. Normally, the ceremony could have been done without fanfare, but the two rich men decided to make a big thing out of it. Since the town was in the know about the open visits of Ayerakwa to Ayowa, their fathers had decided to slow the pace of the whole marital arrangements, in spite of the urgency about it all to Kani, to prevent the townsfolk from suspecting that Benoa and Kani were rushing the affair to conceal something.

By ten o'clock that Thursday morning, many people had gathered in Kani's large house. He had invited members of his extended family and those of Ofosuaa. It was somehow ambiguous, though, since the members of his wife's family were those of Benoa, too. For Benoa also to have a multitude as his entourage, he invited Buaa's people. Flocks of people had therefore arrived in the homes of the two rich men from towns like Asafo, Asikam, Betomu, Ampatia, Begoro, Dompim, Ahwenease, and Kibi.

The sky was all blue, and the sun shone brightly even for a morning. In the patio of Kani's house, the invited guests and their women sat on stools in the form of a new moon. They flanked dignitaries like the chief, his spokesman, Kani and his younger brother from Ampatia, Master Darko and Opong the Asona clan head. They all sat in Windsor or corner chairs brought out from Kani's parlour and the open porch. Three large black earthenware pots of foaming palm wine stood in the middle of the space before them. The seated men engaged themselves in conversations, talking in low tones as they waited for the door-knocking ceremony, which was the same as asking for the hand of the woman in marriage, to begin. Somebody announced that the other party had arrived.

With Mansa in the lead, a contingent of five young women entered Kani's house. They wore similar *kente* wraparounds and they carried on their heads two brass basins with lids on them, two large Samsonite suitcases, and a big rattan basket covered by a white poplin with red and blue morning glories stitched in it. The five young women did not come alone; they brought with them a crowd of noisy curiosity-seekers who stood in a half-circle facing the seated elders and their women to complete a circle. Some people naturally could not see what was going on inside the circle so they went to the stoop behind the dignitaries. Others, like Addo-the-tapper, sat on the short balustrade walls in front of the north and south wing buildings, their legs dangling, and watched the proceedings.

The five young women bearers paraded in a file, going round in the open space. The young men present made amorous noises and whistled as they watched the pretty young women go round. Then, the young women stopped and stood in a line facing Kani and the people seated. Mansa announced that she and the other women were emissaries for her brother and her parents, who had asked them to bring the items to Ayowa and her parents. Kani asked his wife to relieve them of their load, and Ofosuaa directed the girl carrying the rattan basket to the kitchen. Ofosuaa then led the other four into her husband's room. A wave of a murmur suddenly hushed the chattering around. The crowd of onlookers fell back and made way for Ayerakwa, his parents and two of his matrilineal uncles. As they went round shaking hands with the seated people, some others in the crowd made sniffing sounds in appreciation of the fragrance trailing the group from the cologne on them and the smell of their fresh wax print textile.

'Brother-of-man,' Kani addressed Benoa, who stood with his family members. 'As you can see, I've asked witnesses to be present this morning and hear what you promised to tell me. As we all know, when there's a good thing going, townsfolk usually bury their hatchets, and come together for success. So, don't be amazed by the number of people here. It's an indication of how much we're loved. We're listening to you now.'

Benoa took a step toward the seated group, bared his chest and then ran his hand over his dyed black hair, as if in a deliberate effort to draw attention to his youthful looks. 'Distinguished men and women gathered here, suppose you all know why we've met here.' He looked round, beaming. Master Darko cleared his throat quite audibly above the murmurs and asked for his memory to be refreshed. When he had first heard the rumours about Ayowa and Ayerakwa, he was surprised. He contacted Kani to find out about the change in suitors. Kani gave him three thousand cedis to keep his mouth shut, adding, 'When the weaverbird begins work on its nest, the manner of its weaving may look confusing to you at the onset. But be patient. Watch it till it finishes. You'll realize how wise the bird is. Man has control over certain things, but there are others the control of which is in Higher hands.'

Benoa looked at Master Darko briefly. 'Well, as the honourable schoolmaster has requested, I'll remind those who may have forgotten, or haven't heard at all, why we're here this morning. In the past few days, there has been some "they say, they say" about my son Ayerakwa, and Ayowa the daughter of noble Kani. Those of you from this town know that at a certain stage in his growth, my son lived under Kani's roof. It's you our elders who say that for every rumour, there's bound to be some grain of truth. I didn't know at the time Ayerakwa was in Kani's house that my son had designs on his cousin. Well, my son has confirmed it to me now. So we've brought noble Kani a bottle of schnapps to ask for Ayowa's hand for my son. If the nobleman agrees to the request, Ayerakwa would like o marry Ayowa as appropriately as custom and tradition would allow on Saturday – two days from now.' Benoa raised his hand in the air to show the crowd and Kani a large E.K. brand schnapps still wrapped in grey paper with the red wax seal on it.

Kani bowed his head. For sometime, he did not raise it or say anything. Ofosuaa hurriedly trooped to his side, squatted and held a brief mouth to ear conference with him. The people began to talk in low tones. Somebody in the crowd then said above the murmuring that it would be a shame for the nobleman to turn down the offer. Some of the seated elders also leaned over to the others on their sides and engaged them in whispering conversation. The murmurs ceased as Kani stood up to his full height and swathed his *dumas* cloth around him well. His big eyes stared down at Benoa's feet. 'Elders and women of stature who have gathered here,' he bellowed, 'you'll agree with me that one of the greatest honours a father can have is when he's approached in the proper manner for his daughter's hand in marriage.' He looked round at the quiet crowd, let down the folds in his cloth which appeared to be slipping down on their own any way, and flung them back on to his left shoulder, scrunching them up to keep the cloth in place. 'I've been in consultation with my wife. And I'm happy to announce I accept the drink. Ayerakwa can marry my daughter in any way he deems befitting to his status.'

The elders nodded their heads in approval, talking to one another and chortling with mirth. Benoa, together with his wife and son and two other relatives, walked over to the men seated. Having presented the schnapps to Kani, Benoa shook hands with him. Ayerakwa and the other relatives followed, and one after the other, they greeted all the seated people by the hand. Kani turned the wrapped-up bottle of drink over and over in his hands, inspecting it. He then placed it down on his side near his Windsor chair.

Having gone back to his place, Benoa said: 'Well, my

son has just reminded me that he's aware Ayowa and her parents don't live in isolation. They have relatives, too. If they approve of his request, they must share these drinks with him.' Benoa indicated the palm wine, the froth of which was scaling down the sides of the three black earthenware pots.

Addo-the-tapper jumped down from the balustrade wall on which he had been sitting. He entered the middle space, took off his cloth and wound it around his waist like a loin piece so that all his torso showed. This was the moment he had been waiting for, to show off how astute a server of palm wine he was. Reputed to be the best palm wine server at Nkonsia when there was a big gathering, he had determined to do this for some more money from Benoa, who had settled the animosity between them by paying Addo five hundred cedis on the day of the communal labour. Since it was a big disgrace if the palm wine provided for an occasion was not sufficient to go round all the people present, Addo knew that Benoa would give him more money if he asked, for fear that Addo might cause some mischief to blight Benoa's dignity.

'Rich Benoa,' Addo said. 'You have a pouch for me?'

'Yes,' Benoa said. 'Pick it up when roosters come home.'

Understanding Benoa's hint as a dusk invitation to his house, Addo skimmed off the froth and dashed it against the cement floor, rattling incantations in praise of the palm tree: 'Elegant tree no part of which is discarded, even in death, your trunk provides some of the most delicious straw mushrooms.' He poured some of the wine from one of the big pots into a large calabash, carried it to Ayerakwa, whom he handed a drinking calabash. Addo was about to pour him the head drink when Kani's younger brother, who had come from Ampatia, halted the proceedings.

'Wait a minute,' he said, standing up. He was tall, but not as huge in stature as his richer brother. 'Aren't we glossing over something here? If my seniors have forgotten, I wish to remind them that one doesn't make one's bed ready when one hasn't seen the woman one's going to sleep with. Or so it's said –'

'What are you getting at?' Kani asked.

'Where's Ayowa to tell us she agrees to all of this?'

Kani shot up from his seat. The murmurs died down instantly. He had purposely requested that Ayowa be kept inside her room even though Ofosuaa had said all that she could to persuade him that Ayowa's belly was not showing. Kani, however, would not have any of that; he feared that people might think that his daughter's belly was bulging. 'Sit down, will you?' he thundered. 'If my –' and he struck his massive chest '– my own daughter hadn't consented to the marriage, I wouldn't have invited you here. What do you think of me and Ofosuaa? I'm older than you and so know better –'

'You can't intimidate me,' his brother shouted back. 'I fail to understand why all this ceremony should go on over the head of the central person involved in this. I also am her first paternal uncle, if not her father by qualification, and I demand her presence here to say "yes" before me and everybody so gathered here. And I mean nobody here –' and he also struck his big chest '– can drink any of this wine until I hear from Ayowa she wants Ayerakwa for a husband. Who knows if Ayowa has something to say against it? Who knows if somebody has something against the proposal? Who knows if Kani is pushing my niece into it to satisfy his whims?'

'Who are you to hold up these proceedings?' Kani demanded.

'I'm your brother, Ayowa's first uncle. Any questions?'

'You're boring, man. Where did you pick up that?' Kani said.

As the heated argument went on between the brothers, the elders looked on indifferently. Naturally, if there was no opposition somewhere along the proceedings, it would be said that it had been too cheap a proposal. In fact,

Opong the Asona clan head, leaned on his side toward the chief and whispered to him that he believed that the argument was a stage-show. Most of the people in the crowd, however, were astonished about all of it. They felt it did not show solidarity in the family. Master Darko went over to Kani and calmed him down.

'It's for the good of us all that this ceremony proceeds peacefully,' the schoolmaster addressed the two brothers. He put his hands in his pockets and pulled up his oversized white drill shorts. 'I know Ayowa. But for the benefit of those who aren't familiar with her, I think it's only fair that she's asked to come here to quell any doubts, if indeed there are any. Somebody might say that the nobleman is defrauding this rich young man here.' He pointed to Ayerakwa. 'And we don't know if there's somebody in that room. As a matter of fact, we must see the bride-to-be.'

'My man,' Ofosuaa said to Kani. 'Let Ayowa come out. It won't be fair for her if she doesn't get a chance to express her feelings about it.'

Kani looked at Ofosuaa, contracting his greying brows in an expression that seemed to ask whether she was sure. Ofosuaa blinked her eyes in the affirmative, a subtle smile of assurance on her broad face. She knew that her husband was being over protective. So far, she had not seen anything at all about Ayowa to indicate that she was pregnant. 'I'll ask her to come out,' Ofosuaa said and went away to one of the rooms in the north wing that had become Ayowa's private abode.

Kani reclined in his Windsor chair, throwing his head far back and gazing at the clear blue sky, believing that the promising new world he had just stitched together for himself was about to come apart at a delicate seam he had tried so hard to protect. And he wondered why the cause, once again, had to be somebody so close to him. Quite absorbed in his thoughts, he did not notice a sudden hush sweep over the crowd; he only became aware of it when he heard a comment about a woman who should have been the wife of a king. He was surprised to find everyone else looking toward the north wing, and so he also turned his head in the direction of Ayowa's room.

Following her mother, Ayowa was dressed in the cloth dubbed 'the clan is a multitudinous force' because of its dark bluish green designs of quinnate Baobab leaves in clusters. Wrapped around her in the manner of queen-mothers, it exposed her shoulders and the upper part of her breasts, which showed like ripened yellow mangoes. Even the mass of thin corn rows adorned with gold bits could not hide her large ornamental looping earrings that kept clinking together as she walked with Ofosuaa, greeting the seated dignitaries by the hand.

She took deliberate slow steps, as if she wanted noticed her long and fair toes made more prominent by the glossy blackness of her princeling sandals. Some young men under the cloistral veranda began their amorous whis-tling. She paused momentarily, looking at them boldly and smiling, her large eyes made more white by the *kajikaji* applied to her long eyelashes. When she got to her father, she stopped. For some time, Kani could not take his eyes off her, gazing at the eagle-in-flight pendant on her Aggrey beads necklace.

'She's your own daughter,' Ofosuaa said and those around laughed. 'I hope you aren't trying to make me jealous of her.'

'No, no, my woman. I'm just overwhelmed,' Kani said and there was more laughter among the people. 'Now, my princess, if you will please say so, let everyone here know if you want Ayerakwa for a husband.' He pointed at him, standing beside Benoa. 'If for some reason you don't want me to drink the schnapps he's brought me to ask for your hand, please, say so too. Some people think I'm defraud-ing the young man.'

'Thank you, my father,' Ayowa said. 'This is the happiest moment of my life. Ayerakwa and I have always liked each other.' She turned and looked at her fiancé, smiling. 'I have nothing against his marrying me. I agree to become his wife whenever he's ready. I know I'm in love with him.' The candour in her voice would have shamed anybody who might have had qualms about the arrangements. Assisted by her mother and Mansa, Ayowa went round again and shook hands with Ayerakwa and his parents. Then she went back to her father, clasped her hands before her and asked permission to go inside her room.

'Sure,' Kani said, delighted. 'We don't have to display such a radiant woman to public eye for long, especially at this time and stage in her life.'

'If the inquisitive ones are satisfied now, we'll drink the palm wine,' Addo said in an obvious reference to Kani's younger brother. All the people broke into a hearty laugh.

'Yes, now we can share the drink,' Kani's brother said.

Ayerakwa accepted the first calabash, followed by his parents, and then Kani. Aware that most eyes were on him, Kani, after drinking, tilted the calabash and raised it a little while he skilfully swung it in a downward curve toward him and let out the dregs which hit the floor with a pop. 'Epu-o ni! Long life and good health to us all,' he said.

'Congratulations, Nana,' Addo said. 'You make palm wine drinking real fun.' He collected the empty calabash from the rich man and proceeded to serve the members of the two families. When he was done, he called on two other young men to assist him serve all the other people who were waiting patiently for their turns. Suddenly, there started jostling and shoving in the rear flanks of the crowd. As Kani and the other dignitaries looked on, trying to figure out what was happening, Entea pushed his way to the front. Addo and the two young men helping him serve the palm wine grabbed him from behind. They tried to take him away, but Kani stopped them. Dishevelled, Entea demanded to see Ayowa.

'Who is this?' Kani asked.

'Noble Kani, am I not your right hand man? Why –'

'I've had enough of this nonsense.' Kani shot up and

was right in Entea's face before his brother and other men stopped him. 'You should thank these men for holding me. If my hands were free, I would break you in two right here. I promise you this though; if you dare walk into this house again, I'll blow your head off with my rifle.' To Addo and the other young men, he said: 'Please, get him out of here before I lose all my calmness. And to everyone here, Entea has lost any favours he enjoyed with me. He cannot do or contract business with any person in my name any more. I don't know him.'

'That was long overdue, Brother-of-man,' Benoa said.

'Take him away from here,' Kani's brother added.

They soon heard people booing and hooting at Entea outside the house. Addo and his two friends came back to the centre of the gathering and continued serving the palm wine. The ceremony ended a little after noon.

By evening time, a rumour had gone abroad about the gifts Ayerakwa sent his would-be in-laws and wife to-be. Apart from a mat and two woollen blankets he gave Ofosuaa as symbolic gifts to make up for the mother's which Ayowa might have soiled when a baby, it was said that he gave her so much salt that each of the members in her extended family received a cup full. Ayerakwa also presented the nobleman with a briar pipe carved in the shape of a miniature elephant head whose trunk curved beneath the bowl to form the smoke conduit. Ayerakwa topped it with a special type of imported tobacco called King Edward's. And this was so plentiful that the nobleman was able to share it with all the people in his family. Other important presents included ten bales of Dutch wax prints, trinkets, three pieces of kente cloth, Aggrey beads. Never in the whole town and even beyond had a prospective bridegroom presented his would-be in-laws and his wife to-be with such expensive gifts.

In spite of her splendid appearance in the morning, Ayowa was still not at ease. Her preoccupation was not over the marriage arrangements; it was with the baby that she thought was growing inside her. She wanted it done away with. In her view, nothing had been achieved so long as evidence of her pain still lived with her. Would the baby look like Entea? Could she nurture and love it? Could she deceive people forever that her belly belonged to Ayerakwa? She very much appreciated her father's efforts to avoid humiliation, but Ayerakwa was not the father of the baby. In fact, Ayowa had hoped that Kani would seek to destroy the pregnancy. She was disappointed that her father had said nothing about the unwanted pregnancy that was between her and Ayerakwa, whom she was growing to love very much.

She would never forget that late evening when he kissed her. They had returned from Obaa Panyin's, where Ayowa had done the laundry for the elderly woman, then cooked a sumptuous meal with chanterelle mushrooms Obaa Panyin had picked herself when she went to the bush with Ayowa earlier. Ayerakwa had stayed behind and painted Obaa Panyin's sleeping room with fresh paint. The three of them later ate dinner from the same bowl, and after dinner Obaa Panyin told them about how happy she was for them, and that their marriage was an occasion that had to be. She also said that Kani and Benoa were like many people, trapped in time capsules of idiotic ideas abandoned long ago.

On asking what she meant, Obaa Panyin told the young lovers that it was unbelievable that some folks would still subscribe to the old traveller's song of *Okwan tenten aware* that vilified marriages between couples hailing from distant towns when the distance between Great Britain and Ghana had been reduced to six hours by jet flight and zero second by telephone. Then, she added that Ayowa ought to listen to Ayerakwa and not try anything foolish on her own. Both Ayerakwa and Ayowa were not sure of what Obaa Panyin was referring to, but they did not seek to find out; they knew that she was used to making general statements unrelated to the topic of discussion at hand.

When they left Obaa Panyin's they went and sat outside Kani's house on the bamboo pew under the coconut palm. There was no moon, but the night was beautiful; the sky was bright with stars. Ayowa lay on the pew on her back, so that her head rested on Ayerakwa's lap and her eyes remained on the sky. 'Why must we allow something bad to affect our happiness?' she said suddenly. 'That alone distracts from everything.'

'What are you talking about?' Ayerakwa asked, surprised.

'You aren't the father of the child in here –'

Ayerakwa placed his hand over her mouth. 'Had it not been for that child, you and I would never have been together,' he said. 'Let's be thankful to God for our happiness, even if it was borne out of agony and humiliation. I as the man and your husband to-be have no misgivings about the belly. No more talk about this belly. I'll forever be thankful to the baby for bringing you, my love, to me.'

'But it's my belly.'

'What is in there isn't your life,' Ayerakwa said. 'The whole matter has gone beyond the strings of human influence. It's in the realm of God, and we don't have a say in it, my Love.' He smiled at her. She took his hand and squeezed it gently, peering into his face. The white of her eyes was bright and beautiful in the starlit night. He touched her temples and drew his face closer to hers until his lips met hers. He kissed her. After that, she sang him one of her tunes from Odenchey.

> My darling whose love
> Reflects like the mirror
> I'm unable to go to bed
> Unless I hear and see him
> Come wet my lips
> With your sweet touch of love.

'It's cold out here,' she whispered to him. 'Let's go in.'

Sitting in the sofa in her room, they began chewing

roasted peanuts and dry corn called *nchewie* that Ofosuaa
had left them on the centre table; they always ate *nchewie*
in the evening before he left her for his house. She fed a
grain of roasted corn into his mouth, then asked him: 'Do
you know why my mother roasts peanuts and corn for us
every evening?'

Ayerakwa picked the grain caught between his lips with
his tongue, then said: 'I suppose it's to make us sleep
soundly. When we're able to sleep well, we have pleasant
dreams. And we wake up refreshed and ready to work out
of love for the good of the community.'

'That's all nice.' Ayowa giggled. 'But we eat *nchewie* not
for a fantasy world. We eat it for a more realistic pleasant
purpose. It's a women's secret, my mother says. But I'll tell
you. Just because I love you. My mother tells me when
there's love between a man and a woman, it's good and
healthy not to hide things from each other.'

'Why do I have the feeling I'm being set up?'

'Not a set up, but a prep up,' she chortled. 'Are you
ready? We eat roasted peanuts and dry corn to make our
breath sweet when we snuggle up in bed.' She tapped him
on his cheek. He took her hand. Gently, he pulled her
away from the sofa to the bed. And she did not resist in
any way. And for the first time between them, they made
love. Ayowa had come to believe since then that she knew
what true love-making was like. Her contact with Ayerakwa
was nothing like her brutal experience with Entea under
the cassava plants on the Ntanoa farm. When Ayerakwa
left her that night, she decided that she had to get rid of
the pregnancy at all costs.

So, believing that her father would go along with her
decision, Ayowa went to Kani in the evening of the day
Ayerakwa came to propose formally to her. Kani was
relaxing with Ofosuaa in the open porch, listening to the
radio playing Asafo music softly. Kani sat in a wing chair
placed in a corner of the open porch near the gateleg
table. The aladdin stood on the etagere in the corner.

190

Since that infamous night he wetted himself, he had changed some of the furniture items in the open porch, entirely removed the hammock chair which he had folded up and kept under his brass fourposter. The hammock chair was now a landmark in his life, some oath of bitter importance which, in a great exigency, he would touch and point to the sky and swear that 'by the canvas of my hammock chair that prevented my humiliation from trickling before public eyes, I swear to do this and that. . .'

He had now placed in the porch six cabriole corner chairs with burgundy puffs in them, having removed most of the Windsor chairs. Where the hammock chair used to be, he had placed a women's stool with a red velvet pouf on it. He had bought it purposefully for Ayowa. He liked it anytime she joined him and Ofosuaa to chat in the evenings. Ayerakwa had sat with them on a couple of occasions, like the day he and Ayowa were prevented from staying outside on the bamboo pew because of the heavy downpour after Mother Earth had smoked her pipe.

Ayowa and Ayerakwa were behind the primary school building exchanging pink frangipanias dubbed *do not ever forget me* for the five open lobes, when suddenly, their evening was shattered by yells downtown. Going home, they realized that most of the townsfolk were out in the streets, fascinated by a large piece of brown paper a dust devil was whirling high, high up into the sky. It kept going up and up until nobody could see it any more. And it only came down to the ground in the torrential rain that followed. In Kani's home that evening, all attention centred on Ayerakwa as he elucidated in his usual soft voice how Mother Earth lit and smoked one of her rare pipes. At the end of Ayerakwa's explanation, Kani said: 'This is the kind of men we need, those who will use their learning to explain away the elements of superstition tacked onto our customs. I'm happy for you two. I hope you have healthy and intelligent offspring.'

And so, when Ayowa went to him and Ofosuaa the

evening after the marriage proposal, Kani was beaming, delighted that his daughter was going to bring fresh input to their conversation. 'Please, sit down, my Princess.' He indicated the stool with the red pouf on it. Ayowa sat down, pulled down her skirt-like cloth to cover her stretched-out and crossed legs, as an ideal woman would do – so Ofosuaa had taught her.

'I have something to discuss with you. It's about my belly.'

'Is the baby beginning to kick?' Kani asked in jest.

'To kick? I don't want it.'

'It's abominable to think like that,' Ofosuaa said.

'What's more abominable than my experience at Entea's hand? If I had my own way, I'd plunge a knife through my belly. I don't want it. I don't want the child growing in there,' Ayowa yelled. Ofosuaa went on her knees before her daughter.

'Please, don't say a thing like that,' she said.

'Get up and turn off that babbling thing up there,' Kani said. His large lips quivered as he followed his wife with his popping eyes when she went to turn off the radio. Ofosuaa had mentioned to him before, Ayowa's intention concerning the pregnancy, but he had dismissed it as a child's desperate thought. Now, he was beginning to realize it was not anything like that; it was a real threat. Even so, he suspected her of having implanted the idea of abortion in Ayowa's head. He picked up his pipe, lit it and puffed hard at it, then said tersely: 'There's no way we can do what you ask.' His gaze remained on the rising smoke from his lips. 'I don't know what they are, but the spirits won't forgive us if we do anything like that.'

'Where were the spirits when Entea was hurting me?'

'Don't talk like that, Ayowa,' Ofosuaa said.

'But they looked on while I was being defiled,' Ayowa said. 'Any time I remember who the father of the child is, I feel sick. How can I carry such a belly to a full term? This is my body –'

'No, my princess.' Kani interrupted her. 'It isn't your

body. We don't own anything in this world, not even our own children. I see Obaa Panyin in my dreams these days. She tells me her hand is over you. She tells me you're her child. She tells me she loaned you to Ofosuaa and me because we wanted a girl. I believe those dreams. I tell you now, there's something out there. Believe me, there's something out there. It's as if all the painful and frightening experiences in my life were preparing me to become courageous and fearless only for the experience I had the night you told us of your rape. But when the moment came, I still didn't have enough strength for that. Whatever is out there, it's mysterious. It's mystifying. It's awesome.' He just stared at his pipe, held at eye level, as though it held something small but essential to his well-being at that time. And his wife and daughter just stared at him, both astounded by the way he had been talking.

They had never seen him like that.

'Whatever is out there is indeed Absolute,' Kani continued. 'I'm sorry if I'm preaching, but whatever is out there operates on all of us. It doesn't matter what anyone believes in. I was so close to it, yet it remained beyond my reach. And the pain of that separation was horrendous. It was as if I was being held by the legs and being swung against a concrete wall. I tell you, now I'm scared of something. The world isn't what we know it to be at all. We can destroy what we make. What we don't make, we don't destroy. We don't destroy a child's life because we can't make it. We don't even know where it comes from.' His voice was low but firm.

And he did not look at his daughter as he spoke. He just concentrated on the twists of smoke from the burning tobacco in his pipe, his receding forehead frowned in deep thought. 'I'm beginning to question even why I was given *Kani* and no other name. Only I know what I experienced that night you told us about the rape. I'm beginning to accept as good anything that happens to me. I'm beginning to learn the more we do things contrary to natural course of events, the more we complicate life. We make it tough for ourselves.' He sat for a long time without saying anything more; he just kept nodding his head as though he had seen something out there in the patio that held a critical answer to a question he had been pondering for a long time.

'It wasn't your fault that you were subjected to that bad experience,' Ofosuaa said. 'What's more, as you told me last night, it was Ayerakwa that you loved. God in his own mysterious way has brought you two together. Your father understands it. That's why he's gone this far to arrange this befitting marriage ceremony for you.'

Kani's solemn countenance relaxed in a wispy smile at Ayowa. 'I've already spent nearly a hundred thousand cedis to get everything in place so far. You believe me, don't you? And I plan to buy you a car as soon as I've finished building a house for you and Ayerakwa. Just forget about this bad idea.'

'But Ayerakwa isn't the father of the child,' Ayowa said. 'I'm afraid the child will take after the criminal. And people will know that rapist had –'

'Don't even say a bad thing about Entea.' Kani placed his pipe down on the gateleg table. He ran his hand over Ayowa's back and patted her affectionately. 'That child is on loan to us from somebody. God or our ancestors, we don't know. Ours is to take care of him or her. May be, that's why we're here. You don't have to worry about whom the child will take after. You'll spend lots of time with Ayerakwa. His thoughts and mine will influence the child. And remember, your mom and I have the means to take the baby away from you. We'll see to it that it's brought up in a healthy environment. We can see to it that it grows into a responsible person. Could you live comfortably if you killed an innocent child for the crime of another person?'

Ayowa looked down at the floor, biting her fingernails.

'The gods will certainly deal with Entea,' Kani said.

'It's been a terrible experience for me, father,' Ayowa said.

'I know.' Kani nodded his head. 'I've been there, too. I tell you. Certain things happen to make us recognize we always have to answer to a higher authority somewhere. When? I can assure you eternity is long enough. Who is the authority? I can assure you He owns everything.'

'And remember, you're a woman,' Ofosuaa said. 'You're the medium through which the Creator brings human beings into this world. A good woman is never destructive; she nurtures. Just try to give love to the baby. Then, what began in pain and humiliation will end in beauty and happiness. Two wrongs can't make a right.'

Ayowa nodded her head affirmatively. Now, she knew her own mistake. She should not have told her parents about her intentions; neither would ever support her. She knelt down before them. 'I'm sorry, father and mother, to have brought up such an evil issue. A whole lot of things have been going on in my head since the rape. Please, forgive me.'

'Please, rise to your feet, good woman,' Kani said, chortling. He leaned to one side in his chair, buried his hand under the folds in his cloth and fished for something in his pockets. When he brought it out, it held a bunch of cedi bills. 'Here, my princess, this is for you. So you don't have to ask your husband to-be for every cedi you need. Your mother and I love you very much. We know it's a bad friend who counselled you thus. We're here to direct you along the proper path. Please, rise from your knees. You're a beautiful woman.'

Ayowa rose to her feet. She was smiling, but the dimples in her cheeks were small dark hollows in the radiance of the aladdin.

Ayowa gave in to her parents to curtail a long argument. Had she known better, she would have discussed it with only Mansa and sought her help. Together, they could try something that would save her the pain of having to carry a pregnancy she did not want. The next day when Mansa came to visit, as she usually did these days, Ayowa shut the door. Apart from them, there was nobody else in the house. Kani had gone away to Kibi with Ofosuaa to purchase some more items for the forthcoming wedding, but Ayowa did not want to take any chances.

'No music today.' Ayowa stopped Mansa who had begun to work the dry-cell record player on a table in the corner of the room. 'I have something more important to talk about with you. I need your help. Now I realize I should have told you long ago.' She went and sat on the bed. It bounced her up a little because it was the luxury type that had a soft spring mattress called Vono on it.

Mansa looked at Ayowa as though she had to strain her neck to have a good view of her. She had known all along that Ayowa's rush into marriage was all a ploy to conceal something relevant to the questions only *hard* girls knew answers to, questions that Ayowa had asked her on the banks of the Anyinasu stream. Mansa had always wanted to ask Ayowa about those questions, but for fear of her losing the gifts of blouses and cloth and sandals she received from Ayowa, she did not. She sat in the sofa set against the wall and faced the bed. 'How many months old is it?'

'Two, I think,' Ayowa said.

'You aren't sure?' Mansa asked.

Ayowa got up from the bed and paced the room, her eyes fixed on the carpet. It had tinted the white walls a shade of green from a sunlight beam on it through the window whose lace blinds were drawn apart. 'A month and a half after Entea deflowered me, I told my parents about it. And three weeks have gone by since then. But I don't care about the time. Just to get rid of it.'

'One of the *hard* girls says she knows a root and some herbs that can drop a belly,' Mansa said. 'But she'll reveal it only for money. She says she can put them together for another fee.'

Ayowa smiled then went to her bed. She brought cedi bills from under her pillow and gave them to Mansa. 'Here, take these and go to her. You know I love

196

Ayerakwa,' she said and pointed to her belly. 'But as I told you, it isn't his child in here. Your brother is a man, and a strong one, too. I've loved him ever since we were children. In great many ways, I'm happy circumstances have turned this way with him. But I think it isn't fair he's forced to become the father of this child. Ayerakwa can father his own. In a much more beautiful and loving manner.'

Mansa looked at the money bewildered. 'Three hundred cedis?'

Ayowa patted her cousin on the shoulder. 'Relax, sister. Pay that *hard* girl whatever she wants. You keep the change. If she needs more, come and get it. Money is no problem, but we're running out of time. We must get going by sunset.'

'I fear the police might become involved,' Mansa said. 'I heard that one girl from Betomu was taken to court and almost jailed for destroying her own belly.'

'If you don't help me, I'll die.' Ayowa walked away, disappointed. 'If we keep it a secret, how will the police know? The wedding will go on all right, but I don't want this pregnancy. I don't even know if I can love the child. Sister, it isn't a joke. I'm happy that Ayerakwa came along. Will you believe I was beginning to be afraid of, and hate men in general? Ayerakwa is different. It's wonderful being with him.'

'But if your parents find out –'

Ayowa went back to Mansa and placed her hand on her cousin's mouth to silence her. Pulling her gently, she sat with her in the sofa. 'I've thought everything out. My mother has told me about miscarriages. If anybody should see or suspect anything, it could be explained as a miscarriage. There's too much excitement involved in the wedding preparations.'

Mansa smiled at Ayowa's pleasant face over which some of the thin tresses of corn row hair dangled. 'Sister, I never want to lose your companionship. I'm afraid you may die,' she said.

'If we follow the instructions on how to use the medicine, I won't die. Don't worry. Everything will turn out fine,' Ayowa said. 'Just get it. We leave the rest to God, as my mother said.'

Mansa stood up and wandered to the window. She set her dark face against the security bars and looked outside silently. Ayowa went and stood beside her, a head taller. 'After all, everything has happened accidentally so far,' Ayowa said. 'A miscarriage will be another accident that will have happened to me this year.'

Mansa turned and looked up into Ayowa's face. Ayowa nodded her head several times, shutting her eyes tightly enough to prevent the tears from running down her round cheeks. She and Mansa hugged each other. And for a long time, they stood in a strong embrace, sobbing gently in the sunbeam through the window.

# Chapter 12

The sky was turning grey with the approach of nightfall, and the excitement that had begun to pick up since noon time was increasing. It was Friday, the day before the wedding. Kani's house bustled with activity. Two electricians had arrived from Kibi with a transportable generator rented for the occasion. While they were busy hanging wires around the house, many more women – young and old – and even children, kept pouring into the house. They carried fagots or logs of wood. The pile of firewood brought so far almost reached the roof level of the kitchen wing. Other women and girls came with tins and buckets of water. Every container in the large house was full with water, and so some of the women left their containers with water in them behind.

When they had let down their load, they went into the open porch and greeted Ayowa. She sat on her stool, flanked by her mother and Mansa, and other relatives. She had on a leaf-green silk over her head which draped on to her shoulders. Her legs were crossed and stretched out on a green rug.

'Congratulations, my Pearl. I brought a gift.' Obaa Panyin placed a small basket of grapefruits and oranges and miracle berries and avocados at Ayowa's feet. 'Your hand must be sore from the thousands of handshakes you've had today.'

'I'm delighted, Ma Nyamecher,' Ayowa said in her musical voice. 'It shows how much people love me. And I'm thankful to God that all these many people are on my side.'

'Don't be afraid of anything. Only be careful you don't

do anything foolish to shame me.' Obaa Panyin chucked Ayowa under her chin. 'You'll live long. You're royalty where you come from. We'll talk more later. Right now, let me allow others to share in our joy. Bye for now, my Pearl.'

'My ears are breaking with all the blessings being showered on her,' Ofosuaa said. The women around laughed. 'I wasn't this lucky when I was getting married.'

'But then, you weren't Ayowa. You can't be jealous of our own princess,' Nna Asaa the palm wine seller said. She patted Ayowa on her right cheek. 'And where is the noble architect of this masterpiece? I think he also must have his share of these greetings. We couldn't have had Ayowa without his input.'

'He must be somewhere behind the house. And thanks for your goodwill,' Ofosuaa said to the women, who by custom went away to look for Kani and congratulate him also.

That had been the pattern since noon when the activities began. Kani had been busy since his return from Kibi. At the moment, he was too concerned supervising the unloading of items brought from major market areas at Odumase-Krobo, Kintampo, Kumase and Accra, to acknowledge the greetings of the women. Master Darko was with him outside the house beside two semi-trailer trucks and three one-and-a-half ton trucks, all of them Kani's and standing in line, waiting to be unloaded of yams, rice, cocoyams, plantains and vegetables. Two pick-up trucks were already being emptied by young men standing in two long files and passing the crates of beer from hand to hand into the garage turned into a temporary storage. Kani came out of the garage and waved a wad of cedis at the men drenched in sweat. 'Five hundred cedis for you men, if you finish unloading by eight o'clock,' he said. 'I need a truck to go and bring a bull from Kibi.'

Immediately, the hand movements of the young men became faster and more rhythmical, like a conveyor belt with a regulated jerky motion. Kani went back inside the garage to Master Darko, who was keeping track of the beer being stored. 'They're going quite fast,' Master Darko said. He ran his pencil rat-a-tat-tat against the stacked up cases of Star beer. He wrote down the number he had counted on a tally card he held. 'We should finish by eight.'

'It's already dark in here,' Kani said. 'I must check with the electricians.' He left Master Darko and went inside the house. He walked around silently admiring the white bulbs hanging from thin twisted wires in the cloistral verandas and across the drying lines above the patio. He wished the electricians would turn on the lights so that the visitors could see his daughter's splendour in the radiance of the fluorescent tube fixed to the ceiling above the open porch. As he turned round to tell the head electrician to hurry up, he saw Odikuro-the-chief, his spokesman and Opong the Asona clan head enter the house. They greeted him. 'Come inside with us. There's something we think you should know,' Odikuro said. Kani led them through the open porch without saying a word to Ayowa or Ofosuaa and the attendants, and went into his parlour.

'I'm sorry if I have to rush you, respectable elders.'

'You won't go anywhere if you hear me, noble Kani.'

'What is the matter, respectable elders?' Kani asked.

'It's dark in here,' the chief's spokesman complained. He looked around him and then stared at Kani with suspicion. 'We can't talk when we can't see our faces clearly. Bring a lamp.'

'That won't be necessary,' Odikuro said, then he added underbreath. 'Just shut the door, noble one. We came to warn you. I don't know what some young men did to Entea, but he came to my house covered with dirt and swore to disrupt the wedding tomorrow.'

'Whatever you have cheated him out of, please, settle it amicably with him,' the chief's spokesman said. 'We don't want him going on rampage tomorrow, hurting and destroying things we've taken pain and time to build.'

'You know very well Entea rather must have cheated me out of my respect for him.' Kani wandered to the window. His face showed grim in the dusk's light through the window, which by itself looked like a huge eye watching the men in consultation. 'If that confused young man keeps provoking me, I may end up blowing his brains out. What is it with him?'

'He didn't swear by any of the oaths of this town or Akim, for that matter,' Opong whispered, his neck craned forward as if to have a good view of the elders in the partial darkness. 'Entea rattled something unintelligible. But since we don't know the rivers he may have crossed recently, we don't want to take any chances. As we say, if the animal won't bite you, it won't bare its teeth at you. Odikuro has already placed him under surveillance. But we still thought it appropriate to let you know.' He drew up his cloth which kept slipping down his sagging shoulders.

'I don't want to take any chances either,' Kani said. 'You respectable elders wait here. I'll send for Ayerakwa and his parents. We'll perform the marriage ceremony right now. The festivities can wait till tomorrow. I don't want anything to interrupt the marriage ceremony –' He paused to listen, his head cocked to one side as something seemed to rumble in the house.

'What was that?' the chief's spokesman asked.

'Let's listen!' Kani shouted at him.

The spokesman drew closer yet to Odikuro the chief. The spokesman had never been comfortable in Kani's house. He believed that the source of Kani's wealth was by witchcraft. To him, the rich man had a python hidden in a large trunk somewhere in the parlour, and the python puked as much money as Kani desired any time he wanted it. Otherwise, what was the use of the parlour when he had an open porch?

Suddenly, from the patio, a motor sputtered and chugged. The house glowed for a second. Then the motor broke into a smooth run, and the house popped out of the darkness in a deluge of light from the electric bulbs and fluorescent tubes. Wild cheers from outside greeted the flood of light that bathed the house. In the parlour, the four elders stared up at the brilliant naked bulb hooked to the ceiling. Nodding their heads in obvious appreciation they looked round quietly, at the framed pictures hanging down the polished mahogany wainscot panelling with designs like feminine figures that had large breasts and protruding bellies.

'Now, I know,' the chief's spokesman said, his lips parted in wonderment as his eyes remained on the light. 'This is why all the young people yearn to go to the city. They don't inhale any soot from kerosene lamps.' The four men laughed; it was not so much what the spokesman said as the silly look on his haggard face. 'When will our town also have such lights round the clock?'

'Who knows? Maybe when the sea dries up,' Kani said. He brought out bottles of E.K. schnapps and Johnnie Walker Red Label Scotch and a tumbler from a cupboard. He placed them on a round table in the middle of the room. 'Elders, please sit down and relax with these. Nobody is going to stop me from my plans.' He rushed outside before any of the other three elders could say anything.

The elders sat down in the upholstered burgundy corduroy sofa and the mahogany chippendale armchairs with burgundy velvet puffs in them, and began to enjoy the drinks. The chief's spokesman, however, stood before the cupboard for a long time, admiring the small display cabinet that sat on it. The display cabinet held three medals and their colourful ribbons from Kani's days in the Second World War in Burma.

In the afternoon, many young people had gathered in Benoa's house. Apart from Addo-the-tapper and a few others, most of them were Ayerakwa's friends and birthmates. They had arrived at Nkonsia from Accra and Kumase and several other towns, where they had gone to

203

work after leaving school. They chatted excitedly and laughed about the incident involving Entea earlier in the afternoon.

To express their goodwill toward Ayerakwa, they had bought two goats for the festivity. All afternoon, while some of the young men went into the bush to hunt for firewood, others dug a rectangular pit behind Benoa's house. Over it, they would barbecue the two goats whole after the wedding the next day. As they worked, Entea came there. He held his short black stick under his armpit – a stick he claimed to have magical powers that could make the stick fire like a gun. Without saying a word to any of the young men at work, he fetched some of the palm wine they had to refresh themselves. He drank it and fetched another calabash full and gulped that down also. Then, to the annoyance of the hushed young men sitting or straddling in the shade behind the building, he belched loudly and struck his chest. He walked up the heap of red soil and stood at the pit's edge. His muscular hands on his hips, he taunted Addo by saying that he would do well as a construction worker, digging ditches along the highway.

Addo looked up at him from the pit. 'If you don't get away from here the next instant, I'll make you go to bed with your mother,' he said and continued with his work, shovelling out soil.

'I'll have another calabash of wine, then go away in peace,' Entea said. 'After all, occasions like this foster brotherhood. And you can't call food food as soon as it goes beyond the throat.'

'You must do some work to get more wine.' Ayerakwa held Entea's hand. Entea violently flung his hand to shake off that of the bridegroom-to-be.

'Who among you here can stop me from getting the wine?' Entea huffed, looking round him at the young men intimidated into silence. Addo sprang out of the pit and lunged at Entea from behind, throwing him face down. Some of the young men converged on Entea, raining blows on him while other young men hailed Addo. 'Let's bury him alive,' Addo said, laughing. Some of the men then held Entea by the arms and the legs and began swinging him, as he kicked and screamed for help. The men counted one, two, three and on the fourth count hurled him into the shallow pit. They pelted him gleefully with the damp red soil.

Benoa came running from his house, having heard the agitated noise outside. 'Stop it! Quit that ugly game at once!' He ordered the young men. Then, to the frightened Entea, he said: 'If you attend a jollity party with your pugnose up in the air, this is how you're sent away. Get away from here at once.'

Laughing, the young men watched Entea crawl out of the pit, one hand clutching his black stick. Suddenly, he swung it wildly. A muffled explosion, profound in its impact, silenced the men. Stunned, they stared at the white palm wine draining around large shards to fizz into the soft red soil. Before anybody could grab him, Entea bolted, hooting at the dismayed men.

'Who pays for the pot?' Addo was angry. 'That's the only pot I have. What will I use in collecting the wine from the felled trees?'

'Don't worry,' Benoa said. 'I'll pay for it. There's another pot of palm wine inside the house. You can have that to replace this. I'm sorry for all the trouble.'

By sundown, the young men had completed their task for the barbecue the next day. They repaired inside the house to the patio so created by the new walls around the house. Several women guests in the house stood in the doorways breast-feeding their toddlers held to their bosoms and watching the exhausted young men clean their hands. Others had crowded inside the small bathing place, washing the red soil off their bodies. Benoa had provided them with balls of kenkey and ten tins of Exter corned beef, which they had mixed with red hot pepper and slices of tomatoes and onions. Waiting for the others before they ate, some of the men sat on small stools while others squatted, all around three large silver basins containing the food.

Carrying two lanterns, Ayerakwa came out of his room and brought the lamps where the young men sat. Three women brought four enamel bowls and divided the food so that the men could eat in smaller groups. 'Dear friends,' Ayerakwa said, 'thank you all very much for your support and friendship. Please, forget about what happened with Entea in the afternoon. Be assured of a merry time tomorrow.'

'Entea isn't one of the things we're thinking about,' Addo said, squatting before a bowl of food. 'I'm your personal bodyguard. I'll beat him up if he attempts to hurt you.' He struck his big chest and raised his clenched fist to show his muscled arm to the crowd.

'A lot of distinguished guests are going to be in town tomorrow,' Ayerakwa said, raising his hand for silence from the chattering young men. 'I'll appreciate whatever you'll do to prevent nasty scenes that could mar the occasion. It's getting late and you must eat now.'

Just as they began to eat, Master Darko entered the house. He beckoned Ayerakwa to approach him. After a brief consultation, Ayerakwa hurried to his father's room. 'Noble Kani has sent for us,' he told Benoa, who looked up anxiously from the bowl of food before him. Because of the visitors, he was eating inside. He rose and washed his hands in a pot of water on a high table in a corner. He reached for a cloth from his bed.

'I'm sure Entea has gone and misbehaved at the nobleman's house, too,' Benoa said after donning his cloth.

'The police must come and take him away,' Buaa suggested, hurriedly tying on a headgear. 'Why should one person bring a whole town so much trouble?'

The streets were swarming with merrymakers already. Jubilant yells of children rent the already frenzied air as they ran to the roadside to welcome newly arrived relatives. They kept pouring into the town from far and near. Nkonsia was like the eve of some big festival. Young men and women, their hands thrown around one another's shoulders in groups of six and eight, went from place to place, singing. As it was said, it was at occasions like this one that people discovered their life-long partners. They hurled felicitations at Benoa, Ayerakwa and Buaa as they hastened to Kani's. One group actually encircled them. 'We won't allow you to go unless you join us for a game,' the drunken leader said. 'We're in town because of our love for Ayerakwa and Ayowa.' He began a song. The others had to join in immediately because of the leader's terribly parched voice. Benoa, bent on getting away, handed the leader a hundred cedi bill.

'Thank you,' he said. 'But we're in a hurry.'

'This is good enough,' the leader said. 'If you can't dance, your money can. That's fair play. We'll be at your house tomorrow morning. To express our appreciation fully for this gesture.'

Benoa and his family went hurriedly on their way. From the distance, they saw the luminescent haze that domed Kani's house. On getting closer, they found that children were playing hide-and-seek outside among the trucks while the young men still unloaded foodstuff and beer from them. Kani walked to and fro, his hands deep inside the pockets of his long and loose shorts. He did not notice Benoa and his family. 'Brother-of-man,' Benoa called him as he made another return trip near the gate without seeing them.

Kani raised his bald head briefly and signalled them with his big solemn eyes that they should follow him into the house. Then he asked Master Darko to come inside too. When they walked through the gates, Kani quietly bolted the steel cast grille gates behind him. In the open porch, he asked Ofosuaa and Ayowa and all the people there to come inside the parlour, where Odikuro-the-chief and his elders still were, having gone quite far with the E.K. brand schnapps and the Johnnie Walker.

'Noble Kani has decided to have the marriage rites performed now,' Odikuro said to Benoa, who looked astonished. 'However, it's already night. And I can't permit Opong to pour libation.' He got to his feet and so did all the others.

'What we have here is more than daylight,' Kani said. He brought out another bottle of schnapps and handed it to Opong, the Asona clan head. 'The gods of the land don't doze, let alone sleep, so I hear. I want you to marry my daughter to Ayerakwa now.'

'I can't preside over a libation at night,' the chief said emphatically. 'If you like, we can present the couple to be married to each other. And we'll be witnesses to that. Tomorrow morning, we all can meet and bless the union.' He tapped Kani several times on his shoulder. Kani flopped into a wing chair and held his head between his hands. He looked down at the plain brown rug in silence while the bemused men and women talked in subdued tones. From outside, they heard the metal gates clanging, as if they were being banged at.

'Brother-of-man,' Benoa said, 'I think I agree with the chief. All the earth in your house has been sealed with concrete. The drink can't sink into the ground. The spirits won't know our prayers.'

Kani raised his head slowly. He considered Benoa with a sincere knowing look, as if they were at a game of checkers in which he had correctly read Benoa's strategy before he made his move. Like the raven and the vulture, Kani had understood his brother-in-law proverbially. Benoa had actually implied that the gods of the land would not forgive them for a second time if they made the deliberate mistake of pouring a libation at night. Kani stood up, towering above everyone else in the room. He shook hands with the chief, his lips drawn tight and down at the corners as if in deep thought. 'You're the head of this town,' he said in a low voice. 'I won't do anything to disdain your authority. You can finish your drinks while I go with Master Darko to see what's happening outside.'

'There are several other young men in our house right now,' Ayerakwa said. 'As soon as they're done with their meals, I'll ask them to come and help with the work here. I mean the unloading of the trucks.'

'You don't have to go back.' Ayowa walked over to him and took his hand. 'There's something important I want us to discuss in our private room.' The sheen of her silk headgear flashed a soft reflection on the yellowish light panels as she cast a furtive glance at Mansa.

'Well, I guess I have to see to the young men's coming over here myself,' Benoa said in a jocular manner, turning to Ayerakwa. 'It appears to me my niece knows more about marital bond than you, young man. Keep close to your woman now. Somebody may whisk her away before tomorrow morning.' The people around laughed. Soon, they all went out of the parlour, leaving Odikuro and his two elders to finish their liquor.

Outside by the trucks, Kani found that Sanyo had returned from Koforidua where he had gone to get more drinks. He had also brought a giant white bighorn ram which he had tethered to the metal gates. It stood as high as Kani's hip, and its scrotum and its beard came down to its knees. 'I've only seen pictures of such marvellous animal,' Master Darko said. 'I'm impressed by its size.'

Kani patted the ram behind its neck and addressed Sanyo. 'See that it's fed on only fresh cassava leaves. I want it fattened for the first week's anniversary next Saturday.'

'I brought it here to show you, Nana,' Sanyo said. 'I have to take it back to the Zongo and keep it at my place.' He untethered the ram and tugged it to the Mercedes. As he and the other men lifted it bodily into the trunk, the animal gave a loud bleat.

# Chapter 13

Every food item or drinks in connection with the wedding came from a town not fewer than sixty miles away. Even the *akpeteshi* Kani and Benoa bought for those who naturally preferred the local gin to any other brand of liquor, came from Kroboland. There, it was said, the best distillers lived. It was claimed they were descendants of the Scandinavians thousands upon thousands of years ago and that they had the knowledge of distilling spirits in their blood. It was said that unless one was told, one could be fooled by the taste of Kroboland *akpeteshi* and take it for the E.K. brand schnapps. All the palm wine too came from Akim Asafo, the town of legendary tappers whose wine had the reputation of being so potent that a drop of it could crack cement floors. And the loads of plantain for the wedding feast came from Dompim, the town known for plantain, the fingers of which were so large that they were used as bludgeons by hunters long before the advent of firearms in the area. And the cocoyams came from Begoro, the city about which it was said that farmers had to use ladders to reach the *kontomire* leaves which were said to grow as high as seven rungs and as broad as a full piece of *kente* cloth.

By dawn on Saturday, the day of the marriage rites and the wedding festivities, Nkonsia was bustling. In fact, some young men had not gone to sleep at all. They had noisily dragged stringed empty cans and tins along the streets, chanting and singing. And long before sunrise, some women started to bring sunflower tins of water and more firewood into the houses of Benoa and Kani. In the latter's house, the women had raised eight temporary hearths from large stones. They had delayed the cooking till much later because the heavens had threatened to rain. Obaa Panyin said that in all cases, the will of God had to be done. If it was His will that there be no rain, there would be no rain. She said a prayer, asking that the will of God be done. Presently, the clouds dispersed and the women came out to cook without anyone remembering to say thanks to the skies.

The women sat in groups on forms and short kitchen stools, peeling yams and plantain into large silver bowls and steel cauldrons. Others, especially the girls, sat by themselves ramming red pepper, ginger and garden eggs on special granite blocks. Time and time again, peals of laughter rose from the girls about a joke about somebody for having done something funny.

'I hear a young man was buried alive in this town, yesterday.' said a woman stranger. She had been flirting from group to group, not doing any particular work. 'How can some people do such a heinous thing? I thought since a major highway in the country ran through this town, the people here would be more civilized.'

'Will you be quiet and get something to do?' Nna Asaa the palm wine seller said, slicing onions and tomato into a large calabash colander. 'You wouldn't be standing there blathering if somebody had indeed been interred alive. And a word of advice to you. If you don't have anything good to say about a town, you better not say anything at all.' She shoved the large calabash of sliced vegetables into the visitor gossip's hands. 'Do what you will with them.'

'I'm sorry,' the woman apologized. 'I didn't mean –'

'If we don't keep quiet and concentrate on the cooking, by the time we finish it, nobody can eat it. All the food will be full of sputum,' Kapre-the-Radio said. Behind an enamel tray full of peeled yams, she was patiently slicing them up into a medium-sized silver bowl.

Crestfallen, the visitor gossip carried the bowl of sliced vegetables to one of the large stone hearths and poured them into a big steel cauldron that was simmering on the fire. Just about the same time, ten women arrived from Benoa's. They carried trays of fresh beef and goat meat wrapped in plastic bags and covered with fire-wilted plantain leaves.

'Why didn't anyone remember that we had to send some foodstuff to Benoa's house?' Ofosuaa asked, astonished by her own forgetfulness. 'What are the women at that end cooking all this time?' She proceeded to select some women to carry food items to Benoa's place. She did not forget to include the woman who had gossiped about somebody having been buried alive at Nkonsia.

Meanwhile, at Benoa's, it was past ten o'clock. The men outnumbered the women. Most of the women were in the patio, cooking on large hearths raised from cinder blocks that sprawled the courtyard. Buaa, who had been inside her room most of the time, came out where three women stood. They were preparing soup in a large aluminium utensil. Buaa had topped her skirt-like cloth with a lace-adorned pink chemise through which showed her new white brassiere. It superbly held those protruding rubber foam breasts to her bosom. Placing her hands on her hips, she peered at the broth in which chunks of meat tossed around.

'The soup smells great so far,' she piped. 'See how it is boiling. There is so much meat in it that the heat can't turn them all over properly. Maybe we better divide it and use another pot in addition to this.' She brushed off non-existent dirt from the pink underwear. 'I must cover this. The material attracts dirt on its own. Things of these modern times, hmm.'

'It's very nice,' one of the women said, looking at Buaa's chemise with admiration. 'How much did it cost you?'

'It's quite expensive.' Buaa grinned to show her complete set of teeth. 'You can't get it to buy here in this country –'

'I know,' the other woman said, flashing a jealous smile.

212

'Rich men's wives don't shop with the ordinary people. They get their things from Lome and Abidjan.'

'No. This is from *Aburochirey* – the land of the white people,' Buaa said, annoyed by the woman's inability to tell of things from overseas. 'Anything I want, I can just ask for it from the land overseas –' She was interrupted by terrifying shouts nearby. The woman with whom Buaa had been talking dashed away and grabbed her toddler son, who had nearly crawled into a fire. 'This child will kill me!' She screamed and spanked the little boy hard on his bare buttocks.

'You rather must be whipped,' another woman reproached her as the child began to cry. 'Weren't you engaged in just vain talk? Look after your child well. Some day, he may buy you a better stuff than this chemise which the wearer doesn't know she mustn't wear outside the privacy of her room.' She cast an insinuating glance at Buaa, making a prolonged sucking noise with her lips. Buaa hurriedly went inside her room to put on a *kaba*.

There were a few more women outside the house where the men had killed and flayed a bull and four goats. Gathered in groups, some of the men were butchering the carcasses with cleavers and machetes on tree boles while others minced the chunks into basins for the women to carry away. Other groups of men stood or squatted around two rectangular pits above which were two impaled goats, suspended by fork sticks, to barbecue. A young man walked to the place where the butchering was being done and handed a clay bowl to Addo-the-tapper. Already kneeling on one knee, Addo put down his cleaver, and with his index finger cautiously turned over the pieces of roasted meat mixed with slices of tomato, red pepper and onions inside the bowl. Having satisfied himself, he proceeded to eat, walking with the food and supervising the other men. He paused at one of the barrow pits and operated the improvised spit, revolving it at one of the forks that held the impaling stick. He then wandered into the shade where all the drinks were, filled himself a calabash full of palm wine and drank it, pushing the food in his mouth down with it.

In the chief's house, Kani and Benoa sat with other elders. Some dignitaries, like the chiefs of Begoro and Ampatia, had been joining them since morning. Now they were a sizeable group in the cloister-like veranda. They would have preferred the sunny and airy yard outside, to be near the grill improvised from a truncated metal barrel in which chunks of meat were cooking on a metal grid. Chiefs, however, were not to be seen eating in public or the open. Some of the liquor bottles before them were empty; the chiefs had been enjoying them with the barbecued beef and goat meat.

Kani and Benoa and their families had been at the chief's much earlier at sun-up. Opong, the Asona clan head, Master Darko, Odikuro, and the chief's spokesman were also present. Benoa gave a bottle of schnapps for the marriage rites to start when there was a hold up. Amid all the noise and the fanfare that had characterized the prenuptial arrangements, the two families had forgotten about a vital aspect of the whole exercise.

'Has the nobleman accepted your bride price yet?' Opong asked Ayerakwa, opening his eyes wide as if to be able to see the young man well from his deep sockets. Kani and his brother-in-law exchanged embarrassed looks.

'I've only been given the head drink.' Kani exonerated himself. He reclined in the cane wing chair with pillows in it.

'Well, Nana Odikuro,' Opong addressed the chief, his neck stretched forward. 'I can't give my granddaughter away in marriage when her bride price hasn't been paid.'

Benoa searched his pockets but he did not have any substantial money on him. He went outside with his family. 'In the days of old, the bride price was two guineas, which became four cedis and forty pesewas,' Benoa said. 'Now that the weight has fallen off the bottom of the cedi, the equivalent in current cedis won't do. I know Kani.' He collected six hundred cedis each from Ayerakwa and Buaa, and added it to another six hundred cedis he had on him. He then took out four hundred cedis, which he hid in his palm, and pocketed the rest. 'Just in case Kani wants to be tough on us.' He went back to the cloister-like veranda with his family. When they had taken their seats, Benoa gave the money hidden in his palm to Opong, who passed it on to Kani.

'Four hundred cedis? For what?' Kani frowned and gave the money back to Opong. 'Ayowa isn't a commoner, Brother-of-man. I won't accept anything other than the bride price for a princess. It'll be a laughing matter for people when they hear that for all her qualities, I took a meagre sum of money on her head to give her away in marriage.'

'But Ayowa isn't a royal –'

'Shut up your big mouth.' Kani thundered at Buaa, who stepped back. She looked back at Kani, baffled. 'She is my princess.' Kani struck his chest, standing to his full height. 'Send me an appropriate amount for Ayowa's hand. Otherwise, there'll be no marriage.'

'Sit down. please,' Odikuro the chief said. 'We don't have to argue over this, Benoa. If I were Ayowa's father, I could take as much as twenty thousand cedis in bride price for a woman like her, if custom permitted it.'

'The key phrase is "if custom permitted",' Master Darko said. 'We must try not to step too much over the border line.'

'She isn't being sold into serfdom,' Kani's brother added.

'Are you on my side, or what?' Kani asked them both.

Ayowa bowed down her head, embarrassed.

Benoa handed the rest of the one thousand eight hundred cedis in large bills to Opong. He counted and passed it on to Kani, who consulted Ofosuaa and Master Darko. 'We accept it,' Kani said. Opong smiled and rose from his seat. His shoulders drooping as though there was some load weighing them down, he walked slowly to the entrance of the veranda, where the drops of the schnapps would reach the soil of the earth directly. With the two families and all the witnesses behind him, he bared his scraggy chest, stepped on his right princeling sandal and offered a long prayer to God Omnipotent and all His lieutenant spirits. After that, the rings were exchanged and Opong pronounced Ayowa and Ayerakwa husband and wife. The newly-married and their mothers were whisked away in the Mercedes. It had been waiting outside all along.

Much happier that the most important part of the affair was over peacefully, Kani sat spread out in the cane wing chair. The folds in his cloth were on his lap, leaving his massive and hairy chest naked. 'Lest I forget,' he chuckled and extended his hand to Opong. 'Here, the bride price.' Opong took it and shared the money among the three other witnesses, keeping nine hundred cedis to himself.

'I don't mean to spoil a good party, but I want to know something, Opong.' Benoa took out a Consulate from his silver case and lit it. 'Are you still adamant to the request of your elders? Your own granddaughter from whose bride price you just pocketed nine hundred cedis, is in danger because you've refused to cleanse her. She is Asona, and she must be absolved from the bad things Entea has said about the town. Or do you want something bad to befall her or her offspring before you do what you were appointed to do? When will you take away the imprecation in Entea's terrible utterance? Or you've forgotten Ayowa's name translates as a "clay bowl"?'

Opong leaned forward on his seat, and fixed his gaze outside on the crude grill. It fizzled and flared up as the live charcoal in it welcomed the fat exuded from the saucy meat. Then he sat up, turned his head to Benoa and said: 'At sixty-two, I don't think I have anything new to fear. I talked with Master Darko about the shift in responsibility from Entea to me for his misguided statement. Master Darko said I should do what was right not for myself but for the people. I can't save my own skin at the expense of the younger generation. Theirs is the land and its future. Make no mistake, though. It wasn't because of money –' Opong quickly raised his right index finger to the sky in a solemn vow. The elders laughed. 'My responsibility to the Asona clan and the town has always been my duty to God. I'll perform the rites of absolution Thursday under the "tree of threepences".'

'Now, sanity reigns,' Master Darko said.

'I have a good friend in you,' Kani said to the schoolmaster. He poured himself whisky, mixed it with some water and drank it. All the other men did so too. They laughed, happy that a solution had been found to the Entea and Asona clan case. By this time, it was past noon and the men expressed the wish to go to their homes and make ready for the main festivity. Odikuro said that it was in order.

On his way home, Kani noticed that the sporadic pounding noises which had filled the town even from sunrise, had died down considerably. He met several girls and women in the streets, carrying food in baskets and small basins and also in buckets, all covered with poplin or new towels, and hurrying to different homes. Like bad news or good news, it was the custom to share special meals among friends and relatives on festive occasions. The people congratulated him as they passed by him. He waved back at them with a white satin kerchief, beaming. When he got to his house, he found several people eating in the patio. The men had squatted around large enamel and silver bowls. The women sat on stools or upturned buckets and ate in groups of four from clay bowls. As soon as they saw him, they stood up. 'Felicitations to you on your daughter's marriage,' some of them said.

He waved his kerchief in the air. 'You all made it an occasion worth remembering,' he said. Ofosuaa walked up to him from the kitchen.

'My man, you'd like to see the bridal dish,' she said. Overwhelmed by the success of the arrangements, Kani could not help noticing the dancing in his wife's eyes. He drew his kerchief to his own eyes, then rubbed his receding forehead with it, not wanting the onlookers to think he was crying. Ofosuaa took his hand. Together, they climbed the stoop and went through the open porch into the parlour, where she had set a table for the married couple. Some seconds passed and Kani still looked at the dazzling black clay bowl surrounded by sand-and-lime-and-ash scoured pewters on the silk blue covered table.

The lid of the bridal bowl reflected some image that seemed to be his because it moved when he did. Only that the image was too small or too tall or too thin and thus terribly distorted. He remembered many years back when he and Ofosuaa had eaten their first meal together as husband and wife from the same bridal bowl with two lugs shaped to fit ten human fingers. Its beauty had entirely captivated him then, and he kept looking at it while the elderly women presented Ofosuaa to him in his room, saying 'this is your wife' three times, making the bride touch Kani's bed on each occasion with her buttocks. That was nearly thirty years ago. These modern times, brides were not presented to their husbands in that fashion any more, but bridal clay bowls had endured and become heirloom. Ofosuaa had rebaked and repolished hers with palm kernels to glaze. Kani distinctly remembered promising his wife that he would name his first daughter *Ayowa* after their bridal bowl.

'You aren't saying it's the same ayowa?' Kani looked from the bowl to his wife. Ofosuua nodded her head in the affirmative. 'I must have been the luckiest man to have got a woman like you for a wife, Ofosuaa.'

'This bridal bowl has been my most treasured possession, especially since Ayowa was born,' she whispered to him. 'I kept it in a box full of kapok under my bed. And I've patiently waited for this day. To outdoor it again and renew my own marriage vows.' Kani hugged her from behind, making amorous movements with his waist at her back. 'Stop it.' Ofosuaa feigned a protest, yet she responded to him with a backward thrust of her buttocks.

218

'The sofa can carry us both,' Kani said.

'The newlyweds may be returning from the bathing place.'

'It'll be a quick one. Come on, my Love.' Kani insisted, pulling Ofosuaa toward the sofa. 'Can't you imagine what they may be doing now? Have you forgotten how long we were in the bathroom?'

'Times are different now –'

'Spare me the time syndrome,' Kani said.

'We don't want to scare them away with our grizzly pubic hairs. Besides, this isn't our wedding.' She pretended to be pulling away from him, a teasing smile on her face. 'Come on, let's get away from here.' Then, they heard "Hail to the newlyweds" in the patio. Ofosuaa giggled and Kani gasped.

'We have all of tonight,' Ofosuaa said.

'And I caught you from behind,' Kani suggested.

'I'll be waiting in your bed for you, my man.'

'I'll fill up my bottle of bitters with schnapps, my woman.'

They both smiled at each other, and Kani touched her on her cheek. They held hands and walked out of the parlour, through the open porch into Kani's room, where Ofosuaa had set a table for him. Because of all the people around in the house, it would not be appropriate for him to eat in the open porch.

By three o'clock, most of the townsfolk and their guests had gathered at the place of the 'tree of threepences.' The intersection of the two broad streets at Nkonsia had long sheds raised from bamboo poles and palm fronds. The colourful pennants adorning the sheds appeared to be wavering on account of the afternoon frenzy instead of the breeze. It looked as if Nkonsia was hosting a great durbar. The air was full of dust from the feet of scores of revellers dancing to a high-life tune being played by the Betomu brass band. Most eyes of those not dancing were on the lead trumpeter, Kwame Koranteng.

A well-built man whose orange reefer was too small on him, he stood on a packing case before the other musicians, opening his eyes wildly or shutting them tight and bending his body forward and backward as he blared away on his trumpet. The sheds swayed with impact from the milling crowd that jostled to get closer to the dancing ground. Unable to get a good view of the centre area, some people had climbed into the 'tree of threepences.' The branches weighed down precariously.

An old woman sitting in the frontline under one of the sheds got to her feet, threw a coin to the trumpeter and tried a couple of steps. Her legs, however, would not move fast enough to the music. As she sat down, she spoke to the old man sitting beside her. 'This wasn't how we did this particular beat years ago. The beat is different for these times.'

'Our time is long past, my dear.' The old man winked at her. 'Our bones and muscles, our hearts can't stand the pace of today. I'm here so I can have something to describe to my ancestors when I finally go. I swear I could feel the stomping feet in the ground and I could hear the noises in the air at Betomu.'

'I could smell the aroma of the food in the air,' the old woman said and they both laughed. 'I'm happy I've seen a real traditional wedding one more time before I leave the scene.'

The lead trumpeter raised his instrument to the air and played a slow but energetic solo. Then turning round to face the other bandsmen, he let out a couple of long notes. The song ended amid a thunderous roar of applause. Some women flocked around Koranteng, the lead trumpeter and dabbed away the sweat on his hands and face with their cloth. 'Thank you all,' he said in gasps. 'Nobleman Kani has asked us to be here today –' And the applause rose again. 'And you can be sure we'll give you our best till nightfall. Now, the band will take short recess. Thank you again.'

Together with his men, the bandleader joined the

people filing past the platform to shake hands with prominent guests on it. They appeared adorned in shades of red and yellow and green because of the Dacron that sheltered them from the bright sun. Kani and Benoa and their wives sat on the platform, too. They had arrived while the brass band music was going on. Kani and Ofosuaa had on a richly decorated *kente*, the most expensive ceremonial cloth in all the land. Hand-woven on a wood-loom in strips and pieced together, the multicoloured pieces they had on were called *adwini-asa*, implying that particular *kente* comprised all the intricate designs and patterns ever known in the industry. Yellow dominated Kani's, and with a gold chain on his neck, he excelled in glamour the other dignitaries on the platform.

The King of Abuakwa State delegated one of his senior spokesmen. He sat close to Benoa and his wife, and held his golden staff of insignia that bore the Asona clan's totemic symbol of the raven.

'The music was fantastic,' Kani said, shaking hands with the brass band leader. 'There are food and drinks behind this dais for you and your men. Fill up so you can make us happy some more.' The trumpeter took Kani's big hand in both of his and bowed down his head. After the handshake, Kani raised both his hands and clasped them, smiling. He gave a thumbs-up to Benoa, in a beautiful white velvet and sitting on the other side of the platform behind a row of four empty seats, and said: 'The honour is to us both and our wives, Brother-of-man.'

Benoa raised his hands and shook them in the air.

After a while, the dancing ground calmed and cleared. A few people stood there in little knots drinking beer in swigs from the pint-size bottles. Some elders were setting up *atumpan* and *fontomfrom* drums. Three white men placed themselves farther away and took snapshots from various angles of the elders setting up the indigenous musical instruments. The spokesman of the King of Abuakwa State leaned over to Benoa and explained to him that the white men were teachers at the State College in Kibi.

Another band of merry-makers soon began a song. Called the 'Aways' because the group comprised young sojourners, they played *Adenkum* music that was a variation of the swing. Three gourd-stamping tubes formed the principal instruments, and the musicians performed from shed to shed, walking slowly. When they came to the colourful dais, they paused in their stroll. A young woman carrying *donno*, an hourglass-shaped drum, went forward and stood before Kani. Skilfully varying the tone by squeezing and releasing the leather strings on the drum she held in her arm's crotch, she struck with a hooked stick in her right hand a series of rhythmic accents that clearly said: 'This is our affair; a community celebration of prosperity.'

Addo-the-tapper stepped forward from the band, rattling a castanet-like calabash instrument. He faced the woman drummer. Still engaged on their instruments, they bent their bodies far back and started a forward jerking movement toward each other. The crowd cheered as their bellies touched. A man and a woman raced around with some equipment hooked to long cables, shooting pictures of the dancers. Benoa asked the King's spokesman about the equipment with cables attached to it, and the spokesman said that it belonged to the television station in Accra.

Kani stood up. As he went down the platform, Benoa followed him and they each placarded a hundred cedi bill on the foreheads of the dancers. Other people tossed coins on to the dance ground and another member of the 'Aways' group came out and collected all the money from the ground. After they straightened their bodies, the *donno* player drummed a tonal message which said: 'Noble Kani, we thank you.' The group strolled away amid cheers from the crowd.

Obaa Panyin then arrived at the platform. She climbed on to it and shook hands with the dignitaries and Kani.

Pointing at a high chair among four empty ones in the front row, she said: 'I suppose this is the seat for my Pearl.'

'You can tell by the decoration.' Kani laughed. The backrest and the seat had peacock blue velvet poufs fixed to them. 'She should be here any time soon with her husband. There's a chair on this dais for you, too, Daughter-of-the-Land.'

Obaa Panyin went closer to Kani and spoke under-breath to him. 'I warned Ayowa not to try anything foolish. She didn't heed my words. And you couldn't prevent her from it, preoccupied as you are with things of your world. Now, see, Ayowa's chair is soiled with putrid blood.'

'Great One, I don't see any stain,' Kani whispered back.

'You don't have eyes, do you?' She scowled at him. 'And leave him alone, that young man. Stay away from Entea. I don't want anybody to spoil my Pearl's joy, at least what is left of it for the day.'

'Great One, if there's something you want us to talk about, can we do it after the ceremonies, please?' Kani said.

'What will be the use then?' Obaa Panyin said aloud, her countenance changing suddenly to a delightful one. Smiling, she said: 'I better sit behind my Pearl's chair. Don't be disappointed if I leave before the festivities here are over.'

Some music burst forth from one of the streets. Everyone turned in that direction as shouts of '*ayeforo d-o-o d-o-o*, Hail, the newlyweds' followed the music. The procession appeared. Ayowa and her husband were in the lead, followed closely by Opong the Asona clan head, Odikuro-the-chief, and Master Darko in a brown suit. A contingent of well-dressed girls paced beside them. Two of them were fanning Ayowa with pieces of cloth, hailing: 'Congratulations, beautiful bride.'

In their wake came a group of drummers. When they beat high pitched royal drums, Odikuro would halt and so would the others. And they would fan Ayowa even more.

Her hair had been stretched with hot comb and it had the quality of silk sheen from the brilliantine applied to it. Brushed back, it was held in a bun by a sky-blue band. She wore gold chains around her neck and twisted bracelets on her hands, a piece of velvet of the same colour as the headband swathed around her body. Her upper body, above her breasts, was naked but streaked with kaolin paste. She waved at the crowd, smiling. Her dimples were prominent in a grin that revealed her neat set of white teeth. Her looping earrings kept flashing the sun as she turned her head in all directions to acknowledge the crowd, waving.

The high pitched drums sounded and the slow procession halted. Ayowa winced at the sudden stop, as if in pain, but nobody noticed it. Even when she held on to Ayerakwa's hand for support, a bland expression on her face, nobody thought anything of it. The high pitched drums ceased, and the procession moved on slowly again. When it reached the dais, all the people under the Dacron, except Obaa Panyin, rose and bowed their heads. Ayowa sat down on the high chair and placed her feet on a yellow pillow Mansa put down before her. Ayerakwa, Odikuro and Opong occupied the three other seats.

The *atumpan* drums then broke the silence that had come over the crowd with the earlier appearance of the entourage. The sound of the drums gathered momentum when the *fontomfrom* joined in, their heavy throbs punctuating the tonal rhythmic sounds of the *atumpan*. Kani looked up toward the bare-chested drummers who had worn their cloths around their waists like loin pieces, then threw a sweeping glance at the crowd. He began jerking his massive body to the beat of the indigenous drums. Charged, he jumped into the open space and went to place his hands on Odikuro's knees. He bowed down before him, waited until Odikuro raised his arm, a solemn look on his sage face. Then Kani stood up.

He spun round in his sandals, scampered to the drummers and bowed before them, too. Straightening his body, he donned his cloth well, turned to the four points of the earth, and began to dance, the corners of his broad lips turned down. The drums sounded louder the more grave he looked. Moving his legs elegantly, he jerked his torso from side to side, his hands fisted with a finger each pointing outward and weaving symbolic patterns in the air. He would initiate an inward roll of both hands, stretch one hand to the left and the other to the right, his body swaying. He took intricate steps, his hands imploring the skies for prosperity in symbolic gestures. Several women led by Ofosuaa and Buaa skip-danced to hail him, their hands raised.

'Handsome one, slowly. . . slowly. . . short steps.'

Other women fanned him with their pieces of cloth, complimenting: 'Giver of wine when asked for water, well done. What graceful steps, noble one.' Kani danced toward the drummers and bowed down before them again. They acknowledged him by toning down the intensity of the music. Kani went back to his seat, nodding his bald head in response to the cheers of the crowd.

Yes. He was the noble one. Yes. And the noble one never stayed on the dance ground for long. Only the poor did; the poor did not have anything in terms of material wealth to celebrate, and so they wished there was continuous music all the time so they could dance and dance all the time. Sickened to their soul by indigence, they were always hoping for palliatives to lessen their pain of poverty, palliatives that could only come from music to soothe their souls. And so the poor, in an embrace with destitution, danced and danced until they became possessed and transported out of this world of pleasures from liquor and juicy meat and praises of women and a beautiful loyal wife in Ofosuaa, into a world of revelry and madness, ironically reversing the happiness they had initially sought from the dancing. Yes, he was the noble one, the man among men, the man with a shadow, the man who stepped with confidence in his princeling sandals. Who could top his performance on the dance ground? Yes. This was his world. Let us see the man who could top him...

A sudden stoppage of the music jolted Kani from his daydreams of his own glory, and he looked up toward the dance ground. There was a young man in the open space. Wearing a smock encrusted with charms and his face pasted with red ochre and charcoal, the young man held a short black stick which he kept pointing around at the people. He appeared to be chewing something in his mouth. Murmurs rose as he focused his attention on the dais. He approached the platform, walking like someone stalking an animal in the bush. With a wave of his hand, he trained the black stick on Ayowa, rolling his tongue over his lips. Ayowa stood up, leaning back on her chair in fear. Ayerakwa was up beside her in an instant, shielding her with his body from the scamp on the dance ground. Kani just watched the masked young man, dumbfounded. Then he recognized the bloodshot eyes behind the camouflage.

'It's insolent Entea,' he announced.

'Seize him,' Benoa shouted.

'Leave him alone!' Obaa Panyin cautioned, but her warning was swallowed in the simultaneous confusion that ensued as both Kani and Benoa jumped down from the platform. They had, in the process, pushed against Ayerakwa who accidentally shoved off Ayowa, too. Together with her chair, Ayowa fell backward toward Obaa Panyin, who in anticipation was waiting. She caught Ayowa with open arms. Meanwhile, Addo-the-tapper had already tackled Entea and flipped him over so that he lay flat on his back in the open space. Addo stayed on top of him, hitting him with fisted hands. 'Keep him down for me,' Kani said.

He dropped his kente cloth on the ground to be free enough in his jumper to beat up Entea. Leaving Benoa far behind in the race, Kani took long strides in his bid to reach Entea soon, intending to stomp his head into the dust. However, Entea blew hot pepper in his mouth into

Addo's eyes and got away. Kani raced after him, shouting at some young men to catch him for Kani. Then, he tripped in his princeling sandals. And the solid ground rose to meet him. His head and the ground collided in what sounded to him like a thunderclap. And his face scraped against the rough surface of the earth, giving him extremely painful and searing sensation. Yet, he could still hear what seemed like the receding reverberation of a loud report into the woods beyond the outskirts of the town.

Lying prostrate and all spread out in the open under the infinite expanse of the sky above him, he spat out the dust and gravel that had got into his mouth. He slapped the ground in bitterness over and over again with his open palm, wondering why nobody had as yet come to check on him. Did nobody care about him after all? Suddenly, he noticed the eerie silence that had fallen on the crowd and only then beginning to be shattered by shrieks and screams around the corner ahead of him. He rolled over and sat up, propping his massive body with his hands, feeling a little dazed. Looking up, he noticed a small cloud of smoke rising slowly just above the hip roof of the house behind the west shed. What a puff, he laughed, thinking that whoever was smoking must have the biggest bowl ever designed for a pipe. Then he saw a stream of people rushing the other way behind the building, talking in an agitated manner. He began wondering what the matter could be when he heard footsteps approaching.

'Are you all right?' Ayerakwa asked, squatting beside him.

'After such a fall before everyone?' Kani asked.

'Nobody seemed to have noticed you fall.'

'Don't believe it. The people are just being nice to me,' Kani said. He peered into Ayerakwa's face, then looked around. It seemed to him that the crowd had indeed not been a witness to his fall; while most people were crowding around the platform, others were moving away behind the house above which he had seen the small cloud of smoke. 'What is going on there?' he asked.

'It's my wife. She bleeds.' Ayerakwa helped Kani to his feet. Kani kept flicking his hand over his jumper, brushing off the dust while nodding his head, as if he had found the meaning of some nagging problem in what Obaa Panyin had told him earlier: the stained chair, Entea to be left alone. Meanwhile, Ayerakwa was still talking.

'But Entea has been shot –'

'What?' Kani asked. He felt some numbness creep into his legs, and he staggered on his feet. 'Entea shot in broad daylight?'

'In the upper right arm. Behind that house.' Ayerakwa pointed. Kani looked in that direction. The puff of smoke he had noticed earlier had almost dissipated in the air, just as in the complex nature of unfolding events in the past weeks, he had completely forgotten about the promise made him by Entea's father, Bonsra, who had lost a leg while saving Kani's life in the jungles of Burma. Kani felt some pleasant taste in his mouth.

'Aba-kade-wa,' he muttered a slang used to express subdued delight. 'The brave old warrior did it again,' he said.

'What do you mean?' Ayerakwa asked.

'Nothing. Just thinking aloud,' Kani quipped. 'So, is he dead? I mean Entea?'

'He will be if we don't get him to hospital soon.'

'We?' Kani asked sarcastically. 'Hopefully, he'll go on to have a better life in the next world. Let's go and see to the welfare of my Princess, your wife.' He and Ayerakwa hurried to the platform area where Obaa Panyin and Ofosuaa and Buaa had screened Ayowa from public view with Kani's full piece kente that he had abandoned in the chase after Entea. They walked her to the Mercedes. A small group of onlookers had come close to the car and were speculating as to what must have happened. One said that Entea must have fired pellets at Ayowa with his black stick before he was shot.

'How bad is it?' Kani asked Ofosuaa.

'O, my *nobleman*.' Ofosuaa sniffled. Her statement held

all the empathy she could muster for him. 'Our house has no tinder in it, yet Entea has managed to set it ablaze. And broken, my waist beads are spread out in the hot sand before my enemies. I just don't know how to collect them to string again. How do I get my dignity back?'

'You never lost your dignity in the first place,' Kani said, trying to avoid Obaa Panyin's cursory glances at him. 'I'm still the Hawk. I'm still the Buffalo, the grandchild of the Elephant. Humiliation is like hot water. It turns cold as soon as the wind has blown over it.'

'Indeed,' Obaa Panyin interjected. 'But a dead buffalo is good only for the jackals who feed on its carcass. Hadn't you tripped and fallen down the moment you did, you'd have been in the path of the bullet meant for Entea. I have always been so close to you yet you can't hear my voice. You *must* listen to me.'

Stunned, Kani could not do anything, but stare at the calm and wizened face of Obaa Panyin. Those around had also been shocked into silence. Agape, they just looked on as Kani went down on his knees on the bare ground before Obaa Panyin. 'Get up from there,' she said. 'There's no time to waste. Take my Pearl to see the doctor immediately. I'll ask one of your drivers to bring Entea in one of your pickups.'

'Yes, Daughter of the Land,' Kani said in a tremulous voice. 'But send Entea to Bunso hospital. Not Kibi. I don't want him to come to Kibi to distract the doctor attending to my dau –'

'Shut up and go on,' Obaa Panyin silenced him. 'If it's the Omnipotent's will that my Pearl live, she'll survive without the help of a doctor. She needs this trip not for herself, but her children. Now, be gone!' She hurried him away with her hand. Shaking his head in a painful disappointment, Kani got into the car with Ayerakwa, Ofosuaa and Buaa already inside with Ayowa. Sanyo had already started it and he kept gunning the engine. As soon as Kani got inside, Sanyo moved it so fast that the tyres screeched and rose angry dust which whirled in the air and only settled slowly back to the ground long after the Mercedes had disappeared around the bend.

Because it was Saturday, the hospital at Kibi was closed and Kani had difficulties in getting a doctor. In fact, he had to awake the King of Abuakwa State from his siesta and beg him to call a doctor by telephone. Now, he and Ayerakwa waited outside the consulting room. Ofosuaa and Buaa walked about, rocking their bodies, their hands clasped behind them, as they alternately lamented: 'Our bowels, they're on fire. How did we take this path to meet the accursed who dispenses tragedy to other people?'

Ayerakwa sat silently on a bench, his gaze on the open sky. Kani, stunned into silence, stared from him to Ofosuaa. The tiny trails of blood on his face had turned into small black crusts like hardened coal tar. Some moments later, a young man in his early thirties came out of the consulting room to where Kani and Ayerakwa sat. Ofosuaa and Buaa rushed to join them.

'What is wrong with her, doctor?' Ofosuaa asked.

'My name is Myers. Robert Myers.' The doctor shook hands with them, one after the other, smiling. 'Because of the rush, I didn't get the chance to introduce myself to you. I'm afraid it's quite serious, but she'll be all right.' He took Ofosuaa's hand and patted it, speaking softly. 'I gather from what she told me that she's had some traumatic experience recently. I'm sorry. That must have affected her physiologically and complicated her monthly cycles. But she thought she was pregnant and so planted something in her womb to get rid of it. The bleeding has stopped now. I'll have to do a simple surgery on her because it's turned septic. I'm happy it was discovered in time.'

'O, God Almighty!' Kani said. 'Here, Dr. Myers, take this.' Kani offered him a wad of cedi bills. 'Do everything you can to save her life for me. She's my only daughter.'

Dr. Myers chuckled. 'Nobleman, I can't take the money. I'm paid to save lives. She may need a blood transfusion though, and I can take plenty of bribes in blood donation. I need the extra for my blood bank.' Dr. Myers laughed.

'Is that all you need? Look at us, so plump. It's all blood. Take as much as you want from me to get my daughter well again. And take as much as you may want from my wife. Go on, take more from my son-in-law and his mother. We're here for you, Dr. Myers. But tell me something. Can Ayowa have babies later?'

'It's too early to say,' Dr. Myers said. 'But don't be over anxious. Let's worry about getting her well first. Later, when the wound has healed, we can find out if there's another problem. Right now, it doesn't look too bad. Come on. We don't need to waste any more time.'

As they started to walk away, a persistent honking of a truck made them tarry to see what it was all about. The truck pulled up a little way from where they stood. Several young men jumped down. Addo led them, running to Kani and the others. Addo's eyes were still red from the pepper assault on him by Entea. Kani looked at the doctor, a frantic expression on his face. The doctor smiled at him, as if to reassure him that the doctor understood Kani's concerns. 'We wanted to know how Ayowa was doing,' Addo said as the other members of his group reached the consulting room area.

'Ayowa needs a little rest, that's all,' Dr. Myers said. Kani heaved a sigh of relief and smiled.

'I thought I saw Brother-of-man, too,' he said. They all turned to look where the truck was. Benoa lay prostrate on the hard tarmac, one of his legs twisted and still inside the yawning gutter. In their enthusiasm to get to Kani and the doctor, the young men had not noticed Benoa's accident. As Benoa climbed down from the front seat of the high truck, he had not looked and so missed the tread of the step before the ground. His left foot thus went straight into the gutter and he lost his balance and fell forward, tipping over his left leg as if he had deliberately been pushed from behind by an unseen hand.

'Quick, bring that stretcher.' The doctor indicated a

folded cot leaning against the wall outside the consulting room. He was beside Benoa in no time. Coming to, he writhed in pain, groaning. 'Multiple compound fracture.' Dr. Myers pointed to two areas on Benoa's left leg which had perceptibly begun to swell. He directed the young men as to how to lay Benoa on the stretcher.

'I can't believe this,' Kani said in a voice full of apprehension. Subdued, he followed the men carrying his brother-in-law. They went behind the doctor into the building, where two nurses in light-blue uniforms transferred Benoa on to a vehicular litter and wheeled him away.

'Those of you who came later can go away now,' Dr. Myers said. 'You can only stay if you want to donate blood. It won't be painful.' He beckoned Kani and Ayerakwa to follow him. Addo and the men who had come with him hurriedly went outside.

The sun was about to set when Kani and his son-in-law came out of the hospital. The doctor had told them that the surgery on Ayowa was successful. Benoa's leg had been set, but it would stay in a cast for some weeks to heal effectively. There was nothing therefore for the family to stay around for and they should go home and come back the next day when they could talk to Ayowa and Benoa. Ayerakwa insisted on staying behind; he wanted to be around when Ayowa came to. He had some friends with whom he could stay the night. Kani left him and went to the car, in which Ofosuaa and Buaa and Sanyo were waiting, exhausted.

Back at Nkonsia, Sanyo drove Ofosuaa and Buaa home. Kani went on to the festivity grounds. The sheds had collapsed and there were sticks thrown all around, as though there had been a free-for-all stick fight. The *donno* lay broken and battered in a puddle that smelled strongly of liquor. Some people, however, had gathered under the tree of threepences. Kani found it intriguing that they all should have their attention focused toward the centre. On going closer, he realized that the so-called assistant Twafoor priestess, appointed to perform the fetish duties that Obaa Panyin had refused to do, was with Opong the Asona clan head, in the centre of the open space. The old man had just finished pouring a libation, and Addo-the-tapper was getting ready to cut the throat of a white bighorn ram. Kani recognized it was the one he had intended to slaughter for celebration in a week's time. He turned round to go away but a young man approached him.

'Noble Kani,' the young man said. 'You may not remember me. My name is Minta. From Pusupusu. I was here to share in the joy of Ayowa's wedding. But Entea broke up the festivities. I'm sorry about how things turned out. I hope Ayowa gets well soon.' He took Kani's hand in his own and bowed his head.

'Thank you,' Kani said. 'But what happened here? And what is going on there inside the gathering?' He had the look of a man caught in a conspiracy on his face. 'What's all that about?'

'What has happened here defies explanation,' Minta said. 'Entea was shot. When he managed to stagger to his feet, some young men almost tore him apart, but for the timely intervention of Obaa Panyin who sent him away in a truck to the Bunso hospital. The police came but left quickly because ten other men said they did the shooting. The truth is, I shot him –'

'You what?' Kani asked, shocked.

'O, yea,' Minta chuckled.

For a moment, the relaxed manner in which Minta owned up to the deed was so smooth that Kani seemed persuaded that Minta did the shooting. Another part of Kani's mind, however, held steadfastly to the knowledge of what Bonsra, Entea's father, had said to Kani some weeks back. 'Why should I believe you if the police didn't?'

'There are so many of us who love Ayowa dearly. We will do everything to protect her. But don't worry about me;

I'm responsible for my own actions, like anyone else. Excuse me, I have to get closer to the absolution rites being performed here. The town has to be cleansed. I need absolution, too. Don't I? I suppose we all do.' Minta left Kani to join the crowd that was becoming bigger and bigger now. Kani found the throaty bleating of the ram jarring. He turned to go away, but he found Kapre in his way.

'Out of my way, Onions,' he said.

The woman stood her ground and began piping out questions. 'Say, is it true that Ayowa is giving birth to a baby at the hospital? Was the man Ayerakwa? And did –'

Kani swept her out of his way with a swing of his massive arm and walked away. Just as he turned around the next house, he saw Bonsra approaching. In a bluish white kente cloth, he was limping ever so lightly on one crutch, its aluminium stem glistening in the evening sun and sporting adjustable slots near the base where it had a grey rubber buffer. Kani also noticed Bonsra's feet in light brown moccasins. It was abundantly obvious to Kani that Bonsra was enjoying his new scientific leg, and the crutches – or a crutch? Smiling, Kani halted. He expected Bonsra also to stop for a chat or communication of some kind, about the day's events, about the unfortunate turn of events with Entea, about the secret between the two of them – Bonsra and Kani.

However, Bonsra nonchalantly waved a white satin kerchief at Kani. He smiled, revealing his kola stained teeth. And as he stepped past Kani, a considerable distance between them, Bonsra was speaking, as if he found it absolutely necessary to say something so that Kani would not take Bonsra's effusive poise as an insult. 'I don't want to be late for the purification rites,' he was saying. 'The town must be cleansed, you know. I'll stop by later to chat. See you then, buddy.'

Astonished, Kani stood watching him, thinking how dense it was of human beings to believe that they could simply wish away the consequences of their foolish deeds in the bankrupt notion of immolation in any form. He too went on his way after Bonsra disappeared behind the corner of the next building. From the festivity grounds behind him around the bend, Kani heard the Adenkum group start a song. The sound of the *donno* – the hour-glass drum – was missing, but the handclaps were serving as a good substitute. Kani knew the words of the song and so he started to sing it to himself as he went on his way to his beautiful house.

> The Benevolent Giver granted
> The Pangolin a loan in solid gold
> To mould himself an auger
> To dig himself a dwelling
> But Pangolin went and hid
> In the lair of the Odum tree
> And kept the gold for himself
> But the Odum has given him up to us.

**Other titles in the Longman African Writers series:**

**Titles in the Longman African Classics series:**